Camp
Payback

For Katie

J.K. Rock

SPENCER HILL CONTEMPORARY

Contact: Spencer Hill Contemporary, an imprint of Spencer Hill Press, PO Box 247, Contoocook, NH, 03229, USA

Please visit our website at www.spencerhillcontemporary.com

First Edition: April 2014

J.K Rock

Camp Payback / by J.K. Rock – 1st ed.

p. cm.

Summary: Teenage girl is determined to make her last year at summer camp the best ever.

The author acknowledges the copyrighted or trademarked status and trademark owners of the following wordmarks mentioned in this fiction: Airstream, AstroTurf, Bedazzler, Chevy, Coke, Dairy Queen, Dixie, eBay, EpiPen, Ford, Frisbee, Gatorade, Hello Kitty, iPhone, JELL-O, Keds, LEGO, Lord of the Rings, Midol, NASCAR, Nerf, Power Rangers, Scooby-Doo, Star Wars, TED, Tony, Twilight Zone, Twitter, WWE, YouTube, Ziploc

Cover design by K. Kaynak, based on a design by Jennifer Rush

Interior layout by Jenny Perinovic

ISBN 978-1-939392-90-9 (paperback)

ISBN 978-1-93939291-6 (e-book)

Printed in the United States of America

To all of the amazing, talented and hard-working YA bloggers who helped us to find our readers and who made our young adult debut so much fun. Thank you all!

Character List

Martineau Family:
Alexandra
Andrew: Alex's perfect(ly annoying) older brother
Grace: Alex's mother
James: Alex's father

Munchies' Manor: Voted most likely to star in...
Emily (Counselor): viral flash mob to Madonna's *Vogue*
Alex: remake of the movie 10 *Things I Hate About You*...and you...and you...
Trinity: a psychic who shows up on *Supernatural* and dies the next episode without predicting it
Piper: a survival reality TV game show
Siobhan: an episode of *Jeopardy* where her lightning-fast answers short-circuit Watson
Jackie: beach volleyball Team USA Olympic final match-up
Yasmine: an advice talk show with better ratings than Oprah

Divas' Den: Voted most likely to star in...
Victoria (Counselor): live-action version of *Sleeping Beauty* where she sleeps happily ever after
Hannah: 10 *Steps to Squash Your Mean Girl Battitude* infomercial
Brittany: the worst *Buffy* remake ever—Buffy saves vampires and kills humans
Rachel: beach volleyball Team USA with Jackie in Olympic finals—GOLD!

Brooke: *Battle of the YouTube Has-Beens*
Nia: a Broadway hit show about a YouTube star—wins Tony
Kayla: a teen remake of *Home Alone Again...Typical*

The Wander Inn: Voted most likely to star in...

Bruce (Bam-Bam) (Counselor): remake of the movie *Rambo*, without mumbling so people understand lines
Rafael: documentary that follows his win at the World Chess Federation
Julian: a TED talk where he uses *Lord of the Rings* as an analogy for global warming
Vijay: *Jersey Shore: The Movie*
Danny: an episode of *Life in Your Parents' Basement*
Garrett: *Project Runway*, and he never hears the words "*auf wiedersehen*"

Warriors' Warden: Voted most likely to star in...

Rob (The Hottie) (Counselor): any Nicholas Sparks movie
Javier: a top-rated Venezuelan cooking show
Eli: a reboot of *Punk'd* on MTV
Devon: a commercial for an Internet dating site where he's the only single guy
Jake: his own workout video franchise: *Cray-Cray*
Cameron: (Appear on *People* magazine's cover as the 'Sexiest Man Alive'... in a photo-shopped version)
Buster: the WWE; code name: Bust-A-Move

Lake Juniper Point Director:

Mr. Woodrow (Gollum): most likely to star in an extreme medical emergency video where his whistle is surgically removed from his stomach...again

Chapter One

"Martineau family? You're on in ten minutes."

BLISS Network's waiting room door snapped shut behind a tired-looking intern, and my father leaped into action.

"Alex, wipe that goop off your mouth. Andrew, use a double Windsor knot on your tie. Dear, help Andrew. And for God's sake, everyone stay calm. We're going live on national television, so no mistakes." My father stopped pacing, and his eyes locked with mine. I flinched and studied my "gently used," secondhand black loafers. Sensible shoes for raising sensible kids, I mentally quoted from one of their *Wholesome Home* parenting blog posts. Though there was nothing practical about the blisters forming on my pinched toes.

"So the producers think we've got a shot at getting our own talk show?" asked my older brother, Andrew, from the couch. Mom's dress sleeves fluttered as she straightened his tie.

Dad beamed. "Last I checked, our site had over ten million followers and our book is still on the bestseller list, so I'd say yes, champ, we've got a good chance, unless–" His gaze pinned me down again. "Unless anyone breaks our *Wholesome Home* rules. That's why everyone is on their best behavior this summer. BLISS is sending surprise camera crews to check in on each of us sometime over the next couple of months. We won't know until the fall if we're filming a pilot."

I avoided his warning look, grabbed a tissue, and rubbed off my clear lip gloss. It figured that eagle-eyed Dad would notice my small rebellion against his no-makeup rule, which even the studio's hair and makeup team had been forced to follow. What had I been thinking? I crumpled the tissue, chucked it at the trash, and missed. It wasn't like I got away with anything. Ever. Take the long-sleeved shirt and maxi-length skirt I wore. My mother had scoured clearance racks for weeks before she'd found something horrible enough to meet my father's approval.

"Excuse me, young lady." Dad towered over me in a tailored suit, his salt-and-pepper hair clipped a precise quarter of an inch above his ears. "Is this the action of a *Wholesome Home* teen?" He held out the tissue, not bothering to wait for my answer. "Now throw it away properly."

"I was going to pick it up." I grabbed the paper and strode closer to the basket, trying to keep a lid on my frustration.

"What did you say?"

My hand froze over the container. In a few days I'd be at Camp Juniper Point and away from Dad's control, I reminded myself. With friends. Having fun.

"I said that I planned to get it. It's not like I'd leave it there." Would they ever stop blowing every mistake I made into something major? Sure. I made lots of them. But rarely the same ones twice. Or three times anyway. Four max.

Andrew smirked, a mini-version of my father in his dark suit and patriotic tie. My mother paled and mouthed "stop" at me.

Dad stepped closer, frowning.

"When I give you an order, you do it. Got it? No back talk."

Mom joined us and wrapped an arm around my tense shoulders. "She was only trying to explain herself."

"When I want an explanation, I'll ask for one." His flinty eyes sparked my trigger-ready anger.

"And when will that be? You never asked for an explanation about the text message." My voice rose with my temper. "The one that asked if I still wanted to be a virgin." The pent-up words flew from my mouth before I could stop them. And then, suddenly, I didn't want to dam myself up like the rest of my family. Never talking about anything real. Ignoring problems instead of dealing with them. The whole mess simmered inside me, ready to boil over any second.

"Alex, honey, this isn't the time," Mom whispered. "And people will hear you."

"So what if they do?" I scooted away when she leaned close. A kiss would not make this hurt better. "Maybe they want to hear me, even if you don't."

"Pipe down. Now." Dad spoke through gritted teeth.

"Yeah, Alex. Do you want to ruin Mom and Dad's chances for this show?" Andrew tried the reasonable approach, Mr. Perfect Son always taking my parents' side. Never hearing mine.

"Shut it, Andrew." Angry tears stung my eyes. I sounded horrible, yet I couldn't stop myself. If only I was the damsel-in-distress type of girl people rushed to comfort. My instinct was to fight back, which never got me sympathy. I wouldn't be appearing as a cartoon princess anytime soon.

I squared my shoulders to face Dad again. "No matter what I say, you believe the worst. You'd rather send me to a jail disguised as an all-girls boarding school than deal with this or me. "And yes—" A bitter laugh escaped me. "I saw the admissions application on your desk. A New Day Alternative Boarding School for Girls. You're not the only ones who can snoop."

My mother's breathy intake nearly sucked the oxygen out of the room.

Dad's face turned a shade darker than his tie. "Don't tempt my patience." When he leaned close, I smelled the coffee on his breath. "If we didn't already have our overseas mission itinerary set, you'd be locked in your room all summer until we sent you away."

"Honey," Mom broke in. "What your father means is that you should consider these two months a trial. As long as we don't hear of any misbehavior at camp, you won't have to go."

Dad harrumphed. "You will not ruin our shot at a talk show. Got it?"

Oh, I got it all right. Mom wasn't fooling me. There was no trial because I'd already been found guilty. The sentence delivered. Ten months at A New Day School of Torture and Suffering.

I forced myself to speak over the pain squeezing my chest. "Because that's what really matters, right? Your precious career?" I shook my mother's hand off my wrist. "All I am is your personal cross to bear." I quoted from one of the many blog posts they'd written about raising a problem child like me.

In the silence while I waited, stupidly, for my parents to disagree, I flopped in a nearby chair. Emptiness smothered my fire. No matter what I said or did, I would never be good enough. I tugged at the scratchy collar digging into my neck and swallowed past the painful lump clogging my throat.

My parents were the authority on raising wholesome kids. Or *one*, anyway. Every teacher asked me why I couldn't be more like my perfect brother, Andrew. Worse yet, teachers who were *Wholesome Home* fans groaned when they spotted my name on their class list and handed me detention slips for stuff other kids got away with all the time. But that wasn't a mystery. They were all too happy to give quotes about me for the blog. I was a public relations nightmare to my parents. Nothing more.

Well, I was also one more thing: ammunition for their recent bestseller, *Discipline with Love: The Wholesome Home's Answer to Problem Behavior*. At least I had my uses. I rubbed my eyes. No way would I let them see me cry.

The door swooshed open, and a man with a headset and clipboard gestured to us.

"All set?"

"You bet!" shouted Dad, Mom, and Andrew, exhibiting our standard family cheer for public appearances. Only I couldn't join in. Not when I was a prop for the movie set of their so-called perfect life.

"Happy faces!" urged the usher guy as I slouched by him and into the dark hall leading up to the set. My mother's cold hand slipped into mine and squeezed.

We took our seats as technicians clipped microphones to our shirts.

"And we're live in five," blared an announcer, "four..." He held up three fingers, two, then one, followed by a point that seemed to animate *Wake Up America*'s host, Kevin Stiller.

"It's time to wake up, America, and meet the Martineaus, authors of the *Wholesome Home* parenting blog and their most recent bestseller, *Discipline with Love: The Wholesome Home's Answer to Problem Behavior*. Please give a warm welcome to James." Wild applause broke out. "Grace." Louder applause. "Andrew." A few whistles mixed with the clapping. "And Alex." The crowd's hush was punctuated with a few disappointed sighs.

I slid lower in my chair, my damp hands twisting in my lap. Ouch. All the audience knew about me was what they read. And that wasn't pretty. If only I could tell my side of the story.

"So, James..." Kevin Stiller leaned forward in his chair. "Can you give us a quick summary of your *Wholesome Home*'s parenting philosophy?"

My dad's face transformed into a stranger's. His smile was warm, his eyes twinkled. "It's raising your children to embrace traditional, wholesome values such as understanding the importance of hard work, kindness, family, and integrity. We encourage saving rather than spending, helping others rather than helping yourself, faith in yourself and a higher power, and above all, honesty."

The microphone amplified my choking cough.

Kevin Stiller looked at me, stunned, before he faced a lit camera, white teeth flashing against tanned skin. For the next five minutes, my father fielded questions. Then Kevin turned to my brother.

"Andrew, what are your plans this summer?"

"I'm building shelters in Nicaragua." His brown hair, smooth and lacking my red highlights, gleamed under the intense stage lights. The crowd cheered, and a girl yelled, "Marry me!"

Our host held up his hands, and the crowd quieted. "That's wonderful. And will your sister be accompanying you?"

I crossed my arms across my chest, knowing I looked every inch the rebellious teen they imagined me to be. But what the hell? Why hadn't Kevin asked me?

Andrew's expression turned pious and remorseful. "She's going to North Carolina." He hung his head, paused to study his clasped hands, then raised it again, his green eyes looking apologetic. "To summer camp," he added.

The audience's silent, collective disapproval was palpable. I peered into the darkened area and wondered what they saw. An apathetic teenager? A defiant girl? A burden to her deserving family? All of the above?

"And what will she be doing at this camp? Volunteering?" Kevin Stiller prompted, his eyes never straying my way.

I sat up straight, uncrossed my arms and leaned forward, my parents' narrowed eyes on me. Screw this. My family's official talking points about my summer were that I'd be volunteering with younger campers and promoting environmental awareness. Yet that wasn't even close to the full story. If my parents valued honesty so much, then it was time they got some.

"No," I cut off whatever Andrew was about to say, my voice loud in the hush. "*I'm* going to have fun."

My dad looked like he was about to bust a kidney, but I stopped myself from caring. After a grueling year of public appearances to support their book, every interview focusing on me as the bad kid, every misstep dissected on their world-famous blog, they were rewarding me by banishing me from my friends, school, and home.

Someone said the best revenge was living well. If I had the greatest summer ever before they tossed me in A New Day's dungeons and threw away the key, I'd get what I wanted.

Payback.

And if that included the boy who sent me the text, my ex-camp boyfriend, even better.

....

Five days later, when the car rolled to a stop on the huge, horseshoe-shaped driveway in front of Camp

Juniper Point's administration building, I wrenched open the back door.

"Alex." My father coaxed his irritation into a socially acceptable tone in case anyone outside the car could hear. "Wait until the vehicle comes to a stop, please."

What. Ever.

I waited on the sidewalk while they got out of the car. As always, Dad held the door for Mom. They approached me holding hands, a trick they'd taught fans to "present a united front" when confronting your teen.

Little did they know I was about to give them enough material for Volume II on that one. I was already being sent to a school/jail after this summer for crimes that weren't my fault. I might as well commit a few for real.

"It looks like another fun summer, sweetheart," my father boomed loud enough for nearby families to overhear. When a couple rushed toward us, camera in hand, he slid an arm around my waist, my mother automatically stepping to my other side.

"Can we please take your picture?" asked a woman wearing a *Wholesome Home* T-shirt. "I was hoping we'd see you. If you only knew how much you've helped us deal with our Kennedi. Those chapters you wrote about your daughter—"

I gave the pouting Kennedi a small wink, then forced the smile expected of me during family photo-ops. Just a few more minutes and they'd be gone. Then the summer, and my life, would belong to me.

"Your parents are saints," the camera-happy mother said, lowering the apparatus and frowning at me. My insides curled. I hated that knowing, judgmental expression strangers got when they saw me. They only knew what they'd read: one half of the story. My parents' half.

"Yes." I forced myself to return Dad's easy grin. "They certainly think so." It was all I could do not to sprint into the registration building and get this summer started. "Thank you, Dad, for letting me come to camp," I added for good measure.

"You're welcome," Dad said through smiling teeth as a camera clicked. "And don't forget about BLISS showing up this summer." He kissed the top of my head as another family snapped pictures. I did my best to act like that was the most natural thing in the world for him to do. "Use good judgment."

I nodded, my stomach jittery. In moments, I'd see my Munchies' Manor cabin mates, and summer would officially begin. I only had eight weeks to pack in a year's worth of fun. My phone buzzed against my thigh, but I ignored the incoming text. I'd been lucky to keep the phone and didn't want to give Dad any reason to snatch it away.

"Goodbye, Alexandra." It was Mom's turn now. She hugged me and kissed my cheek. I kissed hers, too, wondering how she'd survive the summer with no one to stand up against my opinionated father. His successful books only reinforced his certainty that he was always right. "And don't do anything that will upset your dad," she whispered in my ear so he couldn't hear, "or make him send you away." She looked a little teary, and for the first time, I wondered if she really wanted me home, no matter how many arguments I caused.

I returned her squeeze, feeling it was the closest we'd been to acting real in a long time. But I couldn't make her any promises, not without lying again. Pretending not to notice guys for ten months out of the year was really tough. At camp, it was impossible. But boys didn't top my to-do list this summer anyway. Having a good time did. I smiled and shouted goodbye while hustling toward the administration building.

Hello, freedom!

The pine-log scent of the interior felt like a hug as I pulled my suitcase inside behind me. Tables lined the walls for check-in, with the registration packets sorted alphabetically by last name. I got in the M-R line and waited while my phone buzzed again.

"Alex!" My friends and cabin mates, Piper and Siobhan, rushed over, surrounding me for a group hug. They both looked the same. Piper had a neat braid swinging over one shoulder and a bright T-shirt that said "Recycle This" with a peace sign. Siobhan wore her Coke-bottle glasses that magnified her light hazel eyes and a Hello Kitty tank-top that I was pretty sure came from one of her P.J. sets.

These were the "right" kids my parents approved of. They were smart, kind, and never got in real trouble. But they weren't saints. I could get them into some mischief if I worked at it.

"Did you see Emily's lanyard display?" Siobhan pointed to the other side of the room where campers could sign up early for activities or learn about the special overnight hikes and canoe trips.

"Do I want to?" I pulled out my phone while keeping an eye out for Emily's bright blonde ponytail.

"Right there." Piper turned my chin to help line up my gaze. "Instead of Secret Santa, she's doing a Secret Camp Angel."

I spied Emily behind a hunk of gnarled driftwood covered with dozens of bright lanyards. The Munchies' Manor counselor wore layered neon polo shirts in shades of pink, the collars starched to stand straight up and the sleeves rolled up to her shoulders.

"Secret Camp Angel?" It sounded way too *Wholesome Home* for my taste.

"All the seniors get a lanyard with the name of another camper inside." Siobhan fanned herself with a page of graph paper that looked to be filled with quadratic equations. She did homework year-round and was a shoe-in for valedictorian at her school in Georgia. "You keep the name a secret and do nice things for that person all summer long."

"Emily has a list of suggestions," Piper added as I moved up in line. She caught me up on a few other camp headlines before blurting, "Oh, and best of all! Did you hear there is a movie being shot in Waynesville after the Fourth of July?"

"Are you kidding?" Despite my parents' obsessive tracking of their social media status, I only had access to the Internet for homework. "Any big name actors in it?"

I did know who the hottest male stars were thanks to *People* magazine covers at the grocery store.

"No one I've heard of," Siobhan answered as a group of younger campers entered the admin building in a swirl of sleeping bags and chatter. "It's a historical drama—"

"Ohmigod. Who's that guy?" Piper's voice cut through the buzz. Her jaw dropped, her gaze fixed on a point in the center of the room.

I turned to see. A dark-haired boy prowled among the campers, his hands in the pockets of faded khaki cargoes. An equally faded gray T-shirt stretched over shoulders that had filled out more than most of his peers. A straight nose and prominent cheekbones were probably handsome when he smiled, but right now he scowled at all he surveyed, almost as if Camp Juniper Point was the last place he wanted to be.

"I don't recognize him." Siobhan straightened her glasses. "But we're bound to get a few new campers this year with Matt and Seth gone. I hear the new boy in the Wander Inn is some kind of chess champion, but their counselor said he hasn't checked in yet."

"Of course you'd be keeping your eye out for a chess whiz." I laughed, so happy to be back with my friends. Some of the hurt of the last few days with my family fell away.

"And we'll have a new girl in our cabin now that Lauren is gone this year, too," Piper added distractedly, never taking her eyes off the new kid, who was, now that I thought about it, kinda hot. Super hot, actually.

Lauren Carlson, one of my closest friends, had been admitted to an Aerospace Camp this summer, and I was really happy for her. She'd worked hard to get in. But a part of me wished she was here so that she could enjoy this wild ride of a summer with me.

"Too bad Vijay won't be among the missing," I complained, noticing that my ex had strolled in the registration area—laughing and horsing around with another kid from the Wander Inn cabin. Vijay looked more muscular than I remembered, his lanky body gone. "He must have worked out since last summer."

"I thought you guys were still cool," Piper whispered to me before I got up to the front of the line.

While I registered, I tried not to look back at Vijay. Last summer, we'd hung out and I'd wanted to go all the way. But then I'd gotten cold feet. At fifteen, a girl is entitled, right? Not according to Vijay.

I thought he'd been okay with it at the time, but by the end of the summer, he'd turned downright cold. And more recently? Nasty. I couldn't think about the text he sent me about asking if I still wanted to be a virgin, the message that had turned my life into hell, without fuming. If it weren't for him, I would be going back to my regular school and friends at the end of the summer instead of to problem-child prison.

"We are *not* cool." Finished with registering, I noticed that Vijay was studying his phone before he turned it in for the week. I'd have to hand in mine, too, because we only got an hour of electronics time per week and the counselors held all devices until then. "You guys already handed in your phones?" I checked mine for texts.

"Yes." Siobhan craned her neck to look toward the main door. "Is that Jackie?"

One of our cabin mates must have arrived, but I was too distracted by my messages. The last two were from Vijay.

My stomach dropped.

Still keeping your legs crossed? said the first.

U R a tease, read the second.

Fury whirled inside like a white-hot tornado. I marched over to him.

"Seriously?" I waved my phone under Vijay's nose. "Do you have any idea how much trouble your last stupid text got me in?"

"Got you thinking about me?" He flicked his tongue up and down.

So gross. How could I have ever liked this guy?

"My dad saw it, Vijay." I refused to allow tears to spring to my eyes, but my heart beat so hard I could barely hear anything over the sound of my pulse in my ears. "My parents are sending me to an all-girls' boarding school thanks to you."

We were attracting an audience. I knew I should keep it down, but I was too pissed. Out of the corner of my eye, I saw Emily round the corner of her lanyard display and head our way.

"All girls? Great." He lowered his voice. "Now you can all be virgins together."

His dark eyes were cold and unforgiving. They reminded me of my father.

"What is your problem?" I hissed.

"My problem is girls like you who put on a big show of liking a guy and then turn into a prude when it comes time to put out."

I shook with fury.

"Oh yeah?" I slammed my phone down on the counter to turn it in. "Well, my new boyfriend doesn't think I'm such a prude."

I turned around in a rush of rage and hurt. Unsteady, I marched toward the first guy I saw.

The new kid.

I threw my arms around his neck and planted a kiss on his mouth. Hard. Fast. Wet.

I didn't know him, and I didn't care. Vijay needed to stay the hell out of my way. He'd only ruin my best-summer-ever plans. The yummy kiss I'd just gotten, however, might be exactly the payback I had in mind.

There was nothing wholesome about it.

Chapter Two

Javier

What the hell?

I pushed back from the crazy girl kissing me. I knew better than to touch her, or I'd end up blamed for this somehow. My arms pin-wheeled like a freaking *Scooby-Doo* character as I stumbled backward to break the contact. My arm connected with something and then—*thwack!* Stuff went flying all over the floor.

Crap.

I blinked to take it all in, from the cute girl who glared at me like *I'd* done something wrong to the hyperventilating counselor who was wailing about *lanyards.* They must be the leather strap things spilled all over the floor. I'd hit the display trying to escape.

A shrill whistle cut through the sudden rush of noise, and the camp director barreled through the kids toward me.

"What's the problem here?" the guy demanded, still holding his whistle in one hand. Beady eyes darted back and forth between the girl and me. "Ms. Martineau? Mr. Kovalev? Care to explain this?"

"She kissed me." I pointed at the dark-haired girl who gnawed on her lip, her eyes troubled but defiant. "I was just standing here."

Behind the girl, a couple of guys doubled over in silent laughter. What was that all about? I had a vague

15

sense they were to blame for setting her off, given the dirty look she sent them. But I couldn't think about that now when my job at camp might be over before it began. My shoulders tensed. Fists tightened.

"Is this true, Alexandra?" The camp director–finally letting go of his whistle–took out a notepad from his shirt pocket and scribbled. "Your parents will be disappointed if I need to call them."

The girl's face went white as she nodded. I shouldn't feel sorry for her, but it was obvious that a parent phone call was the last thing she wanted.

"As for you, young man." The guy's attention turned back to me, and he stepped closer and pointed a finger in my face. A crunch under his hiking boot suggested he'd destroyed a few lanyards in the process. "You're off to a precarious start here." He gestured to the mess on the floor and the crowd of gawkers watching him yell at me. "If you want to keep your job, I suggest you look sharp from now on, Javier, or you'll be sent right back to foster care. Understood?"

Fury crawled up the back of my neck at the guy for announcing my status. Not that I cared about fitting in, since that was a lost cause for me. And the only time I'd see the other kids was when I bunked down with them or served them meals. Still. My situation was no one's business.

"Yes, sir," the girl–Alexandra, apparently–answered for both of us while I gave a stiff nod.

I couldn't afford to lose my temper now. But, oh, man. The tic behind my eye was racing at lightspeed.

"Alex, since you are the instigator, you're assigned to breakfast cleanup all week." The camp director tapped the side of his nose. "You'll work with Helena, our new kitchen director, and miss your first activity to fulfill the duty. Let this be a lesson to everyone else about public displays of affection and inappropriate touching." He glared around the room until his eyes stopped on me. "And staff members are reminded to reread page twelve in the employee handbook about appropriate conduct with campers."

My body tensed. Like I'd asked for her kiss? And yes, I'd read page twelve. I had read the entire handbook to make sure I wouldn't lose this last chance I'd been given before being sent to a group home.

The director turned on his boot heel and stalked off after warning me to get my butt to my cabin. I was about to do just that, had even made a few steps toward my bag, when Helena rushed toward me. I wanted to keep walking. But if it hadn't been for her stepping up and giving me a place to stay this summer when my foster parents kicked me out...

I ground my teeth and forced myself to stop.

She clamped a hand on my shoulder and looked into my eyes, her wiry blonde hair showing signs of going prematurely gray. She wasn't much older than my mom, and it killed me to think of my mom going gray before she'd ever get out of prison to have any fun. Saddled with a kid before she could even get to college, Mom had sacrificed everything for me. She would be hurt if I blew this chance at the camp that Mom's old prison friend, Helena, had secured for me until my problems with foster care could be worked out. Again.

"Javier." Her gravelly voice was matter-of-fact, but her face was bright red. "Do you have any idea who you just kissed?"

Around us, activity returned to normal. A bunch of girls surrounded Alexandra. They all comforted her while the counselor tried to resurrect her lanyard display. Every now and then, one of them looked my way, and I glared daggers back at them. Did they have any clue how much their friend might have messed up my life?

"I don't care. Look, I didn't do anything." I wanted Helena—needed her—to believe me.

"Well, you should care. Alex's parents are famous for raising wholesome kids. They write blogs and books about it. Messing around with her is even worse than messing around with any of the other campers. Not only would you lose your job, but the negative publicity would be horrible. Even your mom would hear about it."

I froze. I'd caused Mom enough grief. I would definitely stay clear of Alex.

My eyes strayed to the dark curls waving over her slender shoulders when she picked up a piece of the broken display. "Trust me. She's the last girl I'd be interested in. The only thing I want to do this summer is make money and stay off the director's radar."

Helena made a face. "Well, I hope you have some fun, too. You're only seventeen. For that matter, I still wish you'd reconsider working in the kitchen. You could have picked an outdoor job."

"I like cooking."

Helena sighed. "Maybe it's for the best. Mr. Woodrow told us that BLISS Network is showing up unannounced this summer to film her. You do not want to be the guy caught fooling around with the *Wholesome Home* girl. Understand?"

I nodded, a pang of sympathy making me look up at the cute girl whose mouth I still tasted. Strawberry lip gloss and bubblegum. It must suck to be followed by cameras wherever you went. But like Helena said, even more reason to forget the feel of her soft body and the taste of her.

Helena's fingers snapped in front of my face, and I tore my eyes away Alex. "Stick with your goals, and you'll be able to help your mom when she's released this fall. The last time you ran off to see her, your foster parents threatened to report it and send you to a group home. And if this camp job hadn't come through, that's where you'd be. No more bad reports."

My teeth clenched. "I won't go to the group home. It's on the opposite side of the state from Mom. I'll never get to visit."

Helena's face softened. "We'll sort it out, Javier. But for now, better head to your cabin. Okay?"

"I need to get my stuff first." I'd left my bag near the registration table.

"I'll have it sent over to you later." Helena turned me toward the door. "It's my fault I kept you here talking when Mr. Woodrow asked you to get to the cabin."

I had a real problem with other people touching my stuff. Maybe it came from leaving behind a lot of my things when I went into the foster system.

"It'll only take a sec—"

"Please go before anything else happens." She gave me another nudge. "Mr. Woodrow is about to leave, and I don't want to miss my chance to talk to him."

She hurried after the camp director. I didn't want to upset her for a second time today, so I trudged outside and hoped she wouldn't let anyone mess with my bag. It was all I had. All I could call my own. Home for me was a duffle bag I carried one-handed.

"Javier?" A muscular dude in a fishing hat and camouflage cut-offs called the second I stepped outside. Had to be a counselor.

"Yeah?" I stuffed my hands in my pockets.

"I can show you where the cabins are," he offered.

I could figure it out by the sea of kids streaming away from the administration building with their suitcases, but I figured this was just the guy's polite way of giving me a warning or some advice that wouldn't help.

I shrugged.

"I'm Bruce. They call me Bam-Bam." He offered his hand, and I shook it. "I'm the counselor for the Wander Inn, but you're not on my list."

"I'm sleeping in the Warriors' Warden." I had no idea if that was bad or good, but this Bam-Bam guy seemed all right. "Guess they didn't think I was old enough to sleep in the staff cabin."

"Right. One of the campers cancelled last minute, and Mr. Woodrow thought if you took his bunk, you'd have some camp experience when you're not working. My cabin's right next door." He pointed out a baseball field and a few other kinds of athletic fields nearby. I could see the Nantahala River in the distance, shimmering in the bright afternoon sun.

If I didn't *have* to be here, maybe I wouldn't mind this place so much. But I could almost write the script for the rest of my time at Camp Juniper Point now that I'd been branded as the staffer accused of kissing one of their precious girls. What the hell had she done that for? Whatever her reasons, I wasn't planning on getting too comfortable.

After taking the scenic route, we arrived at the boys' cabins. Apparently, the girls bunked on the far side of camp. The log cabins were different shapes and sizes, as if they'd added on as the camp grew. For the most part, they were in a circle, with the kiddie campers separated by the boys' showers. Now, kids hung out the windows and aired out the buildings. Every now and then a pair of sneakers flew out of a door, or guys wrestled in the common area between the buildings.

"You're over there." Bam-Bam pointed out the Warriors' Warden. "Rob's the counselor in charge. He's a good guy, but if you need anything..." He shrugged. "Let me know."

My guess? Bam-Bam was former military. You could tell by the way he carried himself. And while that was cool and all for him, I wasn't going to be the kid that got recruited out of poverty to earn fame and glory in the service.

I just wanted to keep my head down and get through camp without getting booted. If I could keep my nose clean until Mom got out of jail this fall, then I could get out of the foster system, get a year-round job, and help her go back to college. She'd put off that dream long enough for my sake. But that'd be hard to do if my record showed I'd been fired and sent to a group home—or worse—for discipline reasons.

"Sure." I nodded. "Thanks."

I wanted to get my bag and make sure no one messed with it. Seeing all those sneakers fly out of the cabins made me suspect my bunkmates could be doing the same to my stuff.

When I walked in, a couple of bunks were already made up—claimed by early arrivals. Three guys were sitting on one vacant bunk, the uncovered mattress squeaking as they shifted to see who came in.

Right in the middle of them?

My green duffle.

"What are you doing?" No chance I was going to last out the summer. A girl kissing me...these guys handling my stuff...

There was no respect for boundaries in this place. Tension vise-gripped my shoulders.

One of the guys—a tall, slick-looking dude in a faded red polo—stood. "Just carried your bag up here for you, man. I'm Cameron."

I was less interested in Cameron than the guys behind him, still way too close to my things. I flexed my fingers, trying not to get bent out of shape too fast. "Anger issues" was one of the labels I'd seen in that thick file of mine. But I was working on that. I had to.

"Javier," I informed him, angling to drag the canvas sack toward an empty bed in the far corner. I flung the bag up onto the mattress and folded my arms, staring them down.

"I'm Eli." A squirrely red-headed kid practically leaped to his feet. "Welcome to the Warden." He darted toward the door, nodding at the other guys. "We're going down to the beach before dinner if you want to come."

The other guys fell in line. Cameron and some big, silent musclehead.

I shook my head.

"Too bad." Eli slid out the door. "I'll bet your girlfriend will be down there!"

The other guys snickered while I fumed.

I tossed out some clothes and reined in my temper. If I let things get worse, there'd be a fight before bedtime. Besides, the person I should be mad at was the dark-haired girl.

But as I remembered the look on her face while those guys laughed at her behind her back, I half-wondered if she and I had something in common. At that moment, she hadn't looked like she fit in any more than I did.

Chapter Three

Alex

I so did not want to be here. At least, not stuck in the administration building, crawling on my hands and knees, searching for missing lanyards. I was ready to get the camp party started. If only Emily would let me off the hook so I could scoot over to the arts and crafts building and make over my wardrobe from drab to fab. After Vijay's put-downs and the tornado of rumors swirling around me, I needed to look amazing for tonight's bonfire. Day one of my best summer ever was going down in flames, and I'd have to work fast to correct that.

My fingers connected with a braided leather piece under a desk. Finally.

"Here's the last one." I straightened and waved a tan bracelet with green beads.

Emily held out an overflowing cloth bag. "That makes fifty-two. Thanks, Alex." Her large eyes ran over the shattered driftwood display she'd placed back on the table. "Hours of work gone in seconds. It's hard to believe."

"I'm sorry," I said again, meaning it. It sucked when you worked at making something special only to have it shattered into millions of pieces. Like Vijay did to my heart. I pictured the lanky, endearing boy I'd fallen for last summer and wondered where he'd gone. He used to have a good side—but calling me a prude, asking me if I still wanted to be a virgin and planned to keep my legs crossed...it didn't even *sound* like him.

Emily's eyes crinkled, and she extended a fist my way. "Don't worry—be happy. Right, home girl?"

We bumped knuckles, and I returned her broad smile, relieved she'd forgiven me. Her thin arm hooked around my waist as I hefted my gray suitcase. "You can help pass these out at the bonfire." Emily swung the bag and shook back her tangled blonde curls. "But first I want to hear the dirt on Vijay." She lowered her voice to a stage whisper. "And your new boyfriend, Javier. Fast moves, girlfriend, but be careful there. He's totally quasi-staff this year."

"Can we wait until we get back to the cabin? I need to stop at the arts and crafts building," I stalled. My kissing partner-in-crime had definitely been hot, but he'd been a weapon against Vijay. Nothing more. I didn't need more boy trouble at camp, even if I couldn't stop replaying the feel of Javier's full lips on mine. I planned to pay back my parents by having fun and raising some hell. Not by getting kicked out before I so much as toasted a s'more.

Emily nodded, and we strolled out into the soft purple twilight, following a painted, rock-lined path. An orange moon crested the horizon, a warm breeze off our baseball *Field of Dreams* carrying the crisp smell of freshly mown grass.

I kicked a stone aside, wanting all obstacles out of my way. This summer's good times had to last me through the lonely months ahead at New Day's School of Anguish and Self-Loathing. And nothing would stop my wild plans. Not even Vijay. Especially not Vijay. My mouth tingled as I remembered Javier instead. He had smelled good. Spicy enough to make me want another taste.

Could he be the leading man in my camp drama? Of course there was the teensy problem of how he already seemed to hate my guts. Not to mention that staff (even sort-of staff) and camper hook-ups were strictly forbidden. No wonder he'd looked furious about the kiss. I'd gotten him in trouble, and by the sound of things, he was already on thin ice.

I pictured Javier's sun-kissed complexion and thick-lashed, melt-your-heart brown eyes. Maybe he was exactly the *right* kind of boy for what I had in mind...if we didn't get caught. The perfect candidate for a summer of fun and payback. A slow smile spread across my face.

Fingers snapped in front of my face as Emily pulled me to a stop. "Earth to Alex. Come in, Alex. Didn't you say you wanted to hit arts and crafts?"

I looked up at the pine-sided building. "Oh. Yeah. I just need to fix up an outfit if we have time."

Emily glanced at her oversized, plastic watch. "Will ten minutes do if I help?"

I gave her a quick hug, and we raced inside, my mind full of the changes I needed to make. "Thanks, Emily."

A little later we were back on the path heading home, my wholesome kid look transformed with the help of a pair of scissors and quick-drying fabric glue.

"I hope that passes dress code." Emily eyed my tank as it rode above my cut-offs' waistband. "Didn't think we meant to cut it that much. I'd like to stay on the camp director's good side if I want to have any hope of him approving my field trip idea this summer."

She winked and twirled, throwing an imaginary object—a baton, maybe—in the air and pretending to catch it.

"Field trip?" I hoped it involved something fun and not some stuffy museum.

"It's a surprise," she mouthed in a stage whisper. "Let's hope Mr. Woodrow doesn't see your shirt and nix the trip because he thinks I let you girls run wild." She eyed my outfit again.

I pulled at the front of my shirt so I could read its twinkling red sequins spelling out "Sizzle." It was exactly what I meant to do. At camp, if I wanted to burn red-hot all summer, then I would. I could kiss whom I wanted. Say what I wanted. There were no *Wholesome Home* limits on me here...as long as my parents weren't called.

"I'll throw a sweatshirt around my waist. Gollum will never know." We'd given Mr. Woodrow the nickname forever ago when one of the boys had joked about him loving his whistle like His Precious. "Besides, we don't have much time to change before the bonfire."

"Right!" Emily brightened. "You need that time to spill the deets about what happened at registration. Plus you still have to meet your new cabin mate."

I stopped to tighten a sandal strap. "What's her name?"

"Yasmine." Emily's white smile gleamed in the deepening gloom as we resumed our walk down a smaller path leading to the girls' cabins. "She's amazing. You'll love her. She just moved to Atlanta from Mumbai, and before that she lived in Amsterdam. Can you imagine? Her parents fund charities around the world."

Wow. That did sound cool, though their good-will approach to life sounded a little too similar to my family. Hopefully Yasmine was fun instead of uptight.

When we neared our cabin, the familiar pine trees whispered to me like old friends. I wondered if Yasmine would like our camp. The most exotic we got were smiley-face pancakes on Sundays.

"There she is!" Emily pointed as our porch loomed. "Yasmine!"

The girl's flawless brown skin made her white top seem to glow as she crossed to the birch-log railing. Her waving hand was as graceful as a ballerina.

"Hello, Emily."

I trailed behind our counselor, sizing up this stranger. She was about my height, which was average, but she had about double my curves in every place I needed them. Gold hoops brushed her shoulders, peeking out from silky, flat-ironed hair. Her hooded, obsidian eyes were wide-set and large, bronze eye shadow contrasting with their dark color. Very, very cool. And exotic. Suddenly my "Sizzle" tank felt tacky instead of trendy.

"We just finished picking up those lanyards." Emily turned and gestured to me. "And this is Alex. She used to be best friends with Lauren—the girl you replaced—so now you two can be B.F.F.s."

Yasmine eyed me, her sculpted eyebrows rising. "Are you the girl who kissed the boy who knocked over Emily's bracelet tree?"

I felt myself flush under her scrutiny but forced myself not to look away. Sure that was a dumb mistake. But who was she to judge? Finally, I nodded.

Her delicate nostrils flared, a glittering diamond stud making an appearance. She sniffed, gave me another once over, then turned and disappeared in the cabin without another word.

So much for B.F.F.s. Maybe we'd be B.E.F.s—best enemies forever.

"Friendly," I drawled, following Emily up the stairs.

"Oh, she is. Her parents are travelling in Indonesia this summer and had to drop her off a day early. But instead of hanging out by the lake, she worked all day to help me finish up those lanyards and set up the display." Emily held open the door. "Guess charitable acts run in her blood."

"Emily!" called Bam-Bam from behind us. "Can I talk to you? It's about the new kid, Javier."

"Sure, babe!" she shouted, beaming at her guy before she turned back to me. "Go on in, Alex. The girls are anxious to see you, and you can get to know Yasmine better."

"Saint Yasmine," I murmured as I breezed inside, then raced past upended suitcases and strewn clothes for my bunk. But when I jumped on the familiar mattress, something felt wrong. My hand swept over the soft blue fabric covering it. This wasn't my comforter...

Flared hips filled my line of sight, long, squared-off nails tapping on either side of them. "Are you trying to wreck my stuff?"

Yasmine.

What were her things doing on my bunk? My friends huddled on Jackie's bed, their expressions throwing me silent apologies. My eyes narrowed on them. Traitors. Sure, Yasmine was new here, and we should be accommodating. Still, why hadn't they defended my turf? I'd slept in this spot for seven years.

Taking a deep breath, I reminded myself that I'd battled for my place in my overbearing family lots of times. I could deal with a pushy camper who would have made a perfect *Wholesome Home* kid. I was so not letting her buzzkill my summer.

"You've got the wrong bunk. This is mine." When I stood, Yasmine didn't step back, leaving about an inch of space between us.

"Girls," Jackie warned, but we both ignored her.

I blew a bubble that nearly touched Yasmine's nose.

Her earrings swung as she shook her head. "Your name wasn't on it."

Name? For all her travels, could this be her first time at a camp? Sharing a room? Didn't she know the rules? New people checked with the old before claiming a bed. On top of everything—my parents, Vijay, the bad start to summer—this suddenly felt like too much.

I marched over to my suitcase, snapped it open, and pulled out my glittery pink "A." Back at the bunk, I jammed the ribbon on a nail and watched it swing with satisfaction. There. Territory claimed.

"Happy now?" I looked around for my new nemesis and found her stretched out on my old mattress, a dimple appearing high on her left cheek as she smiled.

"That's cute. My last name is Anderson. So it works for me. Though I don't believe I've had anything pink and glittery like that since I was ten."

Jackie got to her feet in that fluid, athletic way of hers and pulled me in for a hug. "It's only a bunk. Hey, I missed you, Alex, and that's what matters. We're together."

Trinity, another bunkmate, joined in the hug, her familiar, patchouli smell bringing tears to my eyes. This was the homecoming I'd wanted. Needed. Not hassle from Vijay, a week of punishment assigned before I'd finished out my first day, a new roommate-zilla, and a stranger whose kiss I couldn't stop thinking about.

"Maybe it's meant to be. Karma," Trinity said in her faraway voice that reminded me of mystical lands and fairy tales. "Like a tree branch is supposed to come through that window and would have crushed you right there." She pointed at Yasmine, then put a hand over her mouth. "Oops. Sorry."

"It's all right," said Yasmine. "My karma's just fine." She shot me a meaningful look.

"You have a nice aura." Trinity nodded. Guess she didn't notice Yasmine's glare burning my soul to ash.

"Thanks." Yasmine pulled out a necklace with a wooden elephant charm, its trunk pointing upward. "An Indian sadhu gave me this for good luck before we moved. So I'm all set."

Trinity nodded like she knew exactly what a sadhu was...and maybe she did. At least she was trying, unlike me.

Suddenly I imagined Lauren at her NASA camp. What if one of her roommates treated her badly? I'd hate that. I needed to give Yasmine another chance. Girl fights were not part of my thrill ride summer plan.

I pulled out my lavender quilt and tossed it up on the top bunk. "Jackie's right." I forced a smile at the newest addition to Munchies' Manor. "Yasmine—the bunk is yours." My parents would have applauded—and blogged about how it was all thanks to their parenting—if they'd been here to witness.

Trinity's mouth stretched wide. "Your aura just lightened, like, three shades, Alex. Now what happened with you and Vijay? We've only got a few minutes before the bonfire."

Jackie hustled to the door. "I'll watch out for Emily. Looks like she and Bam-Bam are still talking."

Crap.

Really?

Did I honestly just get trapped into this tell-all?

I whirled toward my suitcase. "Later, guys. Got to find a sweatshirt. Plus I don't want to miss out on good seats or the first chorus of 'B-I-N-G-O.'" I raised my head and howled at the vaulted ceiling, my trademark addition to the song. No one laughed.

"Weren't we just playing that game, Truth or Dare?" Yasmine drawled behind me. "Your cabin mates said it's a first-day tradition."

My hands froze, and I dropped my hoodie back in the suitcase.

"That's right." Siobhan clutched Yasmine's arm like they'd been best friends since preschool. "And you were already dared to sing 'Yankee Doodle' on the porch. Now it's your turn to pick the next person to truth or dare."

"Perfect!" Yasmine's eyes gleamed. "I choose Alex."

....

Air rushed from me as I turned. Yasmine smirked from my bunk—her bunk—and tossed a piece of kettle corn in her mouth. I looked to my friends but saw curiosity mixed with sympathy. Crap. I was going to have to choose. And who knew what wild card Yasmine would dare me to do? I took a deep breath. Maybe this was for the best. They'd find out soon enough anyway.

"Truth."

"Why would you kiss a boy you don't know and get in trouble?" Yasmine asked, her dark eyes narrowed as if prepped to see through a fib.

I plunked down beside Siobhan and traced my finger along the hefty spine of her math textbook, imagining it flying at Yasmine's smug, perfectly coiffed head. Despite the surging anger bubbling back to the surface, I kept my voice even. I mean, seriously, did she not sense how close I was to losing it?

"A—I didn't mean to get in trouble and B—since when is kissing someone a crime?" I slid back and pressed my tense spine against the wooden cabin walls.

Yasmine swung her legs over the side of the bunk and crossed them like someone at a Parisian café. La-de-da. "You ruined Emily's display. And you still didn't answer my question."

I popped another bubble, then looked to Siobhan. "I did so answer the question."

Siobhan shook her head, her asymmetrical bob swishing across her cheeks. "Technically, you equivocated which means you evaded the question with a non-answer."

"What?" I pinched the bridge of my nose at a sudden stab of pain. Siobhan was so smart she made my head hurt.

Actually, all the girls in Munchies' Manor were brilliant in different areas. Mine was more in entertainment than academics, my goal to win a Broadway role rather than a Harvard scholarship.

"Come on, Alex. Just answer the question." Jackie peered out the door, then dodged a Nerf football Trinity chucked her way.

"Exactly." Yasmine held up a brush and gestured for Piper to join her.

Who asked Yasmine anyway? And why was Piper hurrying to her side? My fingernails dug into my palms.

"Fine. I kissed him because I wanted to make Vijay mad."

Siobhan pushed up her slipping glasses and peered at me. "What happened? Last summer you were so into him."

"Now, I hate him." The words burst out of me. "He dumped me after you guys left last summer...right before the last bus took us to the airport. He called me a prude because I wouldn't, um, you know..." My eyes flew around the room.

Siobhan's eyes widened. "Because you didn't hook-up?"

"As in *go all the way*?" breathed Piper.

"Aren't you a little young for that?" Yasmine's hands stilled over Piper's hair, a nearly finished French braid angling diagonally across her head.

Saint Yasmine strikes again. Piper grinned ear to ear as she ran her hands over her new style, Trinity looked awestruck, and Jackie and Siobhan nodded at the old-fashioned logic. They already worshiped her, and I felt branded with a scarlet letter "A"—or a pink glitter one at least.

"Some girls are married at my age," I pointed out, just to be contrary.

Yasmine secured Piper's hair with a clip and frowned at me. "Unfortunately true. In some countries I've visited, girls marry as young as twelve. You should be happy that you are free to be a girl as long as you want. Free to do everything a guy can do."

"Whatever," I said, knowing how annoying I sounded but unable to help it. Her little holier-than-thou act was driving me up the cabin wall. She could have been quoting one of my parents' books. Ugh.

"So, because you wouldn't sleep with him, he did what?" Siobhan's pencil rattled along the spine of a spiral notebook. Outside, bonfire-bound campers flowed by our cabin, their laughter filling the night air. If only I could be out there, part of the fun, instead of reliving these painful moments.

"Right before camp, my parents did their daily phone check and caught a text from him before I saw it."

"What did it say?" Jackie looked away from the door as the rest of the group leaned in.

"He asked if I still wanted to be a virgin."

A collective gasp sounded in the cramped room.

"As if your choice had anything to do with him." Yasmine scowled, sliding on wooden bangles in vibrant patterns.

Finally. Something we agreed on.

"I know, right? Thank God my parents don't know the message was from a camper or they would never have let me come. But they are sending me to some horrible reform-type school for girls this fall because of it."

Yasmine's bracelets clanked as she waved a finger at me. "Maybe it won't be as bad as you think. No boys there to cause problems."

I ground my teeth but ignored her for the sake of peace.

"How did I not predict this would happen?" Trinity studied the stars through our window. Our resident astrologer held herself to a high standard of divination, but I was pretty sure that no arrangements of the planets could have predicted what a loser Vijay would turn out to be.

"You haven't heard the rest. While we were waiting in the check-in line, he texted me again, asked if I'd keep my legs closed this summer."

"Shut up," Piper whispered, sounding as shell-shocked as I felt. "So that's why you two were yelling?"

"Yes." I shot a look at the door, then continued. "He's like this totally different person."

Trinity pulled back her dreadlocks and wound a hair tie around them. "And his aura is off. I'll have to do a reading."

"I would have pounded him. What are you going to do, Alex?" Jackie's face was pale against the dark sky behind her.

"Stay as far away as possible. He's a jerk and is definitely not going to ruin my last shot at some fun this summer."

Jackie whistled, and the screen door banged open, a breathless Emily filling the frame. "Sorry that took so long, but we'd better get going or we'll miss out on a good seat. Alex, can you fill us all in later? Hope I didn't miss anything juicy."

"Sure." I hung back as Emily plunged back out the door.

"So you kissed that other boy to get even with your ex-boyfriend?" Yasmine made a disapproving noise and moved to follow Emily, the rest of the girls following like ducklings.

Did we have to be dutiful, good girls all the time and constantly take the high road? Was it so wrong that I had wanted to get back at Vijay for those texts? At my parents for ruining my life?

"It's not like I planned it. Give me some credit. But Vijay isn't part of my summer plan. Javier is."

The girls stopped and turned, their eyes on me.

"What's your plan?" Yasmine asked.

I dropped my hoodie back in my suitcase.

"Fun. Starting now."

A few minutes later, we took our seats on a log behind the Wander Inn boys, including the new-to-camp chess champ Siobhan had been talking about, Rafael Someone-or-Other. Julian, one of Vijay's friends, whipped around and gave me a quick smile.

My breath rushed out in relief. At least Vijay hadn't poisoned all the Wander Inn guys against me. Our cabins had been friends for years, winning capture the flag competitions and cheering each other on in volleyball tournaments. That had to mean something.

I looked away when Vijay glanced over his shoulder, not wanting to see this other boy—this mean version of my old crush. Instead, I poked ticklish Piper who, as if on cue, began to laugh. I joined her, whooping loud enough to convince everyone but myself what an awesome time I was having.

Then I spotted him. Javier.

He stalked behind the Warriors' Warden group, his fierce scowl broadcasting that he'd rather be any place but here. It surprised me he'd come since he technically wasn't a camper. But Emily had explained on the way that, because of his age, Gollum wanted him to participate in activities as much as his job let him.

Suddenly, his piercing eyes met mine, their dark depths glittering in the flickering light. My heart seized, and my fake giggle stopped at his scornful look. Was he still mad at me? When his narrowed gaze shifted away like smoke, I half-regretted dragging him into my personal drama. Either I'd been wrong about him as a fellow troublemaker or he just flat-out didn't like me.

Maybe I should leave him alone. But another look at his gorgeous profile changed my mind back again.

"Alex, would you do the honors?" Emily handed me the lanyard bag. Great. Now everyone would have a reason to stare at Miss Wholesome-Home-Girl-Gone-Wild instead of pointing and whispering like they were now.

I stood. It was the least I could do for Emily. "Sure."

Emily raised her hand, one finger pointing skyward until the group quieted. Bam-Bam stood beside her and gave me a nod that got me passing the bracelets out.

"These are Secret Camp Angel friendship bracelets, in the spirit of paying it forward," Emily announced.

"What's that mean?" called Cameron, one of the Warriors notorious for his unlimited access to camp contraband. "Can we make money?"

Bam-Bam cleared his throat. "It means if someone does something nice for you, you'll do something nice for someone else instead of paying them back. That's paying it forward."

"Right!" Emily nodded, her clip swaying with the overload of springy blonde curls. "So the person whose name is written on the paper inside the band of the bracelet is your secret friend. You are responsible for doing at least three nice things for them without revealing who you are. We'll be spreading camp kindness all through the summer. Awesome, right?"

A few kids rolled their eyes or mumbled, but most looked interested. Quirky Emily...she always came up with good ideas.

Brittany, a girl in the Divas' Den, spoke up. "Can we do more than three nice things?"

"Definitely. That's the spirit!"

I passed Brittany a lanyard, the strip of paper with the name of her secret friend woven into the braiding on the inside. No wonder Lauren had become friends with her last year. In fact, there were a lot of nice girls in the cabin we'd loathed until Lauren brought us together last summer. I even managed a smile for their redheaded ringleader, Hannah, which she didn't return.

"Heard about your lame kiss today," she whispered, snatching a leather strip from me. "Next time, maybe save it for someone who *wants* it?"

"How do you know he didn't want it?" I shot back, my spine straightening.

I spent ten months a year holding my tongue. I had no intention of letting Hannah walk all over me during my camp time. But then—weirdly—Julian turned around and exchanged some kind of look with Hannah and she got all...moony-eyed. What was up with that? Then she sighed.

"Hey, I'm just trying to help you out, okay?" She grabbed two more lanyards and shoved them at other girls from her cabin. "But if you *want* Vijay to keep spreading rumors about you and the cook—"

"Let's keep it moving, Alex!" Emily called, cutting off whatever Hannah had been about to say. "I see some campers who still need lanyards over here."

Hannah was already peeking inside her wristband to see whose name she'd gotten, so I left the Divas' Den girls to pass out the last few bracelets. This problem with Vijay was not going away soon. I planned to become a camp legend because of things I *really* did, not what Vijay *said* I did—or didn't—do.

I thought this would be my summer to get back at my parents. But Vijay seemed determined to make trouble for me—and not the fun kind. Unsure how I was going to handle that, I realized my basket was empty except for one last lanyard.

Mine.

Taking a place at the back of the crowd, I reached in the basket to retrieve my bracelet. The workmanship was nice—a brown-and-yellow weave that hid a paper slip inside. I had to bring the wristband closer to my eyes to see the paper better in the dark.

Javier. Kovalev.

I laughed out loud as I tucked the strap around my wrist and tied the ends tight. I guess leaving the new kid alone was no longer an option. And lucky for me, I'd be seeing him tomorrow when our punishment began.

Cleaning up the mess hall had never sounded so appealing.

Chapter Four

Javier

"Dude."

A voice near my head woke me. It was still dark.

I usually woke up fast from years of foster home B.S. You never knew when you'd get jumped by one of the other kids or have your stuff stolen. But this morning, I was still foggy. It took me a minute to remember where I was. And why the hell had I been dreaming about a girl with green eyes?

But the pine-scented air reminded me. I wasn't fighting for a breakfast, and I hadn't pissed off another foster father. I was at summer camp, and I'd been remembering Alex. And our kiss.

"It's not even dawn yet," I muttered, scrambling to sit up and figure out who was in my face in the middle of the night. My hands groped for my duffle bag, but it was still on my bed, safe between the wall and my body.

Blinking through the dark, I could see the shadow of my counselor, Rob. He stretched out his calves, already dressed in running shorts and a T-shirt.

"I like to run before breakfast. A lot of the guys go with me. You want in?" He switched on the overhead light, and the whole cabin groaned.

"I'm supposed to help with breakfast." I wasn't much of a joiner. And this summer wasn't going to be any different.

Rob frowned. "Gollum told me you could take off from work sometimes."

Around us, the other guys were waking up. The funny one—Eli, I thought—made a snarl of protest as he punched the floor. I figured that must be normal for him because no one paid any attention.

Until Cameron flung an empty pizza box at him like a Frisbee.

"You're dead when I wake up, man," Eli threatened, never moving. "That one had the Greek olives. Pepperoni I can deal with. Olives? You're now my mortal enemy."

"Shut. Up." The big shadow in the corner—they called him Buster, but I had no clue what his real name was—didn't move.

"Come on, Javier," Rob urged, his stretches moving to his quads. "Camp is only fun if you're all in. You've got to eat the marshmallows and do the trust course, you know? Have the full experience."

"I'm here for the girls." Cameron pulled a tank over his head. "I'm getting Kayla back this summer. Hey, new guy?" He turned toward me all of the sudden. "You've been warned, right? We're cool, but no one else hits on my girl."

"The girl who doesn't want him." Eli hurled the pizza box directly into Cameron's back.

"I'm not here to hit on anyone." I lifted my hands in the universal declaration of innocence and pushed back the memory of Alex's arms around my neck.

"Your eyes were all over Alex Martineau yesterday." Eli sprayed enough deodorant on his pits to quarantine the whole cabin.

I ducked, but a few drops hit me anyway.

"My eyes are burning!" Cameron screamed, grabbing a blanket off his bed and tossing it over Eli and the deodorant. He wrestled them to the floor while Eli shouted.

"Idiot! What is your problem?" Eli's muffled protests ended when Jake, a kid who was kind of a Rob-clone, kicked Eli's butt through the blanket.

"Enough, guys. Let's go." Jake had a stopwatch and running shorts, his spiky hair and toned arms all suggesting a fitness buff. "I've got a personal record to beat."

"You sure you don't want to run?" Rob asked me again.

I didn't mind running, but I figured it was probably better to get to the kitchen early and help Helena. Besides, even if these guys turned out to be cool—and the jury was still out on that—I didn't let myself get too close to people. They didn't disappoint you that way.

"I'm good." I grabbed my bag to hit the shower. "You'll probably only see me when I'm not working in the kitchen, which won't be often."

The other guys groaned or shot me sympathetic looks, but I was proud of earning my way. Didn't want their pity. I'd felt lucky when Helena, who travelled a lot looking for kitchen work, landed this job and offered me a chance to come along. If it hadn't been for her going to bat for me with social services, I would have been sent straight to the group home after getting kicked out of my last foster home. She'd said it was the least she could do since her record for writing bad checks, the same crime my mother committed, meant she couldn't be my legal guardian.

So feeling sorry for myself because I couldn't play in a volleyball tournament? Sing a campfire song? Not going to happen.

"Cooking?" Cameron released his prisoner and sat up on the blanket on the floor. "Like making food we'll be eating?"

"Seriously?" Eli clawed his way out from under the blanket. A deodorant cloud wafted out with him.

"Yeah." I shrugged on a clean T-shirt for the trip to the shower. "I like to cook. And it's going to help me save money for—uh—college." I didn't mention my mom. There was only so much these guys needed to know.

Eli's nose wrinkled. "Do you even know how to cook?"

That was his concern?

"I like to use a lot of olives." I said it totally straight-faced, so it took a second for Cameron to crack up.

But he did. I got a high-five out of it, too.

"Good one, man."

Buster, still under his blankets, gave me a shout-out, too.

"If I find olives in my food, there will be deodorant every day!" Eli shouted while the rest of the guys shoved their way out the door. All but Buster and me. "Every day. Do you hear me?"

If it weren't for Alex trying her damnedest to get me kicked out of camp for inappropriate P.D.A., this summer might not totally suck. I planned to ignore her. Keep my nose clean. Helena had bought me a second chance this summer, a place to be for the next few weeks until my mom could finish her sentence and get me out of the foster system. Reclaim me. But that couldn't happen if I made trouble at camp.

Or Alex and her famous parents with their TV show made trouble for me. If she thought she could start anything during our kitchen punishment, she was in for a surprise. I had to stay on my best behavior for two months, and no amount of girl drama was going to distract me.

But dreaming of her—the way her arms had felt around me—had eased something I couldn't put a name to until I'd toweled off later from my shower.

Loneliness.

....

Breakfast went by faster than I'd imagined, and before I knew it, I was alone with Alex in the mess hall, Helena washing dishes in the kitchen area.

I squeezed a rag over the cleaning solution bucket and couldn't resist another look at her. She was so damn pretty in a lacy top that showed off her tiny waist, her lean legs exposed by shorts that just covered her curvy butt.

I slapped my wet towel against the table and scrubbed, wishing I could erase her from my mind that easily. If she hadn't kissed me, would I be so attracted to her? I snuck another look at her soft chin and big eyes. Nah. I'd think she was hot no matter what.

"Javier, I'm sorry about what happened."

Her voice was a low alto that made my insides do something funny. I jerked my chin without looking up and went back to work. I needed to hold on to my anger at her. Otherwise, I might give in to what I was really feeling.

"I mean about the kiss," she continued, her voice louder. Closer. "It was totally my fault because I wanted to get even with this guy for calling me a prude."

My cloth kept moving in larger circles as I neared the end of the table. I'd taken Mr. Woodrow's suggestion and reread page twelve in the handbook. Five times. But knowing that I wasn't allowed to engage in "physical relations" with a camper didn't make me stop wanting to. Even if I was still mad.

"Did you hear me?"

Her question, spoken beside my ear, made me jump and knock over my bucket. Water splashed on me and the floor.

"Oh, I'm so sorry!" She grabbed a dry towel and dabbed at my abdomen, the brush of her fingers making my muscles contract and brain go haywire.

I stepped back and held my clinging T-shirt away from my stomach. How the hell was I going to get through this week with a girl who could make me forget my own name?

There was only one solution. I'd pretend she wasn't there. Ignore her completely, if that was possible.

"Javier, I said I was sorry."

I met her eyes and vowed it'd be the last time this week I did it. Deep green was my favorite color, and their expressiveness made it hard to look away. With any other girl, I wouldn't think twice about passing the time with some talk. But with Alex—a girl who fascinated me more than any other girl I'd ever met, a celebrity with camera crews ready to leap out bushes—I couldn't even take that small risk. No. After I said what I had to say, I'd shut up for the next six days.

"Fine," I muttered at last.

It'd have to do.

....

"Well, I'm sure you can hardly wait to be done serving your sentence with me." Alex slammed another cabinet shut. She put away a serving tray as the mess hall kitchen filled with steam from the dishwashers and the sink full of hot water I'd used to clean the counters and oversized pans.

Just like every other day of her week-long punishment of cleaning up after breakfast, I stuck with my vow and said nothing in response. I'd discovered Alex talked enough for both of us anyhow.

"After today you'll have the mess hall all to yourself." *Slam!* Another cabinet suffered from her bad mood. "You won't have to pretend I don't exist." *Thwack!* A cutting board hit the countertop as she reorganized them largest to smallest. "Or ignore every single thing I say."

Actually, I more than knew Alex existed. Spending this week with her had only made it harder to stop thinking about her. But getting friendly with Alex was out of the question. If only my eyes didn't keep following her around the mess hall. It's like they were magnets pulled in her direction whenever she came into view. I'd almost been caught a couple of times, but I'd acted like I was checking out something else. Smooth. Real smooth.

Plus, her personality had grown on me this week, too. For starters, she wasn't a snob the way I'd expected. She'd worked hard, never suggesting the job was gross or beneath her. Also, she cracked jokes that would have made me laugh if I wasn't still mad at her. Alex was definitely a smart ass. I wondered how a privileged girl like her had learned to be tough and down-to-earth.

"Last day." Things got quiet on her side of the kitchen all of the sudden, and I was tempted to look over there to see what she was doing.

There was energy about her, something that animated her face all the time. It made her pretty in a different way—inside and out.

I kept my head down, scrubbing the faucet handles and getting everything ready for lunch. To me, kitchens were the only place that felt like home. The smell of fresh baked cornbread, the hiss of eggs poured in a frying pan, the salty taste of crisp bacon whisked off the grill a half-second before it burned...it was familiar. Comfortable. I wasn't a misfit or a troublemaker in front of a stove. Here I felt I could do more, be more, than the angry kid of an inmate.

The floor creaked behind me, and I realized Alex was heading my way. Used to her making a lot of noise,

I had a bad feeling about her entering stealth mode. Especially when she was flat-out pissed at me for not talking to her. The first day of our punishment, she'd been friendly and apologized. By day three, she'd spoken only when she had to. By day five, she'd used hand gestures, some of them offensive enough to make me bite back a smile.

Today, day seven, I had the feeling something was going to give in our stand-off. I'd known it the moment she'd stormed into the kitchen with a pile of dishes as high as her head. I thought I had temper issues? This girl could give me lessons.

"Seven days, Javier." Her words were muffled, but I was listening hard. "You've ignored me for *seven* days. You can't take two minutes to explain why, after I apologized, you've been treating me like I've got a disease? I know you are capable of speech since you sing when you cook if you think I'm not close enough to hear. I screwed up, but I'm not a monster."

She joined me at the big double sink, picking up a fresh sponge from the stack behind the faucet. Dragging it briefly through the bubbles on my side, she got close enough that her dark hair brushed my arm. It wasn't flirting though, not with the way she jerked back and started scrubbing the countertops with a vengeance.

"Because honestly? I'd really like to know." Her voice hit a high, unnatural note, and I could hear a new level of emotion from her. Which was saying something, because she was the most expressive person I'd ever been around. More vicious scrubbing.

I felt sick inside because the tone in her voice suddenly made sense. She wasn't just mad. She was hurt. More than anything, I wished her mess hall duty was over. That her girlfriends would take her to whatever was next in their non-stop summer of fun, though I knew I'd miss having her around. As much as

I liked being alone in the kitchen, I looked forward to seeing her in it. Working beside me.

"Can you tell me why, Javier?" She stopped scrubbing, but I swear she practically vibrated next to me anyhow. A live wire of emotions ready to spark. "What is it that makes me so unworthy of listening to? Am I *that* boring? Or stupid?"

Her voice broke now, and I was afraid to look at her —afraid of what I'd done to her without meaning to. I cleared my throat, willing to try something, anything, to stop the tide of whatever was going to come next.

"Because I can't stand another day of talking and *no one* listening!" she shouted right over the top of whatever I'd been about to say. "I can't take another year of carrot cake on my birthday when my favorite is red velvet. Or pretending to be happy about a white nightshirt for the third Christmas in a row when—for the hundredth time—my favorite color is purple."

I turned toward her, not sure what to say, but hoping maybe she'd quiet down before Helena returned.

"*Purple!* Is that so hard? But I get it. No one listens and no one cares. So I give up!"

She threw the sponge into the water, the heavy plop displacing suds that sprinkled my chest and soaked my shirt as she stormed out the door.

Crap.

I took a deep breath and finished up the kitchen on my own. I didn't think she'd go far since she'd be in more trouble if the camp director or any of the counselors saw her ditch her job. But what would I do? Apologize for trying to stay off her radar when she'd caused all the trouble to start with?

Yeah. That's exactly what I was going to do. Because even if I'd had good intentions by not talking to her, my silence hurt her. Weird that she cared what the guy who cooked her breakfast thought. A part of me wished things were different. That I was good enough for a girl like Alex. Someone her *Wholesome Home* parents would welcome instead of blast on the Internet. But who was I kidding? My mother was an inmate, and I'd come close to being one myself with my last foster home fight. People like that set up charities for people like me, but they sure as hell didn't want to associate with us.

But maybe Alex was different.

She wasn't in the mess hall when I pushed through the connecting doors and looked for her there. Didn't answer when I banged on the door to the girls' room. So I walked the perimeter of the building, surprised to find her in the middle of the garden I'd been expanding in my free time. Long dark hair swung around her shoulders, the sunlight finding red-colored strands I'd never noticed.

"You're crushing the carrots." It might not have been the smoothest start, but it distracted her.

She clutched a wad of tissues in one hand, her knees drawn up under her chin. Her ultra-short cut-offs and lean legs were...not where I was going to focus my attention. But when I took a look at the red rings around her green eyes, I guessed she'd rather have me checking out her legs than seeing her cry.

"Wow. You *can* speak. And how would you know a carrot from a cucumber?" she griped before blowing her nose. "Not that I care. And what are you doing out here anyway? Are you enjoying seeing me cry? Well, you can forget it. I'm done with feeling bad about everything. I apologized for the stupid kiss, and if you can't get over it, then it's on you."

Her tough guy act didn't fool me. I'd done it myself too many times. I ventured closer.

"Helena taught me the difference between carrots and the cucumber sprouts." I answered her first question and ignored the rest. I untwined a vine from a pea plant that was trying to strangle a nearby radish. "But if you want to crush the carrots, go ahead. I just scrapped any plans I might have had for a carrot cake."

The snort she made might have been a laugh, but I couldn't be sure.

She scooped some loose dirt around the plant she'd mangled, carefully righting the stems. I watched her in a way I hadn't let myself all week. So much for thinking my interest in her would end if I ignored it.

You couldn't *not* notice her, actually. She was loud and colorful, from the pink streaks she sometimes clipped in her brown hair to the glitter she glued to her clothes. I knew, for example, she'd used something called a Bedazzler to try to write "GIRL POWER" on her tank-top. She'd told me in one of her rants about it breaking down when she got to the "E" and the "R," so her shirt said "GIRL POW."

"And you deserve to be mad at me." I circled the garden, checking on some plants I'd weeded the day before. Not wanting to crowd her. "I shouldn't have ignored you."

She lifted her eyes, and I felt her studying me. "Really?" Dusting off her hands on the back of her cut-offs, she jammed her tissues in a front pocket. "My father claims there's no place for anger in healthy relationships." Her eyes glittered, and her cheeks flushed a splotchy red. "Not that we're having a relationship—healthy or otherwise." She gestured back and forth between us, referencing the lack of relationship.

"I know what you mean." I snapped off some flowers from the oregano plants. They were edible, but any dishes we'd make at camp would only use the leaves. "And I'm going to disagree with your old man on this one. You had a right to be mad."

"Well..." She seemed surprised. "Thanks."

"A blog doesn't make him an expert," I replied, quoting Alex from earlier in the week.

"I know, right?" She stopped twirling a stem and looked at me. "Wait—were you actually paying attention to me this week?" She picked up a stone and chucked it at my boot. "You jerk. How's that for healthy?"

I dropped down to the dirt beside her, careful to avoid the plants, and handed her the oregano flowers, unable to stop the smile she brought out of me. "It's progress."

They were just a few scraggly stems, and she stared at them as if she wasn't quite sure what to make of them. Finally, she reached out to touch a small bloom, her fingertip grazing the back of my hand as she took them.

"They're purple." The wonder in her voice made me feel better than...well, I couldn't remember the last time I'd felt this good.

I guess that's the thing about a mouthy kind of girl. You didn't have to wonder what she was thinking. It was all right there—in her eyes, her voice. I liked that. Respected it.

"Your favorite color." It didn't make up for whatever was going on with her folks. But I liked putting that warm, happy smile on her face, especially when her sniffle reminded me how recently she'd been crying. Some girls cried to get attention. But Alex tried to hide it, and that made me feel worse than anything.

"Not white."

She grinned like I'd just given her something a whole lot better than oregano. "Wow. You are full of surprises, Javier."

"Not really." I wondered why I'd taken a seat so close to her. I stared at her elbow and calculated the number of inches between hers and mine. Less than two. "I just happen to know where to find the oregano in the garden."

"Oregano?" She sniffed the flowers. "Who would have thought a pizza herb would be so pretty? And you just totally proved my point about being full of surprises."

She tapped my arm. I realized she'd only touched me to—I don't know—emphasize a point or something, but even that quick touch made my body tighten, skin warm.

This whole moment with her, side by side in the garden I'd come to think of as partly my own, breathing the herb-scented air, sitting with the sun on our shoulders and finally talking together...I wouldn't forget this anytime soon.

"What?" I asked, trying to hold up my end of whatever we were talking about.

"You!" She laughed again. "You're different. For instance, how do you know so much about the garden and cooking?"

"My mother taught me to cook when I was little." I missed my mom. Normally, talking about her made it worse, but I wanted to share this part of her. "She worked a lot, you know? So I had to fix food for myself."

"Umm. Sure. Most kids make peanut butter and jelly." She tucked her hair behind her ear. "That doesn't explain how you can cook for a few hundred people."

"I didn't like peanut butter." I wanted to make her laugh, and I did. It was easy and a hell of a lot more fun than the slow torture of ignoring her all week.

I hadn't planned on letting anyone get close to me at camp, but with Alex, it felt easy. How weird that the girl I connected with was the one I'd tried so hard to shut out.

"I'm serious!" She nudged me again, and the heat of her seeped into me, making me imagine what this summer could be like if only...

"I wanted to cook food I really liked, so my mom taught me some recipes she learned from my Venezuelan father." I cleared my throat, debating how much to say about that. Then, because Alex seemed interested, I sketched the basics. "They met the summer before my mom was supposed to go to college. He was here on a student visa, but he stayed after it expired and they deported him before she had me so...I've never met him."

"Wow. Really?" She closed her eyes and shook her head, thick strands of hair sliding across her cheeks. "Sorry. Of course *really*. I'm just shocked. That's sad they didn't get to be together."

"Yeah. My mom didn't go to college. It's been tough for her, taking care of me."

"But it's cool she taught you to cook food from your dad's home country." Alex nodded and turned toward me, her green eyes locking on mine. The red circles beneath her eyes were almost gone, her gorgeous face taking my breath away. "That's nice she spent that kind of time with you."

The back door from the mess hall burst open, startling us both.

"Javier Kovalev!" Helena stood there in her white apron, her hairnet slipping, a frown etched so deeply on her face you'd never guess she smiled every now and then. "There you are. It's time to start lunch."

I jumped to my feet and so did Alex. I noticed she kept the flowers.

"Sorry if I wasn't supposed to be here," Alex whispered so Helena wouldn't hear. Then, in a louder voice, she said, "See you around?"

With super-human effort, I didn't allow my eyes to wander all over her. I'd be seeing Alex often enough, even if I tried not to. She was just that kind of girl.

"Yeah." I nodded, thinking maybe I'd go to one of those bonfires. I wanted to see her again when she wasn't mad at me. Even if it had to be from a distance. "See you."

As she walked away, her sequined shirt bright in the sunlight, Helena appeared at my side.

"I'm warning you, Javier. If you start something with her, you won't be risking just your job. You'll be letting me down, too. I vouched for you. Told them you deserved another chance."

I hung my head, visions of what might have been disappearing with the sun behind a cloud. "I know."

"No." Helena pointed a wooden spoon at me. "I don't think you do because if you did, I wouldn't have found you two out here alone. Another girl, maybe Mr. Woodrow might not be so rigid about the employee handbook since you aren't technically older than the campers. But with parents as famous as hers, you can bet he's not going to risk them bringing negative attention to the camp."

I closed my eyes, wishing life gave you do-overs. If it did, maybe I'd ask it not to let me be born. Then my mother would have had a normal life, and my crappy one wouldn't exist. "Fine."

Helena's chin wobbled when she nodded. "Good. If you're going to spend time with the campers, I wish you would hang out with your bunkmates. Or make other friends. Be a kid for once and have fun. Just not with Alex." She grumbled and stomped her way back into the kitchen, leaving me in the garden. Alex had disappeared from sight, but I could still see the imprint of where we'd sat in the empty rows between the carrots and the zucchini. The leaves of the carrot plant she'd resurrected now rippled from a light breeze.

Yes, she'd mangled it. But she'd fixed it, too.

So she'd made some trouble that first day. That didn't mean she would cause problems for me again.

Just once before I left this camp, I wanted to think about something besides my responsibilities and controlling my temper.

I didn't care about swim lessons and obstacle courses. The kitchen was where I'd rather spend summer. But just once, I wished I could sit with Alex again, shoulder to shoulder. I wanted to make her laugh and smile again, like a normal guy. Just once.

Chapter Five

Alex

"It looks like someone got a visit from their Secret Camp Angel," trilled Emily when I returned from a quick, post-swim rinse off.

I toweled my hair and glanced up at the package on my bunk. *Who had my name?* Javier had occupied my mind so much these past few days I'd forgotten someone had been thinking of me, too. I'd contacted my mom on my last electronics day, asking if she'd consider sending me a cookbook on Venezuelan cuisine as I'd suddenly taken a new interest. After some coercing, she'd agreed to look for eBay deals, and I was crossing my fingers I'd have Javier's first present soon.

But now...here was one for me. I returned Emily's smile and reached for it. Who didn't love presents?

"Looks like a book." Siobhan peered up from a periodic table pinned on the wall behind her bunk. "So much better than my gift." She fished a fuchsia-haired troll doll from her backpack and flipped it to Trinity. "Creepy."

The so-ugly-it's-cute figure landed in Trinity's cross-legged lap, breaking her out of her meditative trance.

"So not Zen, Siobhan." She scrambled to her feet and kicked it. The object rolled toward a laughing Jackie, who shot it at Piper with a fly swatter.

"Yuck." Piper picked it up and sniffed. "It smells like a toxic waste dump and looks even worse."

"The worst part was the note," Siobhan said. "What does 'pay the troll and cross my bridge' even mean?"

"Sounds kinky." I waggled my eyebrows, unable to resist teasing my serious friend. I kind of liked her Secret Camp Angel. He or she seemed fun. Speaking of which...fireworks were planned for tonight's Fourth of July celebration, and I intended to have a good time at them...with Javier if I could tempt him out of the kitchen. This was supposed to be my payback summer—the best time ever before being incarcerated at the boarding school. Time to make it happen.

"It's from a children's story." Yasmine zippered her makeup bag and turned from the mirror, her dark eyes smudged and smoky to match her flowing, charcoal caftan. If we'd been friends, I would beg Yasmine to make me over that way. But that was a big IF.

"It's the tale about a troll who guards this bridge and won't let anyone pass unless they pay," she added.

"I know about the fairy tale," Siobhan huffed. "I just don't understand how it fits the gift or why they'd give it to me."

"Maybe you owe someone, Siobhan," breathed Trinity, the faraway look in her eyes. "Karma-wise."

I expected Siobhan to point out that "karma-wise" wasn't a word. So I nearly fell over when she squealed, girly style.

"I'd like to owe Rafael Cruz." She slapped a hand over her mouth, her eyes going wide as if she'd just revealed a state secret.

"Heck yes. He's perfect for you." I took out a fresh pack of gum and offered a piece to all my cabin mates, including Yasmine. "You should definitely be pursuing a chess champ. Talk about karma. Or would that be kismet?"

Even Trinity looked unsure.

Siobhan studied her toenails, her voice low. "I just mean I like him as a friend, guys."

"You should challenge him to a friendly game then, Siobhan." Jackie sauntered over to study the troll doll, and I noticed Siobhan carefully steered the conversation back to the randomness of her Secret Camp Angel gift.

I put down my own present to check out outfit options. If it was a book like my friends all thought, I wasn't that interested. My parents made me read enough of the self-help kind to last me through three reincarnations.

"I think it's a great gift," Emily insisted, hopping into the conversation and holding the troll doll up high for us all to admire it. "Besides, it's not the gift..."

"But the thought that counts," the rest of us finished for her. We'd heard her say that to lots of disgruntled campers this week. While the camp had never been so energized, not everyone was a satisfied customer.

I held up a pale pink gauzy sundress and admired my tan in the mirror. Would Javier like it? My gaze fell to the wilted purple flower he'd given me. It dangled over the side of a half-filled Dixie cup perched on our window sill. He'd barely said a word to me all week, but the bloom must mean that he liked me a little. Or at least didn't hate me anymore. It was a start.

"That's right, ladies." Emily's gums flashed in a toothy smile. "And I've got a big gift in store for all of you!"

The cabin quieted. Emily had been dropping hints about a field trip ever since that first day.

"A rafting trip?" Jackie asked at the same time Yasmine blurted something about a local museum.

"Better!" Emily hopped around in a circle, dangly gold earrings bobbing. "I got permission from Gollum—

that is, Mr. Woodrow—today, and I'm taking you all on the set of *Mine Forever*, the historical movie they're filming in Waynesville!"

A movie? I almost couldn't believe my ears. How could Emily know my secret dream of acting?

Excited talk broke out in the cabin. Piper and Siobhan seemed the most excited, but then they knew more about local history than the rest of us and the movie was based on a nineteenth-century mining incident in the mountains. That part was kind of a yawn for me. But still, it was a movie. Filmed here.

Then Emily hopped up and down more.

"And you haven't heard the best part." She looked out the cabin door, as if she was worried someone would overhear. Then, leaning back in, she lowered her voice. "I think we're all going to be extras!"

"Extras?" Now this was getting good. Really, really good. Before I got too excited though, I pressed for clarification. "Like we'll be *in* the movie?"

"That's the plan!" Emily squealed.

I wondered if my parents would notice me if I was on the big screen. Would news of this trump their Twitter feed?

Distracted, I missed some of the discussion, although I did overhear something about having to get permission forms faxed from our parents if we wanted to attend. As if anyone wouldn't go. I'd probably have to forge a document if I wanted that to happen since Mom and Dad were halfway to Honduras by now. Still, I had to *try* to reach them.

"Okay, settle down, ladies!" Emily called over the din. "I'm not sure how many other counselors are taking their kids—let alone how many are going to help their kids be extras with mad skills like this." She moonwalked a few steps and spun in a circle, showing off her moves. "Not everyone is a fly chick like me, right, girls?"

A fly chick?

While we puzzled out another Emily-ism, she sighed.

"Never mind. Just keep the news on the down-low." She smiled at me. "Now let's see what Alex got."

I'd forgotten about my present in the rush of news. I zippered my dress, twined my damp hair into curls, and picked up the present. A loud rip sounded in the hush as I tore the brown paper loose. My friends crowded around me.

Wouldn't it be cool if I'd gotten the fictional version of that movie that was being filmed—*Mine Forever*? Not that I cared about mining, but I was curious now.

"A *Girl's Guide to Growing Up*," I read aloud, then frowned. What. The. Hell. Of course it was nothing remotely cool. "This is written for, like, ten-year-olds."

"That's a mean gift." Piper turned up our window fan. Its blades stirred the humid air but did little to ease the heat or my irritation. I sprayed a cloud of hairspray to tame my frizz, wishing I hadn't opened the present in front of an audience.

"It's even nastier than the bottle of Midol Hannah got," giggled Piper as she knelt and knotted her sandals' hemp strings.

The mention of Hannah distracted me from the dumb gift. "Hey, did you guys notice she's got something going on with Julian?"

"Hannah?" My cabin mates all chorused at once. Well, all but Yasmine who didn't have the long history with the Divas' Den girls that we did.

"Yeah. I think they're like...a couple or something." It sounded strange to say, but that's the vibe I'd gotten when they'd exchanged looks at the bonfire.

Trinity shrugged. "The Divas' Den girls aren't so bad anymore."

They'd had their moments at the end of last summer when they'd awarded us the dance trophy after a tie. It had been cool.

"The jury's still out on that one." Jackie snorted and swiped on deodorant. "And no matter who Hannah is with, I say the Midol is good for her. She's always P.M.S.ing."

"For her." I held up the book. "But what about my present? I'm sixteen, not ten."

"Act your age, not your shoe size," Emily sang in a falsetto that halted our conversations. She laughed and threw her hands up. "Sorry. Random Prince reference." Her eyes met our blank stares. "You know—the Artist Formerly Known as *Prince*?"

We shook our heads, clueless as ever about most of what Emily said.

"The '80s pop star?" Emily's brow wrinkled. "Anyone?"

Our eyes met one another's, and then we nodded—our trademark way of dealing with Emily-isms without hurting her feelings.

Siobhan's bunk squeaked when I sat and passed the book her way. I crossed my arms and tapped my foot on the floor. Did my Secret So-Not-an-Angel think I was juvenile? Needed to grow up? Past lectures from my father echoed from ear to ear. *How many times do we have to tell you, Alex? When are you going to act responsibly, young lady? Why don't you ever listen?* Only I did listen and what I heard was, "You aren't good enough." I popped in three pieces of gum, chewed until they were soft enough for a bubble, and blew, distracting me from the sound of his discouraging voice. It popped with a satisfying snap.

Maybe Vijay sent the Secret Camp Angel book. The more my mind turned over the possibility, the more convinced I became. He'd called me a prude and a virgin.

Now this book said I was a child. It had to be him, the jerk. If Javier and I hung out tonight, Vijay would think twice about calling me immature. He'd be wishing he hadn't treated me like garbage.

Pages rustled. "Hey, here's a section on dealing with your first period. That could be helpful in a couple of years," Siobhan deadpanned, her hazel eyes twinkling at me. The cabin howled, and I ground my teeth, especially when Yasmine's belly laugh rose above the rest.

Piper grabbed the book and opened it. "This part is titled, 'Growing Up is Normal.'"

"Not when you're living Alex's *Wholesome Home* life." Jackie cackled, then reached for the book, beating me. "Let me see."

"Oh, my turn next!" Trinity jumped and clapped her hands, the bells on her ankle bracelet jangling.

"Enough!" I snatched the book back from Jackie. "Do you guys have any idea how much it sucks growing up in the public eye? Every mistake out there for people to read about and judge?"

"Geez. My bad. Seriously." Jackie squeezed me so tight the air whooshed out of me.

I caught a few pitying glances before my friends got their expressions under control. They knew how much I hated it when people felt sorry for me. "Emily, do you know who left this?"

"Can't say." Emily glanced up from Yasmine's bunk where they'd been comparing nail polish designs. "That's confidential."

I popped a bubble so big it stuck to the slight hook of my nose. That figured. If I had a perfect ski-slope nose like Yasmine, I could blow them as big as I wanted. After unpeeling the mess, I slid into white sandals and headed for the door.

"Are we eating or what?" I grumped, more than ready to get out of the cabin.

Jackie gave the laces on her red hightops a last tug, then leaped to her feet. "Starving."

Piper held out a bag of pistachios. "You could have my Secret Camp Angel gift."

"That's actually a decent gift." Trinity peered over Jackie's shoulder into the pistachio bag. "Wait. None of them are open."

"So evil," Jackie laughed. "We have to re-gift those."

"Girls!" Emily pulled a pink Yankees' baseball cap out of her back pocket and put it on. "That's not in the spirit of the Secret Camp Angel."

"More devil, I'd say." Trinity nudged her Ouija board under her bunk.

"Maybe this wasn't such a good idea after all." Emily bit her bottom lip and rubbed the back of her calf with a foot. "It was meant to help you bond, to feel good about what is—for some of you—your last summer at Camp Juniper Point."

A wave of nostalgia crashed over me. I glanced around the messy room, loving how Piper's overflowing recyclable bins lined the far wall, how Jackie's basketball was always underfoot, how Trinity's tarot cards littered her bureau and Siobhan's books obscured most of her comforter. I'd miss all of this. All the more reason to make this a summer I'd never forget.

My eye fell on Yasmine's impeccable bunk, the corners tucked in, hospital-neat. Now that I wouldn't miss.

"It is a good idea, Emily." Yasmine pulled Emily's ponytail through her hat's opening. "Every day I travel with my parents, they try to teach me about gratitude and to share what we have with others who are struggling. If some of the kids at Camp Juniper Point saw the hardworking children in the countries I've lived in, they'd be grateful for the chance to just have *fun*."

I rolled my eyes but saw only my friends' rapt expressions as they hung on Yasmine's words. Of course, Emily hugged her in her own display of "gratitude." Was I the only one who felt like Yasmine clubbed us over the head with her messages of international wisdom? And what was the harm in pranks? My eye fell on the corner of the purple-and-pink spine peaking over the edge of my bunk. My book was the only exception. That was just flat-out mean. Especially if I was right about Vijay.

"In one village," she continued, hugging her arms around herself, "the women and girls walked ten miles a day just for clean water. Here you have lakes and rivers footsteps away, but does anyone care?"

"I showed my gratitude today by swimming." If this girl wanted to exchange wholesome, happy platitudes, I could totally go there. I heard enough of that at home. I clomped over to the mirror and borrowed some of Trinity's pink lip gloss and mascara. After applying the makeup, I scrunched the ends of my hair to amp up the curl. "And next I'd like to eat and be grateful for the bounty of our fields." I held out my arms like a temple priestess bestowing good will on everyone in the room. Then I quit the act and stuck out my tongue. "Everyone ready?"

Jackie snorted and shook her head. Siobhan tried to give me a scolding frown, but I could see the humor in her expression, too. Finally, I'd won a round with Yasmine, but seeing the way she silently slid into her shoes didn't do much to cheer me.

"I'm so hungry I'm ready to eat these." Jackie handed Piper back the pistachios. "Shell and all."

"You shouldn't have played that pick-up game with the Warriors, Jackie." Siobhan scribbled something in her notebook, closed it, and stood. "You used both free periods, and now you won't have time to get ready before the pyrotechnics show."

Jackie smoothed her Chicago Bulls jersey, then raked a hand through her close-cropped tawny curls. "I think I look awesome."

Everyone nodded. Jackie could wear a paper sack and she'd still look gorgeous, which was one of the reasons the boys always included her in their games— the other being she was a fierce competitor who led her team to victory nearly every time. I added a second coat of mascara, wishing I were a natural beauty, too.

We followed her out the door, my stomach twisting in anticipation. I was hungry, too—craving to see Javier. I couldn't wait to try out my plan to get him alone. What could be more fun, and romantic, than watching fireworks together?

Chapter Six

"Wow. This looks awesome." I examined the steaming spinach, cheese, and chicken strips artfully arranged on a round wrap that looked kind of like a tortilla on my tray. The smell of spices filled the mess hall, making it feel more like a restaurant than camp.

"Thanks, but I can't take the credit." Helena added a scoop of corn on another section of my platter. "This morning's delivery left out the ingredients I needed for the chicken potpie. I was in a panic until Javier came through. He even made dessert."

I followed her nod and stared at the handsome boy serving up what looked like puffs of fried dough sprinkled with cinnamon. Both looked yummy. The flash of his bright smile made my breath hitch.

That smile faded when I stepped in front of him. Despite the encouraging gesture of the flower, he hadn't said a word to me since that time together in the garden. But tonight would change all that. I'd make sure of it.

"Hi, Javier." I held out my tray. "You did a great job. Dinner looks delicious. Are they fajitas?"

"Arepas, actually. A Venezuelan specialty." He kept his eyes fixed on the cinnamon triangles and nodded. "How many do you want?"

I could have wolfed down ten. "Three, please."

"Chocolate or strawberry sauce?" He placed the dessert pieces on my tray. Thick lashes rested on his angular cheeks, his eyes downcast as though a look at me would turn him to stone quicker than Medusa.

Just like he'd been the week we'd worked together, right up until that last amazing hour we'd spent in the garden.

"Can I have both?" *Or a look from you?* I thought Javier and I had found some neutral ground. Declared a truce. Gotten a little close maybe. So why was he back to giving me the cold shoulder?

"What happened to apple pie?" a familiar voice spoke behind me, making my spine stiffen. Vijay.

I shot him a death look, willing him to be quiet.

"Aren't we supposed to eat American food on the Fourth of July?" he added.

Javier slid white containers filled with brown and pink liquid across the counter. I picked up the strawberry sauce and whirled, splashing my ex.

His puffy face twisted, his jaw clenched so tight I thought he'd break it himself. "What the hell, you little—"

"Let's keep the line moving," Javier barked, his forceful voice silencing whatever rude thing Vijay had been about to say.

"But I want dessert," Vijay protested, his thick eyebrows meeting.

Javier leveled narrowed eyes at Vijay. "Looks like we're all out of apple pie."

Vijay's mouth opened and closed like a fish, his skin flushing a deep plum shade. I clapped a hand over my smile to suppress a giggle that would get Javier and me in trouble again. And not just with Gollum.

Vijay jabbed a thick finger at Javier. "Watch it, man," he growled, then marched away.

"Great guy," Javier gritted out between clenched teeth.

I snorted, relieved he was talking to me, finally. On impulse, and because the kid behind me was poking my back, I blurted, "Do you want to watch the fireworks with me?"

"What's the hold up?" someone called down the line.

"Get going," another added.

I stepped to the left and waited for his answer, my heart in my mouth.

Javier's eyes darted to Helena, then back to me. He gave me an apologetic look then placed triangles on the next camper's tray. "I've got to work."

"I'll help you clean up," I said, trying to keep the pleading note out of my voice. My plan had to work. Not just for my summer of payback, but because I wanted to spend more time with Javier.

Javier shook his head and dished more servings to the stream of kids flowing by him, his mouth set.

Knowing it was useless to argue in front of others, I forced a smile and said, "I'll be back."

My stomach did a little flip when the corners of his mouth quirked. "You don't give up easy, do you?" His brown eyes flashed up to mine, then dropped once more.

It was all the encouragement I needed.

"Never." I added an extra swivel to my non-existent hips as I headed to my table.

Our chemistry was real, and we were overdue for a little experimenting. What better time to go for it than while magnesium and potassium (as my science-minded friend Lauren had once explained) exploded overhead in tonight's big display?

Once we were alone, I'd make him admit he was into me. I couldn't stop thinking about the flower and his hand lingering over mine. Something held him back from showing his feelings. I knocked over a salt shaker as I brushed by Vijay's table, pretty sure I knew what it was.

Or *who* it was.

Maybe my ex was to blame. Not that Javier looked like he'd shy away from a fight. The light silver scar that cut through his left eyebrow said he'd been in a few. No. Maybe he wasn't sure how I felt. Once he knew I liked him, he'd open up. Want to be with me for real this summer.

The fact that being together would help me pay back my parents would be the icing on the cake. I glanced at my tray as I set it on the table.

Or the chocolate on the cinnamon triangles.

....

"Alex?" Helena called while I wiped down the last of the tables and stretched my aching back. "Do you have someone to walk with down to the beach for the fireworks show?"

Out of the corner of my eye, I caught Javier's stare and felt a flush of pleasure. He did like me.

"I was hoping you might let Javier walk me."

"The big pots need to be scrubbed, and we need to prep for breakfast," Javier protested, looking incredibly handsome in a white tee that hugged his lean frame and showed off his smooth, light bronze skin. He shoved his hands in the pockets of his low-slung jeans.

The downward lines around Helena's face deepened. "I did want Javier to see the fireworks..." Her voice trailed off, and she looked between us. "You did well today, Javier. Your mom would be proud."

Pink tinted Javier's cheeks, and he smiled, the light-hearted expression transforming him from a smoldering hottie to a cute boy next door—the kind whose name you doodled on every notebook.

"It was amazing," I added. And it had been. The combination of spices with the dark corn wraps and grilled veggies had been inhaled by the campers. Leftovers were non-existent. "You're a really talented cook."

If anything, Javier got redder. "Thanks," he muttered, his eyes focusing on some spot behind my left shoulder. "But I'd better stay here."

Helena waved her sponge. "Javier, may I talk to you?"

I lingered in the now-empty dining space, not wanting to leave him behind. He'd worked so hard and deserved the fireworks show—both the one Gollum planned and the one I'd been thinking about for days.

Helena gestured my way and spoke animatedly. I wished I could hear what they said, but they were too far away. Darn. It looked like they were having some kind of disagreement...about me. Helena kept nodding until Javier stopped shaking his head, a slow smile finally softening the hard planes of his face.

My heart skipped a beat when he headed my way, his long legs eating up the space between us, his expression both intense and anxious.

His deep brown eyes searched mine. "I'll walk you down to the beach so you won't be alone, but then I'm heading right back. Okay?"

"Oh," I said to cover my disappointment. Didn't he want to be with me? Had Helena ordered him to act as my escort? "Right." If this was all the time I had with Javier, then I'd have to make the best of it. Besides, once we were alone, I'd do my best to convince him to stay.

But first, I had the whole walk to find out more about him.

"So...Kovalev." I started at the top of my list of questions. I only had about a million where he was concerned. "Is that Eastern European?"

"Russian."

"Do you have any brothers and sisters?" I asked once we plunged outside. The warm black night wrapped around us like velvet. In the humid air, the electric hum of cicadas trilled, and bushes rustled ahead when Javier's flashlight shone their way. The nighttime scurrying gave me chills.

But walking next to Javier? That gave me goosebumps.

"No siblings," he answered finally. "My mom never married after my dad was deported."

I slid my dress strap up my shoulder and caught his quick glance before he turned his eyes away. My heartbeat quickened. I remembered what Gollum had said about Javier being in foster care. "Oh. Sorry to hear that."

"It's fine," he said gruffly. "I never knew him anyway. Besides, my mom's great."

Did he mean his foster mom? I didn't want to be nosy. But then again, I was interested.

"Do you think she'll visit on Parents' Weekend? I'd love to meet her."

Voices from the beach drifted our way.

"No." His curt tone cut me. Why did he object to that? Were my questions annoying him? Was I? We'd gotten off to a bad start, but I thought we had a bond now after the garden. He'd given me a flower. A purple one, damn it.

My blood warmed. I was over people telling me I wasn't good enough. Even my Secret Camp (not-an-) Angel felt that way if the "gift" was any indication.

"What's wrong with that?" I demanded. "Why wouldn't you want your mom to meet me?" We stepped onto the beach near the kids sitting with their cabins or in couples, the counselors clustered near the tree line.

"Because she's a convict," called Vijay from the shadows to my right. "Didn't your new boy toy tell you? They locked her up and threw away the key."

My mouth dropped open, and I looked from a grinning Vijay to a tense, furious Javier. His face was so fierce I felt a pulse of fear...for Vijay. Would Javier look that angry if the accusation wasn't true?

And suddenly everything clicked. Gollum's comments about Javier, his work in the kitchen, and his relationship with Helena. She must be taking care of him while his mom was in prison.

Sympathy welled for this close-mouthed boy, who must feel as suffocated by his world as I did in mine. We were so different, yet the same where it mattered.

"I'm leaving." Javier turned, but I held his arm a second longer, hating for him to go like this. Stupid, idiotic Vijay. I could kill him. Maybe I would.

Vijay sauntered toward us, kicking up sand as he stopped.

"What's the matter?" Vijay taunted. "Gonna go home and cry to mommy? Oh, wait. You don't have a home...or a mommy."

Javier's arm flexed beneath my touch, so rigid it felt like stone.

"Knock it off, Vijay," one of his cabin mates, Julian, spoke up. He came over and put a hand on his friend's arm but was shaken loose.

"This is between me and Little Orphan Annie over here," Vijay sneered, just quiet enough so the counselors wouldn't overhear.

My head swiveled between an eerily still Javier and a restless, jittery Vijay. While my ex had more muscle, there was something in the coiled intensity of Javier's body language that, deep down, made me feel like Vijay wouldn't stand a chance. Javier could give him the pounding he deserved and, man, did I want that. But even more, I didn't want Javier to get kicked out of camp.

He might have to hold back, but I sure as hell didn't have to. I noticed some of the counselors had joined Gollum down by the shore, while others pointed to the sky. None were looking our way.

The first round of fireworks whistled as they rose, followed by a loud popping that captured everyone's attention. Everyone except the three of us, and possibly Julian, who still hovered nearby.

"Shut it, Vijay." My blood boiled at his stupid smirk. My hand rose, ready to smack it off his face. "You make me sick. Acting like Mr. Bad Ass around people who aren't allowed to fight back. Yeah, that's super awesome of you."

Vijay's face darkened. "You're one to talk, you uptight little—"

"Enough." Javier's steely voice made the tiny hairs on the back of my neck rise. His unwavering eyes held Vijay's. "Not another word about Alex. Ever."

Applause broke out after another flower of fire exploded above the lake, and I could have joined them. Javier was standing up for me. Or with me. For once, I wasn't fighting alone. A round of fireworks went off in my chest.

I glared at Vijay. "Don't you ever call me a prude again." I jabbed him in the chest. "I just have better taste than to hook up with a loser like you."

Vijay and Javier lunged, but before they collided, a bunch of the Wander Inn guys jumped Vijay and dragged him back to the shadowed edge of the forest. Javier stumbled, his unchecked momentum carrying him to the sandy ground. He knelt on the beach, his chest heaving, hands opening and closing in tight fists.

"Sorry about that, guys," Julian apologized, extending a hand to help Javier up.

"Just keep him the hell away from Alex." Javier released a pent-up breath. "Or he's leaving camp in an ambulance."

"So will you, Javier." Julian put a hand on Javier's shoulder. "Don't leave camp over something like this. It's not worth it."

Javier shrugged, his tense face starting to relax.

But I was still fuming. "And tell Vijay if he bothers Javier again—" I threw an arm around Javier's slim waist. "—I'm going to show his text messages to Gollum. He'll know what I'm talking about."

"Um. Okay. That's cool." Julian waved and stepped back. "Later."

"You didn't have to do that," Javier's low voice murmured in my ear once Julian melted back in the shadows. I had to strain to hear him over the crowd. "I was handling it."

"I already got you in trouble once. I wasn't going to let that happen again. In fact, if you want to go back to the mess hall, I understand. I attract problems you don't need."

My shoulders slumped. I may have won the fight, but I'd lost my chance with Javier. I'd practically clawed Vijay's eyes out instead of acting girly and squealing for help. Those were the kinds of girls who got purple flowers. Me—I was the one people ran from. Now it was Javier's turn.

Javier's mouth quirked. "I'll decide what I need." He put a firm hand against my back and led me to a secluded spot. "You attract more than problems."

I looked up into his large brown eyes, loving the red and green fireworks reflecting in their depths. "What else do I attract?" I breathed as we climbed a little higher up the hill, farther away from the campers.

His white teeth flashed in a devilish smile that got my pulse tapping.

"Me."

Chapter Seven

Alex

My heart backflipped.

Or at least, something in my chest lifted and lightened. At the same time, I was struck speechless, unable to think up a comeback for his sweet words. Usually, I don't know when to shut up, but with Javier, I felt tongue-tied. It seemed like saying anything would only shatter this beautiful moment.

"Here." Javier gestured toward the gnarled roots of a tree perched on a low cliff overlooking the lake. We were just far enough away from the rest of the group to give us more privacy. "Let's have a seat up there. Gollum won't see us. I hope."

I hesitated. It was the same place Vijay and I kissed for the first time. But then, as a parachute of red and indigo light popped over our heads in a gorgeous burst of color, I decided I didn't want to waste a second of this time being stupid about the past. I was enjoying the now with a boy who'd just admitted he liked me.

Sitting beside him on the exposed tree roots, I reached for his hand and rested mine on top of his.

"I'm sorry about your mom."

His jaw flexed as another flash of fireworks cast shadows on his face. "She's going to be out in another forty-five days. She'll be all right."

I'd meant I was sorry for *him*, but it seemed sweet he was more worried about her.

"Still...Vijay is an idiot to announce it to the world."

I wanted to know what she'd done to wind up in jail but couldn't bring myself to ask.

"Pretty much." He stared down at my hand over his while the scent of smoke drifted toward us. "When I'm done here, I'll go upstate to pick her up, and we'll try to start over. I can get out of foster care for good once she's got a job and settled. Then I'll be able to help her adjust to normal life again."

"I'll bet she feels lucky to have you." With a twinge of guilt, I couldn't help but picture myself if my mom or dad got carted off to jail. I'd feel bad for them—my mom, at least—but I wouldn't miss them. Not even a little.

"For almost eighteen years, I've done nothing but hold her back, so I'm not sure she feels lucky." He glanced my way, a half-smile kicking up one cheek. "You remind me of her in some ways."

"Really?" Maybe some girls wouldn't want to be compared to a guy's mom. But he obviously cared about his, so it was kind of cool.

A thunderous boom made the kids on the beach squeal. I edged closer to Javier. He didn't make a move to touch me, even though he had a perfect opportunity. Now that I knew he was attracted to me, why did he hold back?

"You're brave and strong. And you don't take crap from anybody."

I laughed, but a pinch of worry twisted my gut. "Strong...as in I come on too strong? My personality is too strong? I've heard those before, believe me."

"No." His answer was firm, and all of the sudden he squeezed my hand. Tight. "You stand up for yourself even when it's not easy. And you stick up for other people, too."

Once again, Javier left me at a loss for words. I had to swallow a ball of emotions welling up in my throat because no one ever saw me like that. Definitely not my family. Maybe some of my camp friends used to, although this year they were all too busy worshipping Yasmine.

The troubled boy beside me—in spite of his secrets and his determination to stay away from me—made me feel more special than anyone I'd ever met.

"I don't feel very brave or strong." I tucked my hair behind my ear as a breeze blew off the water. "When I get like that, I just want to lash out. Hurt the person hurting me. You know?" My heel kicked into the cold sand behind the tree roots, some dirt crumbling loose and falling toward the beach.

My whole life was kind of like that—the ground shifting and falling away from my feet until I had nothing to stand on. I was in my last year of camp, and I'd have a strict new high school to navigate in the fall— probably one where all the girls knew how to say "Yes, ma'am" in twenty different languages.

"Yeah." He nodded. "I get it."

"According to my dad, that's not brave. That's a total lack of control. It's given my parents a ton of blog material, believe me." Frustration gnawed at the back of my neck. "My temper gets entire chapters in their books. And it's gotten me in more trouble than you can imagine at school. When someone gives you a reputation, it has a way of sticking."

"Actually, I can kind of imagine." He tipped his head up as a huge canopy of fireworks filled the sky over the lake. "That's how my life is, too. There's this file on me that every new foster family reads, and they judge me based on what other people write. No one cares about my side of the story."

"Me either. Not until you." Our eyes caught and held, our breaths synchronizing. I scooted even closer to Javier, hoping he'd let me be near him.

"Alex?"

Something in his voice—the seriousness of it—stopped me before I put my head on his shoulder. I didn't want to make more trouble for him.

"Yeah?"

"That first day of camp, when you kissed me?"

My stomach tightened. I wished I could take that moment back. I hadn't realized what serious consequences there might be for him. Actually, I hadn't thought about him at all. I'd been totally selfish.

"You did it to get back at that kid? Vijay?"

So embarrassing. "Kind of. But that's another case where I got a little carried away. He sent me a text about—" I stopped myself, unwilling to share the things Vijay had said about me. "Well, he made me feel kind of low about myself, so I wanted to show him..."

"That someone else liked you."

"I didn't think it through," I admitted. It was weird to think my father had written volumes about me being self-absorbed, and I just felt angry. Javier never accused me of anything, but seeing how I'd gotten him in trouble made me regret what I'd done. "I just—"

"That kid would get under anyone's skin."

"He didn't used to be such a jerk." Right? I didn't have that bad of judgment. "But after we broke up, things turned...ugly. He sent me some gross texts that got me in major trouble with my dad."

"I'm not surprised your dad was pissed. I hope your father raised hell with the kid's parents."

My heart warmed. How cool that Javier would think of something like that.

"Uh, no. Since it wasn't public, he didn't have to blog about it. Our family is up for this TV show, and he doesn't want anything getting out that makes us look less than wholesome. Instead, he punished *me* and reminded me I'm nothing like my perfect brother–"

"Andrew."

I reared back to look at him. "How did you know?"

Javier grinned. "You talked a whole lot that week you had mess hall duty."

"You know all my secrets, and I still don't know much about you," I complained, even though I melted inside that he remembered so much of what I'd said.

"You know a lot more about me than most people." He turned serious again, his eyes locked on mine while rockets and Roman candles whistled in the distance.

But the explosions over the water were nothing compared to the fireworks I felt inside. I'd been falling for Javier ever since he'd handed me that purple flower. And now? I was *waaay* into him. What had started out as a simple scheme to pay my parents back by raising a little hell and having fun had turned into something so much bigger.

"Then you probably don't let many people get close to you."

"I haven't had much luck trusting people." His voice was soft, and I knew I would hear it over and over in my dreams tonight.

His eyelids fell halfway, and the look he gave me tingled over my skin.

"Maybe your luck's about to change." I drifted closer to him as if pulled by a magnet.

His forehead tipped to mine. Touching. "*Alexandra*," he said in a way that rolled the "x" into a soft "s"–a sweetly accented version of my name. "I don't think I could stay away from you if I tried."

Chapter Eight

Javier

And I *had* tried to stay away.

But keeping my distance from Alex right now felt like deciding not to breathe. Impossible. Besides, anyone who said she was looking for trouble didn't know the side of her I knew. Other people saw the fierce girl who didn't take any crap. I saw the hurt that had made her that way.

"I can't stay away either," she said, her green eyes huge.

Her emotions were all right there: attraction, curiosity, and a kind of wonder I'd never seen before. It shone in her eyes as clearly as the reflection of the fireworks. Girls I'd been with before weren't like that— willing to let you see what they were feeling without playing games.

Her hands fluttered around my shoulders and fell there, her fingers resting lightly, as if she might get chased away any second. I hated that she'd doubt her attractiveness for a second when I'd been thinking about her all the time.

"I have to kiss you." I think I was warning my conscience more than her.

"Well, you owe me one," she whispered against my mouth, so close I could have licked her.

But I didn't. I brushed my lips against hers with all the gentleness she deserved—this girl who was more wholesome than she would ever admit and too sweet to understand how badly I wanted this. And how much trouble we'd be in if we were caught.

I touched her waist, one hand on each side of her cotton tank-top. Safe terrain, right? I just wanted to steady her, I told myself.

Yeah, right. And I was going to be Camp Employee of the Month, too.

She tasted like bubblegum and lip gloss, smelled like sunscreen and girl-soap. I wanted to go on like that, breathing in the tastes and scents of summer camp and one of the best days of my life. But then her fingers tightened against my shoulders, short nails scratching into my tee as she deepened the kiss. The fireworks outside were nothing compared to the warning flares going off behind my eyes as she inched closer.

Maybe I should have known Alex would bring the same fire to a kiss she brought to everything else she did. Still, it caught me off-guard and...

"Whoa." I pulled back, taking my hands off her waist and capturing her wrists instead. For my own sanity.

And because I *really* couldn't afford for things to get out of hand on a first kiss.

"What?" Her forehead wrinkled. She looked up at the sky, still flashing from the occasional burst of light. "We don't have to stop. The fireworks are still going on." She looked over her shoulder. "And Gollum is way down on the other end. He can't see us."

"I..." How to put this in a PG way? "I like you, Alex."

She scooted toward me again. "I like you, too, Javier."

I closed my eyes. Thought about the consequences of letting things get out of hand. And steeled myself against the scent of bubblegum.

"I might like you a little too much right now." Gently, I untwined her hands from my shoulders and put them in her lap.

"Oh." She ran a finger over her Secret Camp Angel bracelet. "Sure. I guess we can watch the fireworks."

I breathed the scent of the pine trees deep.

"Is it okay if I..." She bit her lip as a shot of red streaked through the sky with a hissing whistle. "Rest my head here?"

She tipped her forehead to my shoulder and peered up at me. It felt good to have her want to be near me.

"Yeah." I nodded, kissing the top of her head like I wanted to. I needed to get kissing out of my mind. "That's nice."

"Can I ask you something?" She spun the bracelet on her wrist. "Since you know so much about me and I'm still clueless about you?"

On the beach below us, some of the kids were playing flashlight tag on the perimeter of the crowd. The hints of light coming on and off were like lightning bugs around the bushes.

"I guess."

"Where are you from? Did you grow up around here?" Her temple moved against my shoulder, and I smiled because I could tell she was back to chewing her gum.

"My mom moved us all over the place trying to find work until a few years ago when I went into foster care." I willed her not to ask about that. Mom had done the best she could. "I was born in New York, near where she grew up. But we lived in New York and Texas for a little while before we came here."

"North Carolina?" She lifted her head.

"Yeah. Just outside Brevard."

"I haven't met many kids at camp who live near here." She laid her head on my shoulder and kicked her foot so that her flip-flop swung from one toe. "Well, this one kid who used to go here, Seth, his grandparents actually own Juniper Point, and they live close to here."

"Helena has an apartment next door to my mom's old place." An apartment I hadn't gotten to see much when she was in and out of trouble with the cops and I'd been in and out of trouble with school principals and foster parents. If only I'd been a smarter kid, maybe I could have stayed out of trouble longer, but those first couple of years when my mom had been in jail on and off, I'd been mad at the world, exploding on anyone who tried to help me. "Mom thought the mountains would be a good place for a fresh start."

"It is beautiful here." Alex picked a few tufts of grass that sprang up between our knees.

"I wish I could leave when I finish high school." Too many bad memories. Me sneaking out of foster homes to try and visit Mom. Me getting yelled at by various foster parents. Me punching walls, windows, and—one time—a foster dad who'd tried to intervene. I was damn lucky he hadn't pressed charges.

"Really?" She straightened again, winding the long pieces of grass together, fingers fiddling while she snapped her gum. "Where would you go?"

"I don't know." I hadn't thought that far ahead. "Anywhere but here, I guess. But with Mom's parole, I'm pretty much stuck."

"You should visit me in Savannah."

"Georgia?"

"Yeah." She glanced at me sideways and grinned. "You can sneak onto the campus of my new school for 'troubled girls,' A New Day Alternative Boarding School. Save me from whatever torture they've got planned."

"That sounds just as bad as the group home they want to send me to if I lose my job here." Alex seemed too lively and fun to be labeled a troubled girl. It was funny that she and I faced the same future, just with different names.

"It's my punishment for Vijay's text." She rolled her eyes while the light show came to a finale, the lights flashing all over the sky.

"Will you be all right with that?"

"The workload will be tougher." Her fingers paused. "And I've griped about strict stuff, but I'm already used to people telling me how bad I am. What really bothers me about going away is that my parents are doing it because they can't be bothered to deal. They're probably glad to have an excuse to get rid of me."

Shaking her head, she looked back down at the grass she'd been braiding. She laid the green strip on my wrist next to my Secret Camp Angel lanyard and tied her creation beside it. "That sucks. But you might still make some friends here." Her father sounded like a major douche. How could anyone not appreciate magnetic, funny Alex?

"Maybe." She kept a hand on my wrist and tipped her head sideways as if trying to see me from a different angle. Her long, silky hair grazed my fingers. "But school won't have you. That's why I wish we could be together this summer. It's all the time we'll have."

My heart exploded. I wished this stolen moment could be more than that—a point in my life I could shout about from the rooftops and celebrate in public. Alex didn't make me feel like I was any of the things written in my foster record. She made me feel like none of that mattered—that she saw who I really was and liked me for it. Ironic that it took coming to a camp full of entitled kids to make me feel that I might be worthy, too.

Down below us, the campers clapped and cheered for the finale. The flashlights that had been darting around the woods bobbed in the dark, back toward the rest of the group. We'd have to walk back to our cabins in another minute before someone caught us. But right now, Alex shifted closer.

"Camp is turning out better than I expected, too." I cupped her cheek and held her still, memorizing her face. I wasn't sure when I'd get to look at her so openly again.

She studied me before closing her eyes, her mouth curving. We kissed, and I forgot everything else. I didn't think about foster homes or the fact that my mom was in jail. I didn't worry about not having any money and no place to turn if I screwed up at camp. All of it evaporated with Alex. For a few seconds at least, I felt like a guy in control of himself and his future.

Happy.

Inhaling the scent of her, stroking her soft hair, I heard movement in the brush behind us.

A flashlight swung in our direction. It landed on Alex's wide eyes as she pulled away from me.

"What the hell, Alex?" Her ex-boyfriend's voice was as irritating as the blinding light flashing in our faces. I tensed. Fists clenched. So much for that control I was working on. I shot to my feet, ready to break every anger management rule in the book.

Vijay sneered. "Do you drag all of your boyfriends to the same spot to swap spit?"

I froze, and my eyes went to her. She looked away fast but not before I caught her guilty expression.

The jerk-off lowered his flashlight as he swaggered closer.

"You're trying to rub my face in it that we're not together anymore, aren't you?" He shook his head, his features twisted in a snarl. "Is this how you get me back for sending you that text?"

"Is that true?" I asked her in a low voice, sitting up to shield her.

"No." She shook her head fast and inched up beside me.

I wanted to believe her. I really, really did. But a part of me wondered if her kiss on the first day of camp and now here, at her old spot with Vijay, was her way of using me to get back at him. Maybe her parents, too. What better way to piss them off than a good girl like Alex hooking up with a low-life like me?

Nauseous, I stood and held my stomach. Helena was right. Whether Alex meant to or not, she brought a lot of trouble I couldn't afford to get into.

"Give the bastard a break, Alex." Vijay crossed his arms and glared at us. "He deserves to know how much you like to mess with guys' minds. And I'd tell Gollum, too, if you didn't have those texts."

"Shut up!" She leaped to her feet, ready to do battle.

But it was too late. I'd already been cut deep. "Forget it," I told her. "We'll talk another time."

Her friends—and his—were already running up the hill toward us. Alex had other people to protect her. Besides, I needed to follow one anger management rule: walk the hell away. And that meant from Alex, too.

"I've got to go." I strode off, wishing like hell I'd listened to Helena in the first place and returned to the kitchen after dropping off Alex.

"Javier!" Alex called after me, but I could hear the quieter voices of her friends around her, settling her down. She didn't need me. She had her friends and all the attention she seemed to want.

And I didn't need Gollum to catch me with her or, worse, that TV network Helena warned me about. Alex played me, and I'd lost.

Even though I had every right to be, I wasn't so much angry with her. I was mostly mad at my dumbass self.

Chapter Nine

Alex

"Okay, girls, let's move it out!" Emily yanked the bullhorn away from her mouth and clamped a hand over her slipping beret. Its dark color matched her neck scarf, off-the-shoulder shirt, ankle-length pants, and flats. She looked like she'd stepped out of an old-time movie, which was completely in keeping with today's field trip. After getting permission from our parents, our cabin and a handful of other kids were going to be extras in *Mine Forever*. My mother had come through with a fax last night, just when I'd been plotting how to fake her signature and plant a form in the administration office myself. I wondered how much she had ticked off Dad for allowing me to do something he'd probably call "frivolous." But today, I wasn't going to waste time thinking about it.

A current of excitement rushed through me as I dashed down the porch steps into the dawning light. A wind came up and blew out of the woods toward me, carrying with it the chill scent of pine needles, damp earth, and the sweet smell of honeysuckle. It felt like a fresh start, and maybe, after three days of being taunted by Vijay and avoided by Javier, getting away from camp was exactly what I needed.

Javier.

My heart still squeezed up tight when I thought about how we'd parted. I'd made a quick trip to his empty cabin this morning, knowing the Warriors' Warden guys usually went running as a group. Javier, I'd guessed, would be at work in the kitchen, and I was right—the coast had been clear. I'd left him the Venezuelan cookbook my mom had sent me, a perfect Secret Camp Angel gift. He'd probably know it was me, but I didn't care.

What had surprised me about my stealthy mission had been seeing he'd kept the grass bracelet I'd woven for him. It hung around the wooden post of his bed. I hoped it was a sign he didn't hate me.

"I can't believe we're doing this!" Trinity practically skipped beside me, her long blonde dreadlocks bouncing. I couldn't read auras the way she claimed to, but I could tell when someone glowed with happiness. She had a new sketchpad tucked under one arm as we headed through camp toward the mini-bus.

Behind us, Siobhan and Piper tested out their old skills at leap-frog, a game that was working until Jackie came along and practically crushed tiny Siobhan as she vaulted over her back. They collapsed in a pile of giggles.

Trinity pulled her hair back into a bun. "Do you think this will fit under a bonnet?"

I laughed. "A big one, maybe. But it's worth a shot. Plus, the director is going to take one look at you, fall madly in love and say, 'Darling, you must be in all my movies.'"

She laughed. "Are you kidding me? I'm not the drama queen around here."

I peered behind me. "Drama queen? None of those in Munchies' Manor."

That set off more laughter as the other girls caught up to us. Yeah, I got it. They all thought I was the reigning performer in the cabin. They wouldn't even recognize the girl I was back home: Alex the Afterthought. The girl most likely to be swept under the rug.

When we boarded the van, I spotted a couple of the Diva girls and two of the boys from Wander Inn already in their seats. Thankfully, Vijay was not among the small group. Hannah and Kayla were there, and they sat next to Julian and Garrett. Hannah and Julian spoke quietly to each other in the back row.

How did such a great guy end up with the camp queen of mean? It was a mystery I'd solve sooner or later. If Hannah could snag a nice guy, surely I could, too.

"None of the Warriors came?" Jackie observed, dropping into a seat beside Yasmine. "Big surprise there."

"Why?" Yasmine asked, reaching for the box full of paper bags containing our breakfasts as a trio of copper bracelets slid down her arm. "They don't like movies?"

Emily boarded, and Bam-Bam slid into the driver's seat, cranking up the music as soon as the van door shut.

"They're playing sports all day since it's a free day." Jackie took a few of the brown paper sacks and started tossing them to people as we set out for Waynesville. "Jake is determined to win back the boys' volleyball trophy from the Wander Inn guys this year, so he wanted extra practice."

I caught my to-go breakfast and took a big bite of apple, grateful our cabin wasn't devoting every waking second to volleyball this year. The rivalries had gotten way too heated in the past.

"Oh, wow, the breakfast sandwich is awesome," Siobhan sighed. "So glad I'm not vegan. Sorry, Piper."

Piper dropped her apple core in her bag. "Apologize to the chickens. Not me."

"Long live chickens," Jackie agreed, halfway through hers already. "The food is definitely better this year."

Curious, I opened the foil container in my bag and found a still-hot toasted English muffin with an egg and cheese inside. It was a real egg—not the processed slab of questionable yellow that came in fast-food meals.

"I think it's because of Javier." Siobhan polished off her sandwich and wiped the corners of her mouth.

The whole bus went quiet at the mention of his name. Everyone turned to look at me.

"What?" I mumbled around a mouthful of melty cheese.

"Have you spoken to Javier about what happened yet?" Yasmine asked. It was a serious mystery how she could seem to look down her nose at me when we were the same height.

"To say what? I'm sorry my ex-boyfriend is a jerk? I can't help it that Vijay has turned psycho this year." Everyone but the counselors knew about the incident on the Fourth of July because Vijay had made a huge deal about it, calling me out as some kind of two-timer for kissing Javier under the same tree as him. While I hated embarrassing Javier, who'd been nothing short of incredible, I also didn't see why it was such a big deal. A private tree was a rare thing at camp. Could I help it if my options for kissing were limited?

Luckily his friends had kept him from reporting us to Gollum.

"No." Trinity opened up the sketchpad and smoothed her hand over a new page. "But I think it's hard for Javier being new here. Vijay might be a jerk, but he still has a lot of friends because he's been coming to camp forever. Javier really keeps to himself."

I didn't know what she was getting at and had no clue how to fix things with Javier when I didn't do anything wrong. He'd laid low since the incident, but I hoped it was because he avoided trouble and not me. Or was there a difference?

"Believe me, I've gone out of my way to welcome Javier to camp." I liked him more all the time.

Jackie let out a wolf-whistle at that comment.

"But it might help to let Javier know that you kissed him under the tree because you like him and not because you were still trying to make Vijay jealous," Yasmine pointed out.

"I already told him that the first time..." I trailed off, thinking more about how things had gone down on the Fourth of July. "You think that's how Javier sees it? That I kissed him just to piss off someone else?"

Yasmine didn't even bother answering me. She turned to Piper and asked, "Is this girl for real?"

I debated ignoring Yasmine. Taking the high road. But when did *she* ever opt for that route?

"Think fast," I warned, right before I threw one of those squishy balls with floating eyes—Trinity's most recent Secret Camp Angel gift—at her.

I would have pegged Yasmine in the shoulder, too, if Jackie hadn't been sitting right next to her. She caught it with typical Jackie reflexes while everyone frowned at me.

"Real mature, Alex."

Siobhan straightened her glasses. "Did you bring your new book with you?"

Piper winked. "Maybe you should read a chapter on the bus."

"I forgot the *Girl's Dumb Guide to Growing Up*." I faked a yawn to show their comments didn't bother me in the least. "But I do have a copy of a little volume I like to call, *Mind Your Own Business*." I stuck out my tongue at them.

Yasmine rolled her eyes and turned around again, facing forward so she wouldn't have to see me. Jackie hit me in the ear with the ball. Trinity tilted her head sideways, studying me, her drawing charcoal hovering over her sketchpad.

"Can you stick your tongue out again, Alex?" she asked. "I'm having a hard time getting the lines right."

I didn't mind obliging.

....

"Supporting artists report to the tent," Emily announced with uncharacteristic quietness. Her bullhorn had been confiscated ten minutes into our trip to the film set. Apparently her first announcement over the horn—"We've arrived!"—had spoiled a scene in progress two blocks away.

A set assistant had personally sought out Emily to let her know that bullhorns weren't allowed by visitors to the filming. On the plus side, he'd also been able to show us where to go for our work as extras.

He scurried away now, the contraband bullhorn under one arm while he waved for us to follow him through the crush of people trying to get near Waynesville's Main Street for today's filming. I don't think we would have gotten far if not for Bam-Bam parting the crowds.

"Are we supporting artists?" I asked whoever might be listening as I spun in a slow circle on the brick sidewalk, awestruck.

Catering trucks, RVs and Airstream trailers parked along all the side streets that led to Main. There was a small city of Porta Potties, but then I guess they needed a lot to accommodate all these people milling around in period costumes. Everywhere I looked, there were people adjusting makeup in handheld mirrors or fixing elaborate hairstyles from another era. Were these people already hired for the day? If so, there had to be two hundred extras at least. But then, it seemed there were multiple shoots set up. A handful of cameras surrounded a shop front where a group of well-dressed women in full skirts burst through the doors and walked down the steps to the street. Another set of cameras were focused on a group of children playing old-fashioned hoops and sticks, rolling the big iron hoops down the sidewalk. I tried to see everything at once, and it was tough to keep pace with Emily when I wanted to see what everyone else was doing.

"Coming through!" shouted a woman pushing a rolling rack full of clothes. "Make way!"

Piper put an arm around my waist and yanked me out of the way. Brown and gray skirts brushed my bare calf on the way past.

"I need to start sketching!" Trinity wailed, holding her paper tightly. "There's so much to see!"

The atmosphere felt so surreal. It was lights, movement, color, and chaos. I'd never seen anything like it, and yet I felt...home.

"I love it," I announced, wishing Javier was here with me, holding my hand. I was so happy I thought I might float right away.

"Hurry, girls!" Emily called from up ahead, her voice back to normal full volume, which wasn't much quieter than the bullhorn. "The assistant director says we can get in a street scene if we dress fast."

Putting my head down, I pumped my arms and sprinted through the crowd, my eye on the closing gap left by the rolling rack that had just gone by me. For the first time in my life, I beat Jackie.

"Whoa!" she shouted as I streaked by. "Where was that energy during the cabin sack races?"

Sack races? Like that compared with this? The incentive of a free bottle of Gatorade for being first to hop over the finish line didn't compare to the possibility of being on the big screen.

"Are the clothes up for grabs?" I tried to ask the woman who'd been pushing the rack when I caught up to her. Unfortunately, she was on a cell phone in a heated conversation about a problem with the wardrobe budget.

I hung back but not by much, hoping to pounce when she disconnected the call. The huge canvas tent was divided with a large side for women and smaller portion for the guys. We parted from the Wander Inn boys and followed the rolling rack over to our side, where at least twenty other women and teenage girls were in the tent in various states of dress. Most had on old-fashioned clothes already, but a couple of girls were in jeans and tees like us. The inside smelled like new vinyl and sweat, but I was too excited about the movie to care.

The woman with the rolling rack, Cassandra Pierce according to her VIP name tag, didn't spare me a glance as she disconnected her call, while other wannabe-extras swarmed the rack. She was a skinny brunette whose jet-black curls were styled like a forties movie star.

"I need twelve energetic girls ranging from ten to twenty years old, but younger looking is better," she announced, reading off an open document on her digital tablet. "Wardrobe is..." Her finger tracked down the screen "...dark skirts and homespun blouses."

"Alex!" I could hear Emily's voice calling me from the doorway of the tent, but I didn't answer as I dove for anything "homespun." "Are you in there?"

After a small tug of war for a skirt, I had a set of clothes for me and a second set I'd managed to snag before all the dresses were gone. I noticed a few of the die-hard extras had small suitcases with them, however, and had brought similar items from home.

Who had old time prairie gear sitting in their closet in the twenty-first century?

Hugging my loot, I called over the other girls. Even Hannah and Kayla were with them.

"Here." I shoved the bonus set of clothes at Siobhan. "They need people from ten to twenty years old, with preference going to younger people. You look the youngest of any of us."

I didn't really know what was going on, but I didn't mind going with the flow. And my instincts said the best way to get in a scene was to be dressed and ready when Cassandra Pierce said it was time to go.

Siobhan clutched the skirt to her chest while Trinity fussed over her.

"Cool!" Trinity squealed, taking off Siobhan's glasses. "You need to lose the watch and the jewelry, too, so you look historically accurate."

"Smart." I appreciated Trinity's artistic eye as I pocketed my watch as well and shrugged into the blouse. I didn't even bother taking off my tank-top. It hid under the coarse gray fabric of the stark shirt I'd grabbed off the rolling rack.

"Are there any more clothes?" Emily inched toward the rack, sidestepping women bent over open suitcases or seated in small folding chairs while they read a book or checked their phones.

Huge fans moved the stifling summer air, the electrical cords taped down on top of the green AstroTurf floor that had been laid down for the occasion.

"No." I tugged Siobhan forward even as I still pulled my own skirt into place. "I tried, but it was a madhouse over there and I don't want to miss when they call us."

"Wait!" Siobhan tripped behind me. "Go slow. I can't see."

"Sorry." My heart pumped hard, hoping to get picked from the crowd gathering around Cassandra.

I hadn't wanted anything this badly since last summer when I'd wanted Vijay to notice me. And even that didn't compare to the new anxiety level hitting DEFCON 4.

Quickly, I helped Siobhan button the small fastenings on the long shirt sleeves she wore while I backed us into the group lobbying for a place in the street scene.

"We're ready!" I called, waving one hand over my head until I remembered I couldn't button with only one set of fingers.

Cassandra stood nearby, running a critical eye over us while I finished the last fastening.

"Shoes?" she barked, making me look down at my navy blue Keds.

"I don't have any," I blurted, panicking, as I looked frantically around the room. Then, tugging my waistband lower on my hips, I hid them under the dark skirt. "I can keep them under the hem. No one will ever know."

But Cassandra was already shaking her head and moving on to the next extra, a pig-tailed girl who looked all of twelve, wearing scuffed brown suede boots. Heart breaking with the ironic realization that I would have been better off wearing my eBay hand-me-down wardrobe to the set after all, I felt tears of frustration sting my eyes when Siobhan shouted "excuse me!" in that authoritative, adult way of speaking the Munchies' Manor resident genius sometimes had.

When Cassandra turned, Siobhan held up a brown magic marker. "We can color the shoes. As long as we're in the background, no one should see."

I held my breath. The woman ran an impatient hand through her stylized waves.

"Fine. Fine." She waved us off toward five other girls who'd already been approved for the scene.

"Ohmigod!" I hugged Siobhan so hard she dropped the marker. "You're my real Camp Angel."

"Congratulations, home girls." Emily bounded over to sling an arm around each of us. "Represent for the Munchies out there, okay? I'm not sure what scene the rest of us will be in, but look for us in the tent when you're done. If it gets past five o'clock and we haven't met up, head to the bus."

We nodded, and I hugged Emily, too. My emotions were a runaway mess.

"I'm so excited," I squealed like a preteen after her first kiss. "Thank you for bringing us."

"Sistas before mistas, am I right? It was good for you to take a day away from camp." She held up her hand for a high five. "Sometimes, a girl just has to ditch the boy drama."

And the family drama, I thought. It felt good not to be judged or criticized. To be somewhere I fit in. Belonged. Maybe here, I could be good enough.

"Come on." It was Siobhan dragging me now. "I've still got to color your shoes into brown oblivion. You sure about this?"

It was no secret in my cabin that my parents were massively cheap as a method for teaching gratitude. No doubt Siobhan knew I went clothes shopping once a year. Anything I ripped, lost, or grew out of wouldn't be replaced. My sewing skills wouldn't save the shoes.

"Totally sure." I had to stop myself from dancing in place while she applied the marker. "My acting debut is worth crappy sneakers."

Although attending a new school in the fall meant people wouldn't know me, and I'd be judged by what I wore. Ink-covered shoes were never a ticket to

popularity. Javier's work boots came to mind, and I felt
a pang for everything he'd been through.

"So what do we do?" Siobhan asked a few minutes
later, slipping her glasses on to peer around the set
before the cameras started to roll.

We'd followed Cassandra out to Main Street, which
had been turned into an old-time town, complete
with spongy foam covering the road to make it look
more like a dirt street. The director—or whoever it
was filming this scene—paced in front of a camera on
a dolly, talking to three people at once. Mic booms
ringed the small section of street that had been altered
to look historically accurate. The signs had been taken
out of the shop windows. Trash barrels and mailboxes
removed from against the storefronts. Old-fashioned
dark green awnings had been installed over a bunch of
windows. But for the most part, downtown Waynesville
had already looked pretty historic, with the brick
sidewalks and low buildings.

"I don't know." I couldn't take it all in fast enough.
I'd left my normal life and stepped back in time. "Do I
look okay?"

"Um." Siobhan studied my face. My hair. "Yes. How
about me?"

My eye went to her bracelet—the Secret Camp
Angel lanyard Emily had made.

"We have to take these off." I started unknotting
mine while she slid hers off her child-sized wrist.

"Good catch." Siobhan smiled at me, her heavy
frames lifting higher on her cheekbones. "You've got a
knack for this."

"Ready, girls?" Cassandra walked over in her high-
heeled boots, careful on the spongy material covering
the street. "This should be a fairly straight forward
shot. The director is going to film one of our principals

walking out of a storefront with a crowd following behind her. You're part of the crowd."

"Why are we following her?" For the first time, I noticed a young woman with a small entourage off to one side of the set. She wore nicer clothes than us—as if she was a richer woman in the 1800s. She had leather boots with her skirt, the buttons showing when she moved. A white petticoat beneath made the clothes hang better. A wide-brimmed hat shielded her face as a makeup artist dusted powder over her nose.

"She has convinced you all to join her in protesting the conditions in the gold mine," Cassandra explained, moving extras around by the shoulders as if they were oversized chess pieces. "We just need a couple of quick shots to suggest the building momentum of the movement."

"Is this a true story?" I asked when Cassandra moved me where she wanted me—on the top step of a storefront.

"No." She seemed to see me for the first time, her eyes meeting mine. "It's historical fiction but very plausible for the time. When lode mining started, it was extremely dangerous."

"Thanks for choosing me." I was a gratitude machine today, feeling the love for Emily, for Siobhan, and now this total stranger who'd given me the chance to be someone else for a day.

Cassandra smiled at me, her lip piercing winking in the sunlight.

"Sure thing. Just remember to look sort of grim and determined, all right?"

"Got it." I would use the same expression I wore whenever Vijay headed my way.

My game face. My "payback is hell" look. At least, that's what I was going for.

"Places!" The pacing director stood still now, his attention on us.

A thrill shot through me. I looked across the store steps toward Siobhan and winked at her, though I wasn't sure if she could see me with her glasses off.

The blonde actress with the big-brimmed hat came our way and took her place in front of us as if she'd done this a million times. Another girl walked into our little scene with her. She had a hat on, too, but no petticoat.

"Quiet on the set!" the director yelled.

I thought I might hyperventilate. Not that I was nervous. I just loved the idea of becoming someone else. Of creating art in this massive joint effort.

"Action!"

I strode forward with my group, elbows swinging. Jaw set.

The camera moved with us. I could sense it in my peripheral vision, but I didn't look that way. I stormed up that sidewalk like my life depended on my grim determination. I was going to be the best extra in movie history.

And then I did it again and again and again. Siobhan and I marched up that street at least twenty times before the shot was declared finished and everyone took a break for lunch.

"So fun, right?" Emily greeted us later at the extras tent, her beret gone and a dirty straw sun hat in its place. "We haven't done our scene yet, and you can be in it, too. We just have to rush toward a saloon in a big group because we've all heard someone found gold."

"See what I've been working on?" Trinity stood next to Emily in the buffet line, still wearing her camp clothes—denim cut-offs and a purple T-shirt. She flipped her sketchpad toward me. "I've got a lot of touchup work to do..."

"Oh, wow," I breathed, reaching out to touch the paper where she'd drawn the scene outside the storefront. Both Siobhan and I were in it, right behind the two actresses. The other extras were less distinct. "That's incredible."

Siobhan joined me, her glasses back in place. "You must have had a good angle."

"I sat straight ahead of you in a lawn chair behind one of the catering trucks." She pointed out the lopsided green seat. "I could see everything."

"It's great." And I didn't just mean the drawing. I was loving the day. The cool experience of being in a film production.

"I figured it would be nice to remember our five minutes of fame after we go home." She took back the sketchpad as we moved forward in the food line.

My cabin mates talked excitedly about the upcoming scene outside the bar. My heart, on the other hand, had just taken a nosedive, ending up somewhere around my shins.

Five minutes of fame? Ha. I was used to fame in the most negative way possible. But now that I had a taste of people seeing me in a good way, I never wanted it to end.

"What do you want?" Piper studied a tray full of sandwiches.

"It's not on the food cart, that's for sure," I muttered. Grabbing an egg salad on wheat bread, I decided to use the rest of my time meeting everyone I could and learning more about the film business. I'd come to camp to have fun, not regrets. So I might as well enjoy every second before my five minutes of glory were over. For once, I got to play one of the good guys. My summer of payback was finally paying off. If only it didn't have to end.

Chapter Ten

Javier

The camp van rolled up to the curb about an hour after I'd finished in the kitchen, just as it was starting to get dark. Helena had chased me out early, insisting I find something to do besides cook. As if I would just stroll out to a bonfire with these kids and join them for a chorus of B-I-N-G-O. Yeah, that wasn't going to happen.

The Fourth of July had been a good reminder that I didn't belong here. Besides, the next time I saw that Vijay dude, there would be hell. I'd barely kept my temper in check, and I was close to losing it on the dude completely. This was a road I'd travelled before with jerks in other foster homes looking to mess with me, and I knew where it ended—a group home, a discipline record, and no chance of being with Mom when she got paroled.

So, for now, I watched Alex from a safe distance on the porch of the administration building while she stepped off the mini-bus with the other kids who'd made the trip to a local film set. I'd expected her to be the first one out, laughing and talking with her friends. But she came out last, and she looked...sad?

Head down, she scuffed along the sidewalk beneath the light of a security lamp. When her friends slowed down to wait for her, asking her something, she shook her head and the others hurried ahead. Probably going to the beach for the ghost story marathon they were having tonight. Even the counselor chaperones were jogging toward the cabins.

"Hey." I called to her before I'd meant to. Hell, before I'd even decided I should. My heart rate spiked, the traitor.

But then one corner of her mouth lifted, a slow smile curving her lips. Crap. Seeing her smile and knowing I'd put it there made it impossible to do anything besides walk toward her. "Hey, yourself." She picked up her pace, going off the path onto the grass. Her eyes drifted down as she got closer, zeroing in on the book under my arm. "What are you reading?"

A mischievous light danced in her eyes as we met near the trees that separated the administration building from the beach.

"A gift from my Secret Camp Angel." I flashed it in front of her. "Look familiar?"

She folded her arms, trying to give me her best poker face while the night birds chirped and sang. "I have no idea what you're talking about."

"I'll bet you don't." I tucked the book into a camp mail slot outside the building where I could pick it up again in the morning before breakfast. "I'm sure there are plenty of other campers who know me well enough to hunt down a copy of *Traditional Venezuelan Cuisine* for a gift."

She made a point of studying her nails. "There are probably tons of kids who are psyched to have a talented chef working at camp. Maybe someone is hoping you'll make more arepas."

I laughed. For the past few days, I'd been brooding over what had happened on the beach. Blaming Vijay, Alex, and myself. But when I had seen her thoughtful gift, I knew I had to see her again. Maybe I'd judged her too quickly. I hated it when people did that to me.

"That's a pretty good acting job. They must have loved you on the film set." I pointed toward the trees, thinking I should walk her down to the beach before we got caught alone.

Her expression shifted, the glow in her eyes dimming somehow.

"I wish it hadn't had to end. I'll tell you more about it sometime." She gave me a crooked smile, a half-hearted effort at best. "But first, I'm so sorry for what happened the other night."

I shrugged. When I'd seen the book she'd left me, I'd forgiven her. "You wanted revenge, and you got it. I get it. Only next time, leave me out of it."

She touched my arm. "I wasn't playing games. I wanted to be with you, not because I wanted to get Vijay back for being a jerk."

It was tough to follow her conversation when she was touching me. Two heartbeats slugged my chest before I forced myself to take a deep breath and step back. My heel jammed into a tree trunk.

"It doesn't matter." Even if I had forgiven her, it didn't mean we could be together. We might have more in common than I'd thought, but our worlds were too different. We were separated by more than rules in my employee handbook.

"It matters to me."

The fierceness in her voice shouldn't have surprised me. I knew this girl was a fighter. The fact that Alex fought for me—something only my mother and Helena had done before—was killing me.

"Alex, we can't be together." Line in the sand, damn it. I wasn't stepping back over.

"What's stopping us?" She looked behind her, her gray hoodie slipping as she moved. The thin, lace strap of a tank-top was the only thing covering her smooth shoulder. "I don't see any counselors. No Gollum. No obnoxious ex-boyfriends."

Exactly why I needed some distance. I had control issues of a whole other kind around Alex.

"I used the computer lab today."

Her eyes went wide. "You can do that? Campers don't usually have electronics hour until Sunday."

"Helena says it's cool as long as I'm not in there when campers are. After I got your gift, I wanted to read your parents' blog. Know more about you."

Emotions passed over her face in quick succession. Relief. Surprise. Anger. "Excuse me?"

"I read the *Wholesome Home* archives." My chest tightened up, remembering the scroll of endless happy family stories where the problems went about as deep as separation anxiety in toddlers. Of course every story that featured trouble had also featured Alex.

I could relate.

But Alex's problems were nothing compared to mine. She'd never gotten stitches in her hand for punching a window or gotten thrown out of a foster home for fighting with another kid who'd messed with her mother's picture. Those were my issues. Ones I'd been trying to control. I was a work in progress, according to Helena. Alex's family wouldn't begin to know how to deal with someone like me. Especially if I was dating their daughter.

"What does that have to do with us not being together?" She clenched her hands at her side, her whole body tense.

The sound of a twig snapping nearby answered before I could.

Signaling for her to be quiet, I looked. Listened.

In the distance, a flashlight bobbed toward us. I didn't have time to think. We were about to get caught.

I waved for her to follow me, and she did, quick and quiet on my heels. I wasn't just worried about what would happen to me if I got booted from camp. Now I worried about what would happen to Alex back in her "wholesome" home if her dad found out she'd been sneaking around with a guy like me. Or what they'd do to her at that school I'd also looked up. The one with the bars on the windows.

The flashlight swung in an arc closer to us.

"Who's there?" Gollum's unmistakable voice called.

We raced behind the administration building toward the mess hall and into the garden. I knew my way in the dark, weaving through the plants and fruit trees to a tool shed.

I even knew at what point the door would creak, so I only opened it a little way. Enough for us to slip inside. Hide.

Alex was in my arms in a nanosecond. Her arms tight around my waist. Her head buried against my shoulder and her nose tucked into my chest. Her breath came fast but silent, her heart pounding like crazy. As for the rest of her pressed tight to me...

Not thinking about it.

Not thinking about it.

But if I had? She felt good.

Alex's lips brushed against my cheek, and my mouth went dry. I held myself rigid, wanting to crush her against me but knowing if I crossed that line, I might not find my way back. I stepped back, but her body followed mine in the dark, her lips nibbling my jaw. I groaned, my control slipping out of my grasp, especially when her lips found mine.

Adrenaline rushed through me, and my pulse sped. My hands spanned her back, and I gave in with a moan, deepening our kiss. My mouth captured hers in a frenzy to make the most of this forbidden moment. When she stood on tiptoe, I parted her lips and slid my tongue along hers, tasting her grape bubblegum flavor. Her heart fluttered against my chest, and I held her tight, the feel of her soft body driving my senses wild.

My lips traced her cheeks, kissed each of her closed eyelids, wandered to her earlobe where the caress made her shiver. I inhaled the scent of her shampoo, something fresh and tropical, and buried my hands in her long hair. I tugged her head back so I could kiss her neck, my mouth lingering at her leaping pulse.

An arc of light swept across the tool shed floor, startling us apart. We moved deeper into the shadows, and I peered around the window frame. A flashlight swung in searching half-circles, but the sweep moved away from us and toward the van.

"He's leaving."

"That was close." She peered up at me with wide eyes, her chest rising and falling, her breath as labored as mine.

"Too close." I raked a hand through my hair. "What were we thinking?"

"We weren't," Alex sighed.

Unable to resist, I slid a finger along her soft cheek. "You should stay away from me."

Any hope of scaring her off with that comment faded when she grinned, her teeth flashing white in a shaft of moonlight.

"Why would I?" She stared me down. "I wanted a fun summer. And I can't have that if you're not in it."

"But I can't be part of it. Not really. We'd have to sneak around, hide. You deserve to have a boyfriend you're proud of, not someone like me." I had nothing long-term or permanent to offer her when my life was so unstable.

"What if I don't care about that?"

"I do." I shook my head, the air in the cramped tool shed suddenly suffocating. "I'm trying to do the right thing."

"Great," she sighed. "Another person protecting me from my 'bad choices.'" Alex made air quotes with her hands. Her voice sounded as bitter as I sometimes felt. "Well, maybe I'd like to call the shots in my life for a change." She flicked a clump of dirt off a broken tiller blade lying on the tool bench. "Get in trouble if I want. Have the summer I want to have. How about that?"

"How about thinking about the big picture? Beyond the summer. Who you want to be. What you want your life to be like. Or maybe you're just looking for a good time."

She opened her mouth to speak, then closed it.

Hurt by her silence, I went on. "And for that matter, with a camp full of guys, why kiss me? If you're looking for someone to get in trouble with, look somewhere else." Anger simmered inside me, but I knew I'd never let it surface. Not with Alex. Not with any girl. "My life isn't a game, so stop treating me like it is." I untwined her hands from my neck and brushed past her. "Do you *want* me to get booted out of camp? Or are you so determined to piss off your family that you don't care who you bring down with you? What if that TV network, BLISS, had been following us instead of Gollum?"

Shoving out the door, I tromped north toward the boys' cabins for about ten steps before she caught up. Jogging in front of me, she stopped short so that I almost ran into her.

"For your information, Mr. Expert-on-My-Life, I couldn't care less about my parents' stupid pilot. I'm already cast as the villain, so you can skip the lecture." She poked a skinny finger into my shoulder. "As for you?" She narrowed her eyes. "Try and remember it wasn't me who came looking for you tonight."

She had a point there. I dragged in a deep breath to clear my head.

"You're right. I'm sorry." I swiped a hand over my eyes. "You're the only...friend I've made here, and I guess I wanted to see you. Hear how things went during the filming." There. The truth. Or part of it. I'd never see Alex as only a friend. Especially after that kiss.

"Friends, huh?" She gave me a skeptical look, then laughed. "Right. Well, maybe we should just start over." She held out her hand. "Hi. I'm Alex Martineau. And you are?"

I couldn't help but laugh back and take her hand, my dark mood lifting. "Javier Kovalev. Nice to meet you."

Alex nudged me with her shoulder as we walked toward the cabins. "Good. At least that's a start. And the movie was amazing." She seemed to forget all about our argument. I admired that about her—how she could get mad and then let it go. "Best day ever."

Was it possible to envy a movie? I wished I'd been the one to make her that happy.

"I'm going to the *Mine Forever* set next weekend."

She went still. "What?"

"I guess they had trouble with their catering company. They called the camp to see if we could spare any people or kitchen equipment." I'd be cooking for a crowd even bigger than Camp Juniper Point.

"You're kidding." She took a step closer but stopped herself before she put her hands on me.

I swallowed hard, missing the feel and the scent of her hair when we'd kissed. Just friends, I reminded myself.

"I'm 100 percent serious. It's Parents' Weekend anyhow, so it's not like I'll have anything to do here." Most of the kids left the campus to do stuff with their families, so Helena could handle the mess hall alone.

"You're cooking for the *Mine Forever* cast and crew?" She paced in front of me, biting her lip and frowning.

"They only want the best." I grinned. I was looking forward to it. "Helena thought it would be good for me to get away from camp for a couple of days."

I didn't mention that Helena probably wanted me to take a break from seeing Alex, too.

Alex quit pacing. Gave me a level stare.

"You *have* to take me with you."

Chapter Eleven

Alex

"Ouch! Are you trying to hit every bump from here to the film set on purpose?" Although my tongue stung from the last teeth-jarring lurch, riding in the camp van beside Javier felt awesome. In his fitted forest-green polo shirt and khaki shorts, he was handsomer than ever. Better yet, he was all mine...for the day at least. And I intended to make the most of it. This was supposed to be the best summer ever. Payback. Riding with Javier made me feel like that was possible.

His large hands rested on the wheel, his chocolate eyes sliding my way, one side of his mouth lifting. "We just got on the main road and you're already complaining? This is going to be a long day."

"Speak for yourself." I crossed my arms and leaned my cheek against the warm window glass, grateful Helena had let him drive. He was seventeen, after all, and he had his license. Best of all, that meant no chaperone for the whole day.

Even though I was officially spending Saturday helping Javier cater the movie set, I planned to peek in on the filming, too. I'd thought of little else since my last trip there—that and the feel of Javier's strong arms around me in the tool shed.

"So how long before you ditch me for the big screen?" Javier's biceps flexed as he down-shifted, the early morning sun making his bronze skin glow. Saliva flooded my mouth. *Down girl.*

"Sick of me already?" I swatted his thigh, the downy hairs tickling my palm. He jerked away as though my touch was fire.

"Knock it off, Alex." His voice sounded lower than ever, its huskiness sparking the jittery feeling I got whenever he was near. And in the close confines of the van, we were as alone as camp would ever allow. "We're friends, remember? You know we can't flirt."

"Hey, those are your rules. Not mine." I tickled his earlobe until he chuckled and swatted me away. "Besides, this may be the only alone time we get today."

"Don't remind me." Javier cranked down his window, and the fresh, pine-scented air doused us like a cold shower. "How much longer is this ride?"

"Come on, you love it. Why else would you have invited me?" How awesome that I got to go with him. It had to mean he like liked me.

"Because you begged when Helena asked for volunteers." He punched on the radio, and a classic rock song rumbled out of the speakers. His head bobbed along with the bass, rattling the doors, a deep dimple popping in his cheek.

"Details, details." I flicked a gnat away from my shoulder, hoping the gesture would draw his attention off the road and back on to me. Where it belonged. "We were destined to have this day together."

His fingers walked up the side of my arm and stopped to lightly chuck my chin before returning to the wheel. "You're like that gnat—always buzzing around."

"Like a fly to honey." I laid my head on his broad shoulder, loving the feel of his worn tee over hard, shifting muscles.

For a second, it felt like he leaned his cheek against the top of my head, but another bump sent me sliding away.

"You did that on purpose."

"Maybe it was destiny." Laughter filled his voice.

I waved back at a couple of roadside vegetable stand owners, then glanced at his smirking profile. But so what? I was glad for the day of freedom. This wasn't just freedom from my parents and *Wholesome Home*. Today was freedom from everything. I'd even ignored a letter I got postmarked from Honduras. So not ready to deal with whatever my parents had sent.

I curled my legs beneath me, the vinyl seat sticky and summer-slick while the folded envelope shifted against my thigh pocket. "Whatever. How much longer until we get there?"

"Seriously?" His grin was open, wide, and ungodly hot.

I blinked up at him, loving the way he'd lost his battle not to have fun around me. I never made anyone laugh at home. Usually it was all disapproving glances and lectures.

"I kind of need to pee."

A long breath made his chest rise and fall. "And you didn't take care of that before we left?"

"Maybe if you hadn't rushed me—"

"Fine. We can stop in Waynesville. I was planning to anyway to take my mom's weekend call." He held up a cell phone. "Helena's number is on her approved list at the jail."

"Then you'd better speed it up. I think my grandfather could have lapped us on his walker."

"Don't make me pull this van over, missy," Javier growled, his fingers tapping on the steering wheel to another classic tune, the streaming sunshine spinning his profile into gold.

Goosebumps rose on my arms. "Say that again!"

He shot me a surprised look. "Don't make me pull this van over?"

"No—missy. It helps me get in character in case they need an extra. Don't forget, I'm just a poor mining girl from a hundred years ago."

"There's nothing poor about you, Alex."

I shuffled my scuffed shoes. "What makes you say that? I don't have anything nice."

"At least your family's together. If you get in a fight, you go to your room or something. If I get in a fight, I get kicked out of the house and I'm onto a new family, new school, new rules." He shook his head.

"So what's the deal with your family? Why is your mom in jail?"

Javier's lips turned down, and suddenly I wished I'd kept things light.

"Sorry. You don't have to talk about it." This time when I placed my hand on his knee, he didn't shy away. One-story houses began to appear between the thinning trees, an occasional business flashing by.

After a long moment of silence, his hand slipped down to hold mine. It felt warm and clammy at once.

"Bad checks. She couldn't keep up with daycare, babysitting, and all her other bills on a waitress's salary. Eventually she wrote some checks she thought would clear but didn't and they took her away. After a few times, it's a big deal." Javier cleared his throat and was quiet for a while before he spoke again. "She'd been fixing up our apartment in September when they arrested her this last time. It would have been my first time out of foster care in a while."

"That sucks." It seemed so inadequate, but it pretty much summed everything up. How weird that all Javier wanted was to have a home and all I wanted was to get out of mine. "So do you guys ever see each other?"

"Yeah." Javier hit the brakes when a couple of bike-riding kids wove in and out of our lane. "I visit, and she calls every Saturday morning."

"You must miss her." It was hard to imagine since I couldn't wait to get away from my family, but Javier's voice sounded so wistful it made me wish I had that kind of bond with my mom, too.

"Yeah. But we'll be together when she's paroled. I hope." My heart ached for him. It sounded like he loved her so much. "I've got to maintain good behavior and keep my nose clean at camp since Helena really went out on a limb to have me here. If Gollum tells my caseworker I haven't caused any trouble, I'll be able to be with my mom at the end of the summer. Although, technically, I'm not allowed to move in with her until she finds a job and a place for us."

"Maybe that won't take very long. She has waitressing experience." I gripped my seatbelt as a weird idea struck. Mom. One of her good works was helping to rehabilitate women coming out of rehab, abusive homes, or jail. Could she help Javier's mom when she got out?

"Yeah, but she's also got a felony charge she has to report on every job application. It's not easy for ex-cons to get jobs." Javier blinked up at the ceiling, then back down at the road. "Basically, I'm the reason her life sucks."

I winced at the wound in his words. How could anyone as awesome as Javier make anyone's life bad?

"Bet she doesn't think so."

Javier took his eyes off the route long enough to give me a half-smile. "She says that all the time. How did you know?"

My breath rushed out when he faced forward once more, his cut jaw and straight nose making him look like an actor instead of a chef. Javier was hotness times a million from any distance. But this close, he was gorgeous times infinity.

"Because anyone who knows you knows you're special."

His hand squeezed mine, then returned to the wheel. "That's the nicest thing anyone's ever said to me."

"I mean it."

"I believe you."

"Finally." I biffed him on the shoulder. My stomach rumbled as I spotted a Dairy Queen. Time to lighten the mood. This was my fun summer. Fun. And Javier could use some as much as me. "Hey, can we stop for a Peanut Buster Parfait?"

"It still doesn't mean we can be a couple." The cords on his neck shifted as he shook his head. "And we can't stop yet."

"Grinch. And again—your rules."

"You're impossible." His low, rumbling laugh sounded in the cramped space. "Has anyone told you that before?"

"My parents. Every day of my life. How about a banana split?"

"For breakfast? And wow, that sucks."

"Yeah. Like why is eating ice cream for breakfast wrong? I totally would if my parents would buy anything with refined sugar, but—"

"No." Javier was sexy when he smiled. But his warm, sympathetic expression stopped my heart. "I meant that being criticized all the time sucks."

"It's hard not to believe what you always hear." A salty stinging pricked the backs of my eyes. I rubbed my temples and stared out at a man watering his front lawn. It was as useless a gesture in this heat as my mini-rebellion. But darned if I'd give it up.

"Then believe this." Javier slowed for a stop sign and paused a second to look my way. "I think you are amazing."

My mouth dropped. "I think you are, too," I whispered, my pulse tripping over itself in its rush to flood my heart.

Javier's lips twisted, and his eyes swung forward as he accelerated again. "Tell that to the judge. Nothing special here."

"Duh. You're like the most interesting thing to happen at camp in forever. And if you loosened up a little, you'd even look like you were having a good time. Try not to work so hard and act more spontaneous."

"Fun, huh? Spontaneous?" His thick dark hair slid forward as his head banged to the squealing guitar solo blasting from the speakers. "Like this?"

"Only if you want to look like a total loser."

We cracked up, the sound shaving a hundred pounds off the mood. "Just don't always do what people expect," I added.

"Right. Like that's a choice." A tinge of bitterness entered Javier's voice. His hands tightened on the wheel. "Everyone expects a convict's son will wind up in jail, too. I have to act better than everyone else because I always get judged."

A car dealership full of gleaming Fords and Chevys blurred by us in a rainbow of colors. "I can relate. My brother Andrew is like the golden child, and I'm devil's spawn."

"Devil's spawn?" Javier tucked a strand of hair behind my ear, the gesture making my spine tingle with electric warmth. "An angel's more like it."

For a moment, I sat in stunned silence. Now *that* was the nicest thing anyone had ever said to me.

"Wow. Guess I *can* stop the chatter for a minute."

My heart pounded. "Say that all day, and I won't say a word."

"I wish I could, but we're here."

Was it my imagination, or did he sound apologetic? The blinker clicked on, and we turned left into a gas station parking lot. "My mom should call soon." He pulled out Helena's cell phone. "I'll talk to her while you're inside. Okay?"

I nodded and wobbled out of the van's cab, mind reeling from his beautiful compliment. Was there any chance he meant it?

Chapter Twelve

Javier

I watched Alex sashay across the parking lot in that exaggerated way that made me want to laugh and kiss her at the same time. Damn. In her tied-up white tee and cut-off jeans, she was devil and angel. That gold strip of flat belly above her low-rider shorts was hot.

When she disappeared inside the wood-varnished store, the world rushed in on me again. A horn honked to my right, and I jogged to a nearby bench, the gravel crunching under my work boots. Why was I letting this girl mess with my head? I knew what the plan was. Understood the stakes. Yet here I was, drooling after Alex like that panting bulldog tied up under a nearby oak. The dog stood, lumbering over to greet me.

Time to focus on my goal of getting Mom's life back on track. I needed to graduate high school and find a decent job to support us and pay her bills when she got out of jail. It was the only way to guarantee we'd stay together and she wouldn't go back to prison. But if I got kicked out of the foster system or moved too much to graduate on time, my permanent record would follow me around like a red flag with the message "TROUBLE." Who'd hire me then? I had to be there for her.

I stared down at the black reflective screen, willing it to ring. Nope. There wasn't a chance I'd risk letting down Mom, no matter how much I liked Alex. And, yeah, I could admit that now. I knew she wasn't just trying to play me. She was real and down-to-earth and sexy without even trying. But her parents were practically national treasures. Hooking up would cause major problems for her. She was a *Wholesome Home* kid, and I was anything but.

The phone buzzed in my hand like a trapped bee. I raised it to my ear.

"Mom?"

"Hi, Javi. What's new at camp?"

Since I'd come to Camp Juniper Point, Mom couldn't hear enough stories. It sucker-punched me to think her interest in the great outdoors came from never getting to see them herself.

"I'm not at camp today." A wet nose rubbed against my calf, and I ruffled the bulldog's short ears.

"Are you in trouble?" Mom's voice rose. I could hear her fingernails tapping against the payphone at the jail, a babble of voices in the background.

"No. No. It's good. I got a temporary job with a catering company this weekend. It's for a movie." My chest swelled a little at that. It still felt unreal to be picked to cook alongside professionals.

"Wow. Big time. You always loved learning those Venezuelan recipes I taught you. There was the *perico*—those eggs you used to make me for breakfast when you were twelve, remember?"

My throat closed around itself. How could I forget? It was the last full year we'd lived together. She'd taken off for work in the next state over, and I'd been stuck alone all the time, wondering when she'd return. It had been right after we'd moved to North Carolina and she'd moved next to Helena, a friend she didn't think would mind checking up on me every now and then. But that year, things had started to fall apart. Two years after that, she was in jail again.

"Javi?"

"Yeah, Mom." I rubbed my eyes. The sun was too bright so I strode under the tree, the dog on my heels. "I remember."

"So how's that camp director doing? What'd you call him?"

"Gollum." I plucked off a broad oak leaf and fanned the panting dog. If I had a breath mint, I would have slipped him one. He reeked, and his gooey saliva kept landing on my ankles.

My mother chuckled. "That's right. Did he swallow that precious whistle of his yet?"

"Mom."

"It's a joke, Javi. Sheesh. Always so serious. Now. Did you go on any canoe trips? Mountain hikes? No, wait. Didn't you say there was a camp scavenger hunt the last time we talked?"

I paced, hating to make up stories. Lying about working felt wrong, but she'd vetoed the idea when Helena called her with it. Out of options, we'd told her I'd accepted a scholarship instead of a job. If she knew I was cleaning dishes instead of having a wild, fun summer, she'd be sad. Mad even.

"We had to hunt for things that started with the letter 'S,' so first I had to find a spoon, which was easy because I was already in the kitchen."

"Hey," my mother interrupted, her voice harsh. "Trying to talk to my kid here so wait your turn."

"Mom, do you need to go?" I tossed the bulldog's soggy ball and took my first odor-free breath when he ran for it on his long lead.

"No, but this lady's going to be taking a hike in a second if she keeps bugging me. Go ahead, sweetheart. So what else did you have to find?"

"Then we had to find a shell." A small breeze lifted my hair off my sweating forehead. I should have gotten a buzz cut before summer started. "So I went down to the beach—"

"When did you go on a scavenger hunt?" Alex snorted behind me. I held in a swear word that would rile both Alex and Mom.

"Who's that?" My mother's voice rose.

"Uh..." I stalled, then turned and walked away, cupping my hand over the cell. "No one." My voice broke like a preteen.

"No one?" Alex practically screeched, her long, reddish brown hair aflame under the glaring sun.

"That sounds like a someone to me. Put her on."

"What?"

"I want to talk to the girl who's spending the day with my boy. And maybe more. Make sure she's not trouble."

I almost choked on that, but arguing with my mom was useless. Kind of like arguing with Alex. I handed the phone over. An enormous bubble nearly engulfed her small round face before it popped.

"Mom wants to say hi."

"To me?" Alex's eyes widened before she snatched the phone. "Hello, Ms. Kovalev—Okay, Sofia. I'm Alex. What? Yes. It's short for Alexandra. Um—I don't know if it's Russian. I got it because my parents wanted a boy."

There was a pause, and then my mother's laugh came through the phone, followed by Alex's giggle. How did I know these two would get on like instant B.F.F.s?

"Your son? He's behaving too much. He hardly ever leaves that kitchen. What? Hikes?" Alex's surprised glance flew to me, and I shot her a pleading look.

She wagged a finger, and I steeled myself for the worst.

"Oh, yes. *Javi* does those things, too, of course. In fact, we're doing this thing, Secret Camp Angel, and he carved this awesome hobbit out of soap and gave it to another camper named Julian. He's like this total *Lord of the Rings* fan and—"

My shoulders lowered in relief, even though Alex now knew my nickname. Wow. She'd covered for me. Crisis averted. Lucky for me she'd helped deliver Julian's gift before we left this morning. After a few more exchanges, she handed the phone back.

"That's a very nice girlfriend you have there, sweetheart. Don't mess it up."

"Mom." I walked a few steps away and lowered my voice, hoping an idling diesel truck would cover the sound of my voice. "She's just a friend."

Another argument broke out on the other end of the phone before she replied. "I doubt she's 'just' anything. Look, I've got to go, but enjoy yourself, okay? Knowing that you're having fun is what keeps me going. If we can make it through another month and a half, things will be good again, all right, Javi?"

I put a hand on the rough tree bark and leaned. Wow. I knew she liked my stories. Never understood how much she needed them, too.

"Right, Mom. I'll talk to you next Saturday."

"I love you, honey. Goodnight, Irene."

Irene. I pinched my eyes shut, willing back the wetness. Since I'd hated saying goodbye to her as a kid, we'd made up a special code word for it—my favorite childhood song.

"Me, too. 'Night, Irene.'"

When I punched off the phone, a soft hand fell on my arm.

"Are you all right?" Alex's eyes were large and deep. I wanted to fall into them because for the first time in a long while, I felt like someone might actually catch me. But I squared my shoulders instead.

I wasn't going to get Alex mixed up in my problems. "Sure, let's go."

Chapter Thirteen

Alex

"More cilantro!" Javier shouted over the hum of the commercial-size blender.

We'd been working in the cramped quarters of a mobile catering unit just off Main Street in Waynesville for two hours already, and we hadn't even hit the noontime rush yet. I was sweaty from playing gopher girl and filling orders at a take-out window built into this kitchen-on-wheels.

"Cilantro?" I juggled a couple of vegetable fajitas for an impatient old guy, trying to remember what category of food cilantro fell into. "That's a spice, right?"

My eye roved the built-in wall of seasonings near the dry goods cabinet.

"Excuse me, darlin'." One of the other women working in the catering truck, Marianne, squeezed past me. "I'm taking a smoke break, but I'll be back in five. You'll be okay?"

"Fine!" I lied brightly, knowing twenty people would show up requesting fancy coffee drinks from the espresso machine I couldn't work the second Marianne left.

"It's the green plant, Alex," Javier called. "There are bunches of it in the back of our van."

"I'm on it." I shoved fajitas at my customer and dashed out of the truck toward the nearby van.

The set had gotten busier since we'd first arrived. I'd heard some buzz at the take-out window that a big shoot-out scene was being filmed today, and I hoped I'd be able to see some of it from our spot.

Grabbing a tray of green herb-looking stuff from Javier's food stash, I slid the van door shut and dashed back toward the mobile kitchen. I edged around a couple of guys carrying big sacks of weapons—antique rifles with the occasional bayonet mixed in.

I set down the herbs in the prep area near the sink. "Want me to wash this for you?"

He nodded distractedly. Javier was so cute with a hair net holding back his dark waves. He filled plastic dishes with homemade salsa while another guy working in the kitchen chopped tomatoes and onions.

For Javier.

It hadn't escaped my notice that my seventeen-year-old crush had taken over the cooking. I hadn't seen him do anything to put himself in charge other than get right to work the second we arrived. He'd organized the food we'd brought; asked how we could help; and then turned on fryers, griddles, and ovens. He'd put together salads, cooked eggs, and grilled chicken. I'd seen him making crepe batter, kneading dough, and roasting vegetables.

It was clear he knew what to do in a kitchen. Which was why the fifty-year-old guy with a chef's apron hustled over to take the cilantro from me and prep it for Javier.

"How'd the salsa turn out?" I asked, hurrying over to help some girls at the counter who ordered "double dry" coffees.

Did that mean they'd just eat the Styrofoam straight?

"Fantastic," the older guy answered my question, even as Javier shook his head and said, "Needed more jalapeño."

The older guy grinned at that.

A chime went off, and Javier moved toward the wall of ovens. "Stand back," he ordered, pulling open two of the doors.

Steam wafted out, along with a scent so intoxicating I couldn't inhale it enough. Moist heat filled the mobile kitchen.

"Oh, wow," I breathed, drooling over rows and rows of stuffed crepes on baking sheets. "What's in them?"

"Gorgonzola and porcini mushrooms," Javier answered, pulling out the trays to cool. "Can you add that to the chalkboard menu out front?"

"Consider it done." Grabbing a stub of chalk, I hurried outside and erased the morning's special—bran muffins that had been imported from some organic L.A. bakery—and wrote in "Fresh Salsa with Chips" on one line and "Gorgonzola Crepes" on the other. I had a crowd around me before I was done, but I think it was the scent that brought them and not my partially legible script.

"Allie!"

I turned, expecting to see Marianne returning from her smoke break. I found a brunette with jet black curls instead.

Cassandra Pierce.

"It's Alex. Hey." I gulped, accidentally swallowing my gum. I also dropped the chalk. A coughing fit ensued.

Not pretty.

"Can we get a drink?" Cassandra took my arm and ushered me back into the catering truck through the side door. "You must have water around here?"

Javier looked our way while his kitchen helper tossed me a bottle of water. I took a seat on an empty orange crate tucked near the pantry. Thankfully, Marianne returned to handle the sudden crowd at the window. Half the movie town wanted to try the homemade crepes.

"Sorry," I croaked after a sip of water, careful not to cough on the assistant director lady anymore. Amazingly, my *Wholesome Home* manners flashed into my brain when I wanted to be very well-behaved for once.

"It's fine." She studied me as I drank more, tipping her head one way and then the other. "You had a signed release from a guardian when you were here last time, right?"

I nodded, and behind us, Marianne rushed between the counter and the crepes, selling Javier's specialty while he went back to work at the mixing bowl.

"Good." Cassandra straightened. "We lost an actress with a small speaking role this week, and now that I see you, I think you're sort of similar to her from certain angles."

"Really?" I think I would have sold my soul and moved to Hollywood at that moment if she'd asked. I could already see myself at my first movie premiere...

"Could you be in a couple of scenes that actress was supposed to be in? Non-speaking, of course."

From across the kitchen, Javier turned off the mixer. I could tell he was paying attention. I felt special. Grown up.

Too bad I already had a job I was supposed to be doing today. Heart sinking, I couldn't imagine how to say no to this.

"Why 'of course'?" Javier asked Cassandra. "Alex could do the lines." He wiped his hands on his white apron and walked closer.

Hope fluttered in my chest. Or maybe it was happiness that Javier would stick up for me like that.

"I'm sure she could." Cassandra hit a button on her buzzing cell phone and checked the screen. "But we'd need a different release signed, and she doesn't have a guardian on site. Plus, we're shooting the scenes this afternoon. We're cutting it close on time as it is."

"I'm supposed to be helping Javier." Standing, I glanced behind us at Marianne who collected cash and poured drinks.

"We'll handle it." Javier put a hand on the back of my shirt and gently propelled me toward the door. "I'd rather see you on the big screen."

"You're so busy—"

"Go," he urged, his expression stern, arms folded. "I mean it."

"Helena's going to kill me." I hung back long enough to kiss Javier on the cheek. "But thank you."

"Great." Cassandra held the door for me. "We'd better hurry if you're going to get to wardrobe in time."

She didn't have to tell me twice.

I raced down Main Street at her side, gathering intel on my character as we went. The scene we were shooting was the emotional aftermath of a shoot-out, and—the best part of all—I'd be *dying* on screen. The scene would be set to a musical score, and there would be slow-motion close-ups of characters falling to the ground. Later, they'd add in the main characters' reactions, but today, I would get to fall to the ground like I'd been shot. A close-up of the original actress could be interspersed with my scene.

But for today, I could be Juliet. Cleopatra. Ophelia.

A big deal.

I nearly chewed a hole in my cheek. When I got in the wardrobe tent and changed into my costume, my parents' letter fell from my pocket. My mom's handwriting on the envelope felt like disapproval. I'm sure she would have been disappointed in me for ditching camp to help Javier. But then ditching him for a chance to be in a movie? They'd call that self-centered and attention-seeking. Like they should talk.

I forced those thoughts aside, stuffed the letter back in my shorts' pocket, and pulled on my long skirt. By the time I buttoned a faded cotton blouse, I'd started to relax. I was lucky to have another chance in front of the camera. No way would I let my parents' past criticisms ruin it, especially when they were half a world away.

I had a quick once-over in hair and makeup that amounted to scrubbing away all traces of glitter lip gloss and adding dark smudges under my eyes to make me look gaunt and tired. As I began to look the part of a turn-of-the-century miner's daughter, I started to *feel* the part.

It was weird. And cool.

"Alex, we're ready for you!" Cassandra called through the front flap of the big wardrobe tent.

I hurried outside into the sunlight, following the assistant director toward a green hillside behind Main Street where the close-ups would be shot. Lights and cameras on dollies were already set up. Other machines I didn't recognize ringed the patch of grass where a few actors stood around getting last-minute adjustments from stylists.

And that's where I headed. Center stage. Where all the lights were shining. A thrill shot through me. Because for a few hours at least, I didn't have to be me.

Chapter Fourteen

Javier

The rest of the day disappeared as fast as the steam from our food tent. My homemade salsa impressed the caterer so much he even offered me a job as a *commis*, the lowest level cook. Lots of chopping and prep work but still...a start. Even my last foster family would have been impressed. But more importantly, the extra income would help my mom when she was released. It wasn't until one of the other cooks swatted me with a spatula that I wiped off my goofy grin and got back to work. I didn't see Alex again until I'd nearly packed up the truck.

"Sorry, Javier," she called. I whirled, more excited to see her than I wanted to admit. "I didn't mean to leave you so long." She bounced on the balls of her feet, her cheeks flushed. "But it was amazing." Her head tipped skyward, and her eyes out-sparkled the lowering sun. "Can't believe I got the job, even if it was for only a day. Plus the assistant director, Cassandra, said I have potential. That maybe I should audition for this performing arts school she went to."

I forced myself to look away and hefted another container into the back of the van. Car doors slammed and engines revved as the milling cast left the lot. "That's amazing. And I got offered a job, too."

Arms wrapped around me from behind, and my muscles tightened, my brain in a tailspin. Friends, I reminded myself. Just friends.

"That's so great, Javier! Maybe you'll have a cooking show someday. *Javier: Hot and Spicy.*" Her giggle vibrated along my spine. "Looks like we both found out what we're good at. The assistant director said I have potential. Can you imagine?"

I turned. Imagine it? She was already a star. "Yeah. It's too bad you can't do more."

Alex twined her hands in mine. "Who says I have to stop? I've got a plan." She nodded to a waving group of extras, then leveled her megawatt smile on me.

My fingers curled around hers. Traitors. "Why do I have a feeling this includes me?"

"You're going to be the star. Next to me of course." She popped a bubble, the grape smell making me want a taste. My eyes dragged themselves off her lips. "I'm going to convince Gollum to let us do a camp-wide production with sets, makeup, costumes—everything. How do you feel about playing Tony in *West Side Story*?"

"Like I'd rather swallow Gollum's whistle. I'm not an actor. Or a singer."

"So let me teach you." Alex leaned against the van door beside me, the brush of her shoulder electric. "Plus, you sing when you cook, and I happen to know you have a fantastic voice. If Helena gives you the time, you'll do it right? The rehearsals should be after dinner."

I stared at my shuffling feet. I'd forgotten she'd overheard me. "I'll help. But that's it."

"Yes! You'll make the perfect Tony to my Maria." She patted my cheek, then trotted to the front of the van and slid inside.

Her smiling profile appeared in the side mirror, and I couldn't help but grin, too. She was incorrigible. There. I'd actually used one of those S.A.T. words Helena had me studying. But Alex was also irresistible. How could I say no?

But spending more time with Alex...that was definitely a game-changer.

The ride home was quiet. I checked Alex out a few times to make sure she was okay...and that her shorts were as short as ever. A "hell, yeah" on both counts. But her faraway look meant she wasn't thinking of me. I should have been happy, but I missed her non-stop chatter.

"I'll help you unload the pans," she offered when we stopped behind the mess hall. The deepening dusk washed the camp grounds in shadows. The faint sounds of kids enjoying some free-time filled the evening air, laughter and muffled shouts followed by long shhhs and giggles.

"I'm fine on my own," I insisted, wanting it to be true. The door squealed open, and I shoved the keys in my pocket as I hopped out.

Alex met me at the back of the van, her fists on her narrow hips. I wondered if I could span them with both hands, then pushed the thought away.

"Let me help, Javier."

I jerked open the rear doors and kept my eyes on the dim interior. "Thanks, but I've got this. Hang out with your friends. You worked hard." Spending so much time with Alex had destroyed my will to resist her. I was a breath away from kissing her.

My pulse sped when she stepped closer. I should have known rejection would have the opposite effect on her. My tingling fingers knotted behind my back. Look, don't touch. Don't touch.

"So did you. Besides, I want to be with you." Her white teeth glinted as she smiled.

She was so freaking close. I felt the warmth of her body and her exhale as she adjusted a slipping tank strap. How the hell could I say anything when my only coherent thought was, *I want you, too?*

Her palm flattened against my pounding heart, her words flowing over and through my overheated brain. She was hot. But more than that, she was goofy, smart, talkative, spontaneous, stubborn, and a serious pain-in-the-ass. And she'd gotten under my skin in the worst way.

It was only until she quieted that I realized I was staring. She rubbed her foot against the back of her calf but didn't look away.

"I want you, too," I finally admitted, then pulled her soft body against me. Amazing how it held so much steel. I cupped the back of her head and gave her the kiss I'd fantasized about all day. Oh, hell.

Her arms wrapped around my neck when my lips opened hers. She tasted like berry sorbet on a hot summer night. I couldn't get enough. My hands plunged into her long waves and crushed her closer still.

My breath came hard and fast, my pulse speeding. We were already in a remote spot, but I turned us so that I hid her from view, her body as light in my arms as the wind ruffling the swaying trees.

Alex tasted as sweet as cotton candy, and she shook against me like an autumn leaf. I held her with one hand and slid the other across her smooth stomach. When her fingers tugged up my shirt and wandered up my chest, it was my turn to shake, though I tried to hide it.

When one of her legs wrapped around mine, I snapped out of my red fog. She might want to play with fire, but I wouldn't let her get burned. I pulled away and peered down at her. With her lips parted in surprise, her eyes wide and face flaming, she'd never looked more beautiful. Or more wounded.

"I'm sorry." And I was. Alex might be playing, but life was no game for me. I shouldn't have led her on, let her think I'd be the guy she needed for her last, wild summer.

"Don't be." She marched to the back of the van, her spine straight. "I came on to you, and you didn't like what you got. I get it. You just want to be friends."

I touched her arm and ducked in front of her before she could grab an empty container. "No. You don't get it. Look. The truth is that I like you. Too much."

The corners of her lips lifted. "Oh."

"Oh." I couldn't resist returning her slow grin.

"So, what do we do about it?" Her question sounded more like a challenge. And I could never resist one.

In this case, however, I had to. "Nothing. This can't happen again. Ever. Okay?"

A light sheen covered her forehead. "No. Not okay. Who said you get to decide what happens to us?"

"There is no us." I flinched inside at how cruel that sounded, but I was pissed at myself for letting things go too far.

Again. When was I going to control myself? My feelings? I could blame it on my age. Hormones. But I felt older than boys my age. Had been through more. So why did Alex get past all my defenses?

"Right," she snorted. "You won't even fool yourself with that lie."

True, but I forced my mind off what I wanted and focused on my mother. She needed me. If Alex's famous parents found out about us, they'd turn me into a bad boy and go viral with it. Not that they could mention my name legally. But some of the campers would post about us and everyone would know anyway. It'd make Gollum mad enough to send me away and, worse yet, Alex would be in trouble, too.

"'Signs your child is dating someone undesirable: Your child is acting differently. Your child is keeping secrets.' Sound familiar?" I intoned.

Alex scowled. "You spent way too much time on my parents' blog."

I crossed my arms. "Yep. I don't think I'd make the *Wholesome Home* cut, do you?"

Alex scuffed the dirt so hard it rose around her shoes in a brown cloud. "Like that matters?! I'm sick of living by those rules, and I came here to get away from them. And now you're enforcing them? When do I get to call the shots in my life? I thought you of all people would get that."

I caught her neatly by the elbow when she spun hard enough to stumble. Helena opened the back door with a trash bag in hand, spotted us, then eased the screen shut. I sent her a silent thank you.

"I do get that. But we're no good for each other. Besides, that TV crew is supposed to show up and film you any time. If they caught us together...there's too much against us."

"Then why does it feel right?" When Alex brushed away a tear, the backs of my eyes pricked. I hated that I'd made her cry. Plus, she had a point. I'd been forced to follow other people's rules all my life and so had she.

"Can we just hang out—take things slow? Friends with—uh—potential?"

Alex blew her nose and shot me a speculative glance. "Doubt it. But at least we'll still see each other."

I held in a groan. Spending time with Alex and keeping us from going too far...it'd be an impossible feat. But I couldn't deny how much fun we'd had today—both together and separately—and that I didn't want it to stop.

"So you want to help me with these pans?" I tossed a small one to her, then ducked when she pantomimed hitting me over the head with it. "What the hell?"

"I thought I'd knock some sense into you." Her sassy grin was back in place.

"Good luck with that." I stacked a couple of containers and headed toward the lit kitchen, Alex hot on my heels. There was nothing sensible about "us." Maybe I needed that blow to the head after all.

....

A half-hour later, we stopped in front of the juniper trees that guarded either side of her cabin. The smell of fresh earth and decayed pine needles hung heavy in the humid night air. It was one of those moments that felt as still as a snapshot, and I kind of wished it was. Next month, I'd want this mental picture of Alex, her eyes flashing as bright as her smile, her hands gesturing for emphasis as she described her *West Side Story* plans. She'd been thrilled when Helena gave a cautious thumbs-up to the idea of me joining the group. Especially when Alex mentioned it'd be supervised.

"So you get to do this whole fake death scene, and I'll be crying over you, and then..."

"Hello," called Alex's friend from the porch. She had dark hair and thick glasses, but I blanked on her name. "How was cooking for the rich and famous?"

A guy named Rafael sat across from the nameless girl, a chessboard set up on the table between them. I'd met him a few times around camp, and he seemed cool. He wasn't one of those tools who tried to make me feel like a loser for working in the kitchen.

"Hey, Siobhan!" Alex called, answering the mystery of her friend's name. "It was hot and sweaty. Lots of work." Alex grabbed my hand and tugged me up the stairs. Like a friend would. A friendly friend. The kind of friend that makes your knees weak when her small fingers wrap around yours. Friends with potential.

"Sounds fun." The screen door banged as another girl wandered out on the porch. I knew this one because the guys talked about her a lot—Jackie. She wasn't Alex-hot, but I guess she was hot in a way a lot of guys notice. The bigger reason they knew her, though, was that she could kick most of their asses on a hoops court. Jackie glanced down at the checkered board. "I'm not an expert, but it looks like she's got you in check in, like, three moves, dude."

"Concentrating," Rafael said through clenched teeth, his thick eyebrows knitting over his prominent nose.

Siobhan leaned back with a smug smile. "Did you guys get to have any fun?"

"If Alex is involved, I don't doubt there was mischief," another girl called from the window, then peered at our clasped hands long enough to make me let go. That piercing stare of hers made me think of Helena.

A huffy breath sounded beside me. "F.Y.I., Yasmine," Alex began, "today was totally legit. I helped Javier cook until the assistant director asked me to do a non-speaking role.

"Still concentrating." Rafael tapped a pawn against the side of the table.

The guy clearly took his chess seriously.

"It won't do you any good. I've got this one." Siobhan's voice rose. She stared at Rafael like no one had ever bested her before at anything.

Hadn't she heard Rafe was a chess whiz? I barely hung out with most of these kids, and even I knew that.

I cleared my throat, wanting to see Alex get her due. "The director told Alex she has real potential."

"Really?" Another girl—there was no end of them on this side of camp—rushed outside and hugged Alex, her blonde dreads swinging. "I'm so proud of you." She stepped back and studied Alex. "You have a rainbow aura tonight. I think you've found your life's purpose."

I wasn't exactly sure of the aura stuff, but Alex did kind of glow as she explained her plans to get the camp involved in the musical.

"*West Side Story*? Great message about intolerance." Yasmine pushed a brightly patterned head scarf over her forehead as she joined us outside. "I'm in."

There was a brief quiet moment. Almost as if all the girls had been waiting to see what Yasmine would say. Then they all spoke at once.

"Me, too," they chorused. Now that they'd stopped teasing Alex, they looked as excited as she was.

And suddenly I was, too. I'd never seen myself as the kind of guy that'd do something like this. But I knew it made Alex smile, and I couldn't do that enough.

"Me three." Their counselor jogged up the stairs, her bushel of blonde hair wilder than ever. "I love musicals. Nearly played *Annie* on Broadway until my final audition with Sandy the dog ended with an EpiPen and an ambulance ride. So much for my name in lights," she sighed.

Rafael twisted around in his seat. "Still concentrating."

"Focus on how you're going to carry my meal trays all week because I'm going to win." Siobhan laughed along with the group.

"Not exactly." Rafael slid a piece diagonally, captured one of Siobhan's pawns and announced, "Checkmate."

Yasmine whistled, and the rest of the group leaned over the board.

"No. That's—that's not possible." Siobhan stood, her eyes wide behind her thick lenses. "I had him."

"So had him." Jackie nodded and patted Siobhan. "I never saw that one either. Sorry, champ."

"She's not the champion anymore," chortled Emily. She pointed her index fingers, cocked her thumbs, and curled her fingers toward her palms. "Looks like there's a new sheriff in town. Pow pow."

"But...but...," stuttered Siobhan. If it wasn't a game, I would have actually felt sorry for her. She looked like she'd lost more than the chess match.

Rafael stood. He was compact and so thin the porch rails were thicker than his calves. He pointed at Siobhan, one side of his mouth quirked. "I like hot sauce on my scrambled eggs. See you at breakfast. Good night."

Had to hand it to the dude, he had style. I returned his grin, then winced when Alex elbowed me.

When Rafael stepped off the bottom stair, two middler kids raced up the path, their flashlights bobbing like police search lights.

"Fight! Fight!"

My gut twisted.

Emily leapt off the porch, going into Power Ranger mode. "Where? Who?"

"Vijay and some other guy," gasped the boy, holding his side.

"Where, Emilio?" Rafael squatted down, their resemblance suggesting they were brothers. For a moment, I felt a pang and wished I had one, too.

"Down by the dock," a high voice rang out, the girl who'd run with him. "And one of them has a bloody nose, Piper. Gross. We saw them on the way to outdoor movie night." All of the sudden, her voice wavered, and she ran into what must be her sister's arms.

"It's all right, Leila. Shhhhhhh."

"I'll take the kids with me and find Mr. Woodrow." Emily already had the pre-teens in hand. "Meet me down there but don't do anything stupid, like get in the middle of it. Talk them down if you can."

Alex's friends all took off—Rafael, too. But I held Alex back before she could spring off with them.

"We should find another counselor." I looked at the other cabins, but they were either dark or—if the lights were on—looked empty inside.

"There's no one else." Alex tugged me forward. "Come on."

It wasn't like me to play Switzerland and be all neutral, but I knew I skated a thin surface around here.

"I'll get in trouble—"

She sprinted toward her friends and raced along the narrow forest path, giving me no choice but to follow her. Damn it. Damn it.

Our shoulders and hands collided as we careened off each other in the dark, catching up to the others. After a moment, we burst onto the beach and took in Vijay and Jake wrestling on the sand. Even in the dim lighting, the red flow from Jake's nose gushed bright.

My pulse thrummed. I'd seen and been in way too many of these fights to count. It was easy to see that Jake was about to get his ass handed to him. He covered his wet face with his hands and twisted uselessly to the side. But that's what happened when you went up against a kid who fought dirty. Knowing Vijay, he'd probably thrown sand in Jake's eyes.

"Stop it, Vijay!" Alex screamed. Before I could stop her, she lunged at her ex and grabbed his swinging arm.

What the hell?

I was in motion before I could stop myself. Toward her, toward him, toward trouble.

Vijay's momentum hurled Alex into the sand, and I heard her teeth rattle as she landed hard. I saw red. Intentional or not, no one hurt Alex. Especially this douchebag. Anger management could kiss my ass.

I grabbed him from behind and put him in a headlock that gave Jake enough wiggle room to escape. In three steps, he stumbled into the forest and disappeared. Now I was the one left holding the bag—two hundred pounds of raging Vijay who was pissed to see his opponent get away...and all too happy to see me take his place. A jack-o-lantern grin split his bruised face.

"Let go, asshole." Vijay squirmed, but I tightened my hold and dug my heels in the sand.

"So you can throw around more girls? Yeah. Super tough, man."

Jackie stormed to my side, and Alex joined her until I waved them back. No more collateral damage. Besides, I had this. Vijay might outweigh me by thirty pounds, but it took brains as well as muscle to win a fight.

Vijay kneed me in the groin and ducked out of my hold when I doubled over. I took an uppercut to the jaw before I shoved him hard against the chest.

"Don't want to fight you, man," I rumbled, forcing myself to step back and give him a chance to calm down. Not that my temper was going away. I wanted to pound him. Grind his ugly face into the ground until he learned to stay away from Alex for good.

Vijay crouched, ready to spring. "I bet you don't, you puss—"

I dove for his legs and grunted in satisfaction when the jerk-off crashed backward. Adrenaline pumping, I leaped to my feet, then stared down in amazement at an immobile Vijay, his head resting on a rock the size of his head.

Damn. Was that blood by his temple?

"What in the name of Camp Juniper Point is going on here?" Gollum thundered, his whistle emitting a powerful shriek.

A flashlight shone in my eyes, blinding me. Without thinking, my arms rose in the air.

Emily knelt beside Vijay and gently tapped his cheeks until his eyes slid open. The snake.

"You're in a lot of trouble, young man," hissed Gollum.

Helena was going to kill me for letting her down. Again.

"Tell me something new," I muttered and followed Gollum back to the main office.

Chapter Fifteen

Alex

Teeth chattering, I danced from one foot to the other to stay warm in the dark outside Warriors' Warden shortly before midnight. I'd been waiting for Javier to return from the meeting with Gollum for almost half an hour.

I jumped up and down in between the juniper trees, sticking to the shadows since a few lights stayed on around the perimeter of the boys' camp at night. Had the temperature really dropped into the fifties or was I just shivering from fear? I knew a storm was coming, and I'd even worn a hoodie. But I think most of the chill came from the inside.

Javier was going to get booted out of camp, and it would be completely my fault.

At the sound of a twig snapping, I flattened myself to a tree, heart racing. There were wild animals out here. Dangerous ones.

But as I searched the dark woods, the tree bark biting into my cheek, I recognized the sound. Someone walking toward the boys' cabins without a flashlight.

"Javier?" I shout-whispered. "Is that you?"

The walking stopped. The shadow stilled. I swallowed my tongue because whoever it was stood tall enough to be a counselor.

"What if it wasn't me?" the voice shot back. Javier's voice, thank you, God.

He sauntered over while I peeled myself off the tree, my knees shaky.

"What happened?" I could see him fine when he got close. "They didn't kick you out, did they?"

I reached for him before I could stop myself, my hand landing briefly on his bare forearm. Tense. Muscular. Warm.

I stepped closer. He stepped back. Pulled away. It hurt me to see how much he wanted me to stay away from him.

"They didn't kick me out. Yet." His white teeth flashed in a grimace as he flexed his fingers.

"Are you okay?" His knuckles looked scraped.

"It's nothing." He stuffed his hand in his cargo shorts pocket. "Look, thanks for checking on me, but everything's fine."

My teeth clenched. How easily he brushed me off like I meant nothing. Like my concern meant nothing.

"What did Gollum say? Did you tell him the fight was between Vijay and Jake? That you only went... because of me?" I squeaked out the last part, the guilt choking me.

"Bam-Bam intervened. He'd heard what happened from Emily and..." He took a deep breath and stared off in the direction of the moon, still kind of low over the lake where we could see it through the trees. "Bam-Bam went to bat for me. Really fought hard to make Woodrow let me stay. He told him I'd do some kind of overnight intervention thing with him."

I silently vowed to be extra-nice to Emily for the rest of the summer. "He seems like a good guy. I just hope they kicked Vijay out."

"As if. Vijay hasn't used up all his chances like me. His punishment is to have an activity period taken away so he'll sit in the mess hall for an hour a day." He shook his head. "Right where I get to look at his ugly mug."

I was stunned. "You're kidding? That's all he gets while you're given the third degree? I just can't believe you'd get in trouble *at all* when you didn't even—"

"Alex." Javier stared me down, his chocolate eyes fierce in the moonlight. "Don't make excuses for me. Hitting him was wrong and I'm not getting dragged into situations where I can't control myself anymore."

"I didn't make the drama—"

"But we let him drag us into it. The kid's not right in the head, and the sooner everyone else realizes it, the sooner he'll get help. Until then, I'd suggest you stay away from him, too." He stepped toward his cabin, but I couldn't let him go yet.

Not on that crap ending note.

"I'm sorry." I put my hand on his chest to stop him, but then I pulled back. "I should have listened to you and stayed away from the fight. I'm sorry."

"It's not your fault. I make my own mistakes, and now I need to take that trip with Bam-Bam this week. He told me we were lucky that TV show of yours wasn't around to catch that on tape, or it'd be a lot worse. Oh, and I'm also supposed to hang out with the guys in my cabin more. Like we're going to suddenly all be pals." His jaw tightened. "It's all B.S. But I've got one last chance here, Alex. I can't screw it up."

I nodded. "I know."

"My mom—" He swallowed hard. Shook his head.

Nearby, a screen door banged from one of the cabins. Javier put an arm around me and guided me behind a thick tree trunk, and it was all I could do not to lay my head on his chest and feel his heart beat against my cheek. I could do it, too. We were so close.

"I don't want anyone to overhear us," Javier spoke against my temple, his words soft against my ear.

I nodded and—against all instincts—stepped back.

"I'm so glad you're staying." I snapped a twig off the pine tree, the sticky sap smearing on my fingers. "I'll try to respect what you want."

Maybe if I gave him space for a few days, he'd miss me. Besides, we'd be working on the play together. I could see him when he was Tony and I was Maria.

"It's safer for both of us." He reached toward me, and I closed my eyes.

Hoping.

His lips found mine in a kiss so light I could have dreamed it. He touched my hair, stroking down the side of my head and twining a finger in one lock before he let it go again and stepped back.

"Night, Alex." He spoke softly, and I pretended it was tenderness I heard in his voice instead of goodbye.

I had to lick my lips before I could get any words out.

"Goodnight, Javier."

I walked away before I said how I really felt. We might come from different worlds, but we were the same where it mattered. With him, I didn't have to try so hard to be accepted, didn't have to try at all. He liked me for who I was, and that was more precious to me than any payback summer.

....

"Where were you last night?" Trinity's soft voice startled me awake the next morning.

She perched on the edge of my mattress, making me wonder what time it was. It seemed too dark to be breakfast time. Since most of the Munchies were gone, they must be at the showers. Jackie, however, was still in her bunk on the other side of the cabin, softly snoring.

"I have no idea what you're talking about." I yawned through my lie, not ready to sit up. Last night wore me out in too many ways to count.

Javier.

I missed him, even though I knew we'd be together soon. I'd really, really blown it the day before.

"Don't be ridiculous. You left, and I didn't rat you out. That means you tell me what happened."

Trinity wore her glasses instead of contacts, a sure sign she'd just rolled out of bed. The funky purple frames had zebra stripes on the arms. Her nightshirt had a screen print of some Dali image on it—a fact I'd never have known if she hadn't explained it to me once. The melting watch had something to do with surrealism, I think. But I personally equated it with the way time slowed down at camp. Less focus on the cyber world. No discussions about Twitter feeds and what was trending in social media—especially when that trend was me. The year when I'd first gotten my period, I'd thought the Internet would implode from the comments on my parents' blog post about it.

Total humiliation.

"I had to see Javier and find out what happened after Gollum dragged him off." Reluctantly, I elbowed my way to a sitting position, blinking against the gray light and noticing it was pouring rain outside.

No wonder it seemed so dark. The earthy, loamy scents of camp really came to life in the rain. I inhaled the cool, wet breeze that floated through an open window above my bed. It hadn't warmed up since the night before.

"And?" Trinity waved her hand in a circulating motion—to get my story moving.

"Bam-Bam stuck up for him and said he'd take Javier on an overnight thing—like some kind of 'scared straight' thing maybe. So Gollum said Javier could stay, but it's his last warning. If he messes up again, he's done here."

Which meant I needed to make sure that didn't happen. I didn't want to stay away from him, but if there was really no other way...

"That's not fair. Oh, hey, check this out!" Trinity climbed down the ladder, pulled her suitcase closer by the leather handle, and dug through the tangle of colorful tees and shorts. She pulled out a paint-by-numbers velvet canvas of Elvis Presley. "Does my Secret Camp Angel know me or not?"

I examined the dusty, dime-store gift. "Ummmmm. Not." We both laughed.

Trinity pulled a bra on under her sleep shirt. "So how come Gollum will acknowledge that Vijay was in the wrong, and then still give Javier the third degree like it was his fault?"

"Because life sucks." I smacked the flyswatter against the window screen, scaring the snoozing moths that hovered on the other side.

I would have vented more, but the screen door banged open and Emily charged inside, her red-and-black ladybug umbrella spinning water droplets everywhere as she tumbled in out of the rain.

"Raining cats, dogs, and pine needles out there!" she huffed, tossing aside the umbrella while Piper and Siobhan rushed indoors. "Girls, you'd better hit the showers if you want to make it to breakfast on time."

There were more grumbles from Jackie's bed, and she tossed a wadded-up gym sock in the general direction of the noise but it landed with an ineffectual plop on top of the blue duffle bag emblazoned with her school's name and volleyball team's logo.

"I agree with Jackie." I made no move to get out of bed. "Who cares about rushing to breakfast only to hear we'll be stuck inside all day doing some dumb activity Gollum pulls out of his butt?"

"Someone needs to remember her Kindness Cup manners!" Emily chirped, waving the big pink painted chalice she'd made the year before. "No wonder we're halfway through the summer and there's hardly a chip in sight." She rattled it meaningfully, stirring just a handful of poker chips she'd painted with daisies or covered with unicorn stickers.

It was tough to think evil thoughts with those unicorns staring up at you with their big, blue anime eyes.

Piper rattled a worn box beside her bunk. "We could stay in and play with my Secret Camp Angel gift."

Jackie squinted at her. "Why would someone give you a *Star Wars* LEGO set?"

"Maybe they think she's really an alien." Siobhan stopped toweling her hair and headed to the mirror.

"Or nine years old," I added, laughing as I forced myself out of bed.

"Wait until you hear about today's rain activity," Siobhan called over the top of the whirring hairdryer she'd plugged into the socket near her bed. She smoothed her dark hair with a round brush, making it shine blue-black even in the dull gray light.

I was glad to see she'd recovered from the chess loss the night before.

"I'm afraid to ask," I said, bored already as I rummaged for a piece of gum to tide me over until I could brush my teeth.

"It's going to be a whistling, hog calling, lip-syncing, stunt contest," Emily blurted, bouncing on her toes and spinning around in a circle for good measure.

We all stared. Even for Emily, this seemed over the top.

"What?" I shook my head to clear my ears.

Piper scrunched up her nose and squinted, as if seeing Emily better might help her figure this one out. Behind Emily, Yasmine strolled into the cabin, drenched to the skin and not seeming to notice. She hummed to herself, in fact. What was wrong with that girl?

"A whistling, hog calling, lip-syncing, stunt contest!" Emily counted out the name on her fingers, her nails decorated with American flags and military stars that were probably some kind of ode to Bam-Bam. "Mr. Woodrow may not remember, but he put *me* in charge of back-up activities and named me the official Rainy Day Director in a planning session last spring."

"I'm sure Mr. Woodrow appreciates your creativity, Emily." Yasmine smiled warmly at our counselor.

I tried not to roll my eyes at the obvious suck-up since Gollum had probably wracked his brain to find some task to give our over-eager counselor that wouldn't wreak havoc on his camp.

"Aww!" Emily grabbed the Kindness Cup and held it out to Yasmine. "Score one for Yasmine being so sweet!"

Somewhere, a unicorn lost its horn.

"Emily?" I toed open my suitcase and scrounged for something clean. "What exactly is hog whistling?"

"You'll love this." Emily shoved the Kindness Cup back up on a shelf over her bunk. "I looked up rainy day activities in a book after Mr. W. assigned me the position. And I saw a bunch of silly little stuff, like a whistling contest. An animal sounds contest. A knot-tying contest."

Jackie sat up and yawned.

"Exactly!" Emily shouted, pointing at Jackie. "Yawn, right? But if we combined them..." She peered around the room, her smiling growing wider and wider until she was all teeth and gums. "We've got a fun day of stunts and talents and silliness that will have us all laughing. It's going to be great!"

She cranked up a contraband radio and started dancing to the beat. Talk about being high on life.

I still had no idea what hog calling involved, but as I slogged out of the cabin and into the rain toward the showers, I wished I could at least sit next to Javier during the event. As friends. A shared laugh would be good for us, even if I wasn't his girlfriend/friend with potential anymore.

Then again, maybe I never had been.

Javier had one more chance at Camp Juniper Point, but it seemed like I'd already used up mine.

....

Tough to share a laugh with the boy you like when he doesn't even bother showing up. And watching Buster–one of the Warrior guys–actually compete for a bird call prize was fairly entertaining. His turkey call might be dead-on accurate for all I knew, but the contortions involved in drawing in his cheeks and clucking in his throat had potential for hysterics.

While he gobbled and cooed on stage, I slumped in my chair at the rainy day extravaganza and wished Javier had at least come out of the kitchen after breakfast. But I'd watched the double doors for a long time while helping set up the mess hall with a stage and something vaguely resembling theater seating, and my handsome Russian-Venezuelan kind-of-boyfriend had never made an appearance.

"Are you all right, Alex?" Emily slid into the empty seat beside me while the acts changed and a ten-year-old camper in pigtails took the stage with a hula hoop.

"Yeah." I tried to force a smile. "You did a great job on the event."

"You have to admit Buster's hog call was great!" Even Emily couldn't quite pull off that fib. Her toothy grin seemed a little lopsided.

"It was a turkey call," I told her, smiling for real this time.

"Oh! Well, that explains that." She bit her lip hard because—true to her Kindness Cup and Secret Camp Angel roots—she wasn't the snarky type.

And Buster's turkey impression would test anyone's anti-snark powers.

"Emily?" If I didn't ask her now, I'd lose my nerve. And I needed a favor to distract myself from what I was feeling about Javier.

"Mmm?" Eyes on the stage, she pumped her fist in the air and whooped as the pigtailed hula-hooper spun the neon green ring on one arm.

"Will you ask Mr. Woodrow about doing the play this summer?" She'd seemed excited about it the night before. "We could do it instead of the talent show. You could direct it."

The play could distract me from Javier. Or it could bring us together, since he had agreed to be Tony in the production. I really, really needed that play to happen.

Emily forgot about the hula-hooper, her eyes meeting mine while the audience applauded politely.

"Me?" She was already shaking her head. "No way, missy. You're the expert on acting, and this is your idea. You should be directing."

"I'm just a camper!" What was she thinking? Gollum had barely let Emily direct the rainy day activities. What made her think he'd let me direct *West Side Story*? "Gollum will never put me in charge of something so big."

"So adapt it and just do a few scenes from *West Side Story* as a skit. Camp Juniper Point needs a Skit Night, and I've been telling Mr. W. that very same thing since last summer." She sat straighter in her seat as a couple of guys from Wander Inn dragged old wooden ramps out onto the stage. "Look, girls! They're making a half-pipe!"

How could Emily do this to me? I'd hoped to do an entire play, maximizing my time with Javier.

Siobhan and Yasmine slid closer to us on the table bench.

"Did you hear who's back at camp?" Siobhan whispered while the whole mess hall buzzed with some kind of gossip.

Something was definitely going down.

"Not really," I shot back glumly, not caring so much about gossip these days.

"Remember Nick Desanti?" Siobhan prodded, pointing to a cute guy with dark hair who strode out onto the stage in some kind of colorful athletic suit like a biker might wear. Or a NASCAR driver. There were patches on the knees and elbows. Sponsor names sewn on the sleeves.

"He used to be in Wander Inn a long time ago, right? Then he started snowboarding. Won some medals." My gaze landed on Kayla West, who'd dated Nick once upon a time. Well, *date* the way you do when you're little. Which is to say that they held hands during bonfires until her friends convinced her Nick wasn't good enough for her—or any of the Divas.

He'd left camp after that and hadn't been back since.

"Right." Siobhan spun her magenta-colored Secret Camp Angel bracelet around and around her wrist.

Jackie leaned forward, animated. "I can't believe he's back. Amazing."

"He used to be so short," I blurted.

Yasmine sighed dreamily, for once not frowning at me. "He's hot."

I followed her gaze and agreed Nick was cute. Not brooding-Javier-sexy, but definitely good-looking.

"He can't snowboard here," I pointed out as the volume level in the cafeteria got louder and louder.

"It looks like he's going to do a skateboard trick instead," Siobhan explained, pointing to a board propped on one side of the stage. "Did you see where Rafe went?"

"Rafe?" I had no idea who she meant.

Her cheeks went pink.

"Rafael Cruz." Her voice caught as she said his name.

I'd never seen someone advertise a crush so clearly.

I couldn't hold back a giggle. "Oh, so it's Rafe now?" I shouted loud enough to turn a few heads our way. "Siobhan, you've got it bad."

She bolted out of her seat and rushed away.

"What did I say?" I wondered. I hadn't been making fun of her.

Yasmine tsked at me and slid back down the bench seat, putting a few feet between us like we were junior campers and I had cooties. For crying out loud.

"Rafe is Siobhan's first crush. I don't think she wants it advertised," Emily pointed out kindly, getting to her feet. "I'm going to go announce Nick's act."

I nodded, hating that I'd embarrassed Siobhan. Geez, if Emily was more sensitive to someone's feelings than me, I was seriously falling short in the emotional intelligence department. My parents had blogged about that topic once, and I remembered thinking they were both pretty emotionally clueless. I would *not* let myself turn into them.

"Alex, I want you to organize that skit night, okay?" Emily stared down at me with her hands on her hips, all serious-like.

"Really?" I swallowed hard.

Who would put me in charge of anything?

Yasmine had scooted as far away from me as the seat would allow, and I'd just embarrassed one of my oldest friends. Oh, and the guy I was crushing on didn't want anything to do with me since I, apparently, threw gasoline on simmering drama. It was shaping up to be a real banner year at camp.

"Yes, really. This is a good idea. You take it and run with it." She pointed her finger at me, the American flag on her finger making me feel like it was an order directly from Uncle Sam himself. "I'm telling Gollum to set aside a Friday night slot for a scene from *West Side Story* presented by the senior campers."

Would Gollum even listen to the camp Rainy Day Director and let us do a skit night? I gave Emily a shaky nod, not sure if I should be thrilled at the opportunity or scared to death.

Chapter Sixteen

Alex

"Fire!"

My fingertips vibrated on the quivering string as my arrow flew at an archery target. I squinted in the morning sunshine at the untouched yellow, red, and blue circles.

Darn. A total miss again. There should be a prize for not hitting the target at all. It took hard work and dedication to suck that bad.

"Alex, sight the target. Look before you release." Jackie raised her elbow to eye level and pantomimed pulling back on an invisible arrow. She straddled a white powder line that ran the length of the field. The rest of my cabin mates ranged along the chalk boundary with Jackie to my left and Trinity to my right.

"Yes, ma'am." I fake-saluted her. Like I cared. Although it was nice of her to give me pointers on my least favorite activity. I raised the unloaded weapon.

"And keep your elbow still when you pull back." Jackie leaned over and steadied my straining arm. I couldn't help it if my skinny guns didn't pack any muscle. I'd give anything for Jackie's toned biceps.

"Got it. Thanks." I tried to keep my aching limb from shaking, then dropped it. We'd been at this for over a half an hour. How much longer until lunch? And Javier?

"You can do it, Alex," called Piper from farther down the line. Her blonde hair was twisted in an elaborate knot, two patterned hair sticks holding the improbable bun in place. "Try to hit the target at least once today."

I pulled my hair off my heated neck, wishing I had an elastic band. It might only be 11:00 AM, but the temperature had already kicked into high gear. If anything, the muggy air was a thick soup full of swimming gnats. "I think I hit Trinity's."

Trinity's laugh rang in the still, humid air. "That doesn't count and you know it."

"It's our last shot of the session," Yasmine put in. A lime-green scarf encased her hair, the crisscrossing fabric looking like it might engulf her head. "Plenty of time to redeem yourself."

It was practically encouragement. Sometimes Yasmine wasn't awful.

I glanced past her to Siobhan. Her small shoulders were stiff and squared, her jaw set as she stared down the field. Usually she'd have something to add about angles and trajectory lines, but she'd been quiet around me all day. I shouldn't have teased her about Rafe and needed to find a way to make it right. I used to think it was just having a temper that got me into trouble. But it was my lack of filter, too, apparently.

"Clear down range!" barked our activity director. Everyone was safely in line and out of danger.

I stiffened my stance, aligned my hips and shoulders, and planted my left foot over the white powder streak.

"Nock!"

I inserted an arrow and brought up my trembling arm.

"Not clear! Not clear!" One by one we lowered our bows and stared as a tall, older boy ambled out of the bushes behind our targets. He pulled up short at the sight of so many armed young women. A short gust blew his longish, dark blond hair off his face, and Trinity gasped as fear turned my stomach inside out.

Had BLISS Network caught up with me at last? Despite my brave words to Javier, I wasn't ready to face the reality of my parents' world and the crappy role I played in it.

"It's Seth," Trinity whispered.

Seth? I blinked through the sunlight and realized she was right. A former Wander Inn camper, Seth had dated my B.F.F. for years until an outsider swooped in and stole her away. I'd always liked Seth, though. We all did.

"Hi, Seth!" Trinity shouted, waving. All the other Munchies did the same until he grinned and waved back.

"What are you doing here?" she called again. Mr. Barry, the archery instructor, shushed her.

"Working!" Seth shouted back. "I'm staying at my grandparents' house." He lifted a hatchet before he waved again and stalked out of sight.

"Who is it?" Yasmine asked.

"Seth Reines, a former camper," Siobhan said as we all took up our positions again at Mr. Barry's command. "His grandparents own Camp Juniper Point, so he must be down here visiting them for the summer and helping out."

"I heard he's doing some volunteer work to rebuild the old gazebo area out by Crystal Falls where we used to picnic," Jackie chimed in. "Some of the Wander Inn guys are signing up to help him during their free period."

"Cool." Piper stretched her arms over her head. "It's great to reuse those building materials. It's just been sitting in a heap for years."

"Ready!" Mr. Barry shouted. "Aim."

I tried to concentrate on my target even as Trinity whispered, "I wonder if anyone can sign up to help?"

"Fire!" came the command.

The air reverberated with the collective release of our arrows and Trinity's deep sigh. We all knew she'd had a secret crush on Seth since forever, but he'd been off-limits because girl code wouldn't let her poach on Lauren's guy. Except...Seth wasn't Lauren's guy anymore.

"I can't believe he's working here." Trinity shook her still-stinging hand. "Isn't it weird to have him so close by and not have him hang out with us?"

Siobhan and Piper nodded. But then, we'd spent a lot of time hanging out with the Wander Inn guys. Until this mess with Vijay, I had, too.

Jackie jogged closer to thump me on the shoulder. "Good job, Alex!"

I'd almost forgotten about my shot. I smiled at the arrow sticking on the left edge of the board.

"Isn't that Trinity's?" Yasmine retied the ends of her head scarf.

"Oops," giggled Trinity. "That is my yellow-stripe. Guess I was distracted. Sorry, Alex."

I shrugged. At least I had one arrow on my target, even if it wasn't mine. Done and done.

"All right, ladies, retrieve your missiles, we're finished." Mr. Barry gave the order that set us free.

Hallelujah. I stumbled down the field after my cabin mates. Because we weren't stopping at our cabin on the way to dinner, I'd worn my three-inch wedge sandals to class. Definitely not the most steady footgear on rough terrain, but they added the height I needed to catch Javier's eye.

"If Jackie's right about some of the boys helping Seth during a free period, you ought to be able to do that, too, Trinity," said Siobhan when we reached our targets. "You should ask Emily. You know she always fights for girls to be able to do anything the guys can." She plucked arrows from her archery board as I scanned the ground for mine.

Trinity dropped her nearly full quiver and had to start over. I helped her scoop up some, surprised to see my normally Zen cabin mate looking so flustered. Hopefully that meant she was going to make a play for Seth.

"You should go for it, Trinity," I encouraged her.

Piper handed me one of my red-tipped arrows. "Let's all sign up."

"I'm in." Yasmine pulled another arrow from her yellow bull's eye. What did that make—eight? Not that I was counting.

"I can't." I grabbed the last of my missed shots and stuffed them in my quiver. "I've got to get the skit organized, and as much as I want Trinity to have her chance with Seth, I really need the rest of you guys." They were so not bailing on me.

"And why should your friends do what you want them to all the time?" Yasmine's hoops swung as we headed back to Mr. Barry. "Maybe they have their own dreams to explore and stars to follow."

"Thanks for the life lesson, Yoda," I shot back, earning a scathing look from Yasmine and a giggle from somewhere behind me. "But I'd like to think I would help them if they were put in charge of something that was really important to them. I can't make all those costumes or sets by myself."

A lean arm settled around my shoulders, the faint smell of patchouli tickling my nose. Piper.

"We can do both. Okay? No worries."

Easy for her to say. It's not like Emily put her in charge —set her up to look like an idiot when this turned into a colossal fail. But how could I turn it down? Now that I'd acted, I couldn't wait to do it again. Besides, Javier had promised to help—a guarantee I'd see him again, whatever our status.

"Girls!" Emily dashed our way, her hair wild, cheeks a bright pink. "You will never guess who is going to be leading a very special new initiative at camp."

"We know!" Trinity exclaimed, then mouthed "Seth" at me. She handed Mr. Barry her quiver and spun in a circle that made her gauzy skirt billow around her calves. "And we absolutely can't wait. It's going to be awesome."

"Yes!" Emily fist-pumped like a New Jersey D.J. "Knew I could count on my home girls to help with my personal development and growth workshop."

"Wait. What?!" Trinity stopped so fast that Piper ran into her back, making them both stumble.

Emily reached to steady them. "I know. I've got to work on that title—something more catchy. How does 'Don't Be a Teen Statistic' sound? More to the point, right?"

Jackie chuckled. "It says it all."

"I liked the first name," Yasmine said. "And I want to help."

"Wait." I sprinted ahead and turned to face my friends, halting their progress. "So now you're all going to rebuild the gazebo with Seth and do Emily's workshop? Hello, what about my skit? I need you. Where are your priorities?"

"Where are yours?" a cool voice shot back with the same level aim that made her the best in archery.

I gave Yasmine a dirty look, which she returned with a smug smile. Who did she think she was, Gandhi?

"I'm trying to create something special for camp and no one cares," I huffed, falling in with the group as we continued our trek to the mess hall for lunch.

Yasmine pointed a finger at me. "Are you sure that's all you're trying to do?"

I started to object, then stopped when Javier came to mind. How the heck did she know I wanted an excuse to be around my camp crush? But I also wanted to act again. A passion and talent all my own. This was supposed to be my best summer ever. If I couldn't have Javier as a boyfriend, I could still make him my leading man.

Jackie nudged my shoulder with hers. "Fess up, Alex. We all know it's about Javier."

My cheeks warmed, and my neck prickled. "F.Y.I. we are not hanging out anymore."

"Then what do you call last night?" Trinity whispered loudly.

I elbowed my friend-turned-traitor. "Fact finding." Luckily Emily couldn't hear us since she'd dashed ahead when Bam-Bam came into view.

"If you care about Javier, you don't want him to get kicked out of camp for good," Siobhan said matter-of-factly. It was the first thing she'd said to me all day. "Maybe Yasmine has a point."

Trinity scooped up a flat piece of wood. "This would be great for a sign over the new gazebo. And, Alex?" I pushed on my sunglasses to hide my hurt and nodded. "For what it's worth, I agree with Siobhan. I know you care about Javier. But maybe the best way to help him is to cool things down for a while."

My friends sounded like Mom and Dad...

Did that mean I should listen? I stuffed down that thought. My so-called friends needed to mind their own business. They were just looking for excuses to bail on skit night.

"That's right, girls! Focus on yourselves and don't become a teen statistic!" Emily exclaimed as she rejoined us.

"We were just telling Alex she focuses too much on herself," Yasmine said. I caught a couple of glances exchanged amongst the group. They'd never openly agreed with Yasmine because they were my friends first. Still...did they think I was selfish? Hadn't I just offered to help Trinity fix her T-shirts? What did a girl have to do to get some credit?

Then again, I'd been raised in the glare of social media. Was I too used to the spotlight to let someone else take center stage? It was too horrible a thought to believe.

"This is about the skit, not me." I leaned down and mopped my forehead with the hem of my shirt. "And I need your help, not your insults, thank you very much."

"It's nice to see your polite side, Alex." Yasmine arched an eyebrow, her sparkle eye shadow catching the light.

"Maybe one of these days I'll see yours," I shot back, firing off the words before I had a chance to think about them. Sometimes, it just felt good to say what you meant. And damn it, wasn't I walking on eggshells all the time lately?

"Girls, let's not waste our feminine energy fighting with each other. Instead, let's use it for our enlightenment and empowerment." Emily put her hands together and stopped to bow. "Namaste." She gave a half-laugh, half-snort, then jogged to catch up to us. "I'm so using that in my workshop. Genius, right?"

"Right," I muttered, stuffing my hands in my jean cut-offs—the ones that made Javier's eyes stick to my legs like glue. "Could you share some of that genius with me and the skit?"

Emily waved away my question like she was swatting a mosquito. Speaking of which...I slapped at one when I felt a sharp pinch on my shoulder.

"About helping you..." Emily gave me an exaggerated pouty face. "Victoria is going to work with you since I'll be in the computer lab most nights. I need to research material for my workshop. But I know you two will get along great."

"Victoria! She's—she's—" My engrained *Wholesome Home* manners kept me from saying what I really felt about my elder. Darn it. The Divas' counselor was known for being totally useless. Between my friends signing up to help Seth and Emily ditching me for some lame-sounding girl power workshop, I was really and truly on my own.

....

The sounds of scraping chairs, chattering campers, and clanging utensils against dinnerware filled the mess hall. The talk around our table was all about Seth and what Trinity should do to get him to notice her. I was glad for her. Really glad she would have a chance to flirt with a boy she'd always liked. But did anyone remember I had a huge skit to organize? Did anyone care that it meant a lot to me?

Finally, I couldn't take it anymore. My fork clattered on the table. "I can't believe everyone is ditching me."

Trinity lowered her juice and blinked at me. "We would never do that."

I sucked in my lower lip and shook my head, more hurt than angry. No way would I look weak in front of Yasmine. Plus, I was trying to be more even-tempered. Less ruled by my emotions. If Javier could do it, so could I.

"Really?" I wanted to believe my friends would always have my back. But this summer, I'd felt more alone here than I ever had before.

"But we only have one free period," Siobhan said logically. She dabbed at her mouth with a napkin. "It's either help Seth with the gazebo or work on the skit."

Okay. Siobhan was clearly still mad at me. But would the others join me?

A very attractive, very single old friend versus doing a musical skit. My shoulders slumped. There was no competition, no matter how close we were.

"Oh! I forgot to tell you the best part." Emily pushed back her chair and stood. Her fork banged against her glass of milk until all of the campers quieted and looked our way. What was she up to now?

"I'd like to announce an exciting new dramatic arts activity for the senior campers, available for next week only. It's led by Victoria and Alex." She gestured toward me, and I sat up straighter. Everyone looked at me. Well, everyone but Javier. It would have been a perfect moment if he'd glanced my way, too.

I couldn't resist a fist-bump to the sky. Not a self-victory cheer or anything, although I could kiss Emily for solving at least one of my problems. I did it to get the crowd hyped for the new skit night. Emily had to talk louder over the excited whispers going around the room.

"A sign-up for it is posted on the bulletin board. Space is limited so don't delay. Thank you." She sat down with a huge, gum-exposing smile and leaned forward. "See? You can sign up like a regular activity. So no conflicts, right?"

"I was doing the skit anyway." Jackie shrugged her tanned shoulders and dug in her sherbet cup with her wooden scooper.

A round of agreement followed, and I suddenly felt sorry for having doubted them. The relief on Trinity's face meant she'd been planning a way to divide her free time between me and Seth anyway. It meant a lot.

And my warm fuzzy feeling continued when I finished the salad I'd had for lunch and checked out the nearly full sign-up sheet on my way out of the mess hall.

"Why is Kayla's name crossed out?" Weird. What would have changed her mind?

"Look—there's Nick's name under hers." Piper tapped his scrawling signature. "He'd be a perfect Tony."

"Do you think she crossed out her name because of him?" Trinity ran her fingers over Kayla's name. Was she looking for some kind of karmic vibe? "Remember how the Divas made her stop hanging with him when she moved into their cabin?"

"Yeah." Jackie crumbled her third sherbet cup and tossed it in the trash. "But now they're all over him because he's an Olympian. Classy."

"Poor Kayla. It must be weird." Siobhan turned and hurried off to collect Rafael's dinner tray. Even though she'd lost their chess bet, I could tell she looked forward to seeing him by the way she rushed over the minute he stopped eating.

I scratched at the red bite forming on my shoulder. "I'm casting Javier as Tony, not Nick."

Yasmine reattached her loose Camp Angel bracelet. "You can't do that."

I bit my tongue to keep the sigh from exploding out of me. I counted backward from ten. "Why not?"

"Because he didn't sign up, and..." She added her name to the bottom of the list. "...there aren't any more spots."

I gasped and checked and double-checked the names. Sure enough, Javier wasn't on there. How could he? He'd promised. Betrayal soured my stomach. I knew he wanted us to stay apart, but I never thought he'd break his vow to me. When I peered over at the serving counter, I caught Javier's eye before he turned his back and hurried through the swinging kitchen doors. Ouch.

"What'd I miss?" Siobhan asked when she rejoined us, her face glowing from more than the exertion of dumping one little tray. I should feel happy for her. Was happy for her. If only my romance could be that easy. Was that why I'd teased her? Was I jealous?

"Only Javier bailing on me." I couldn't keep the bitterness out of my voice. "What else is new?"

We walked out into the noonday heat, the sun disappearing behind rapidly shifting clouds. A bolt of lightning snaked between the trees across the lake. The air pushed hot and heavy against us, a sticky wet feeling filming our skin.

"Maybe you should stop worrying so much about Javier and Vijay," said Jackie, her voice steady while the rest of us huffed and puffed on our race back to the cabin. We didn't want to get caught in another summer rainstorm. "This is your chance to take charge. You always complain that your parents never let you do anything, and here's the perfect opportunity to create something yourself."

Thunder boomed the moment we jostled up the steps and into our cabin. The purple-bottomed clouds let loose as our screen door banged shut, rain ricocheting off our roof like a nature shootout.

I bolted up my ladder and flopped on my bunk. Jackie had a point. This was a chance for me to show everyone what I could do on my own. Create a world the way I wanted it—not my parents' version. Only, how could I show Javier—the one I really wanted to impress— if he wasn't a part of it?

Something dug in my back, and I yanked out a pink tissue-wrapped package.

"A Secret Camp Angel strikes again," Piper called from across the cabin.

Great. Just what I needed. Another mean-spirited gift. I shoved it under my pillow.

"Come on, Alex." Emily climbed a couple of the rungs and tickled my feet. "Get in the spirit and open it. Besides, your last gift was awesome. It's what inspired me to pitch my workshop idea to Mr. Woodrow."

"Fine." I sat up and crossed my legs Indian-style. The girls gathered around my bunk, all except Siobhan. "But only if Siobhan accepts my apology for teasing her yesterday. I'm really sorry."

Siobhan's glasses rose as her smile pushed her high cheekbones even higher. "I accept. And I don't like Rafael. Not that way."

I bit back a laugh at her transparent denial.

"Are you opening it or what?" Emily pulled at the present's magenta curling ribbon. Now that I looked at it, the package was pretty. Maybe the first present was a fluke?

I tore off the wrapping paper and sucked in a breath when I saw my surprised face reflected back at me. A mirror. I turned the black plastic handle and examined the back. No markings and no note. My mysterious camp devil had struck again.

"Oh, that's pretty!" Emily grabbed the mirror, smiled at herself, then picked a piece of lettuce out of her teeth.

"A mirror? I don't get it." Piper tilted her head as if to see it from a new perspective.

"Maybe Alex needs a closer look at things." Siobhan lifted her eyes over the spine of her textbook, then lowered them again.

"Some people can look and still never see," added Yasmine. I felt the bunk shift as she ducked onto the bed beneath me. My old spot.

"Give her a break," Jackie chided. "She's trying, dude."

The other Munchies seemed to murmur in agreement. And as much as I appreciated them getting Yasmine off my back, I still felt frustrated I wasn't getting the message of the dumb presents. Did I really need a stupid mirror? How would taking a closer look help anything that had happened this summer? As it was, I already lay awake in bed at night trying to think my way through problems that didn't seem to have solutions. I couldn't be with Javier. I had to ignore my dreams of acting to fit a mold my parents were determined to cram me into. And as much as I felt resentful about my life, I hated that Javier's was even harder. He'd never met his dad. His mother had struggled so hard to be with him, and he'd still ended up in crappy foster homes.

Taking a closer look at things just magnified how much they hurt.

"Here." I handed the mirror to Emily. "I don't need it."

Emily passed it back. "Rule seventeen of the Secret Camp Angel policy—you cannot return a gift given in good faith."

"How is this good faith? Someone is trying to be mean."

"Maybe they think you're just really pretty. It could be Javier." Trinity sat on her bunk and smoothed her skirt, a small smile—the first really happy one I'd seen on her in a long time—appearing. Had she already searched her star charts for signs of a good time to approach Seth?

I glanced in the mirror, trying to imagine that Javier had picked it out for me, then shook my head. These gifts were coming from someone who was trying to tell me something. Someone who felt like they had me all figured out. This just wasn't Javier's style.

Emily climbed back down the ladder while Jackie and Piper surveyed the clouds out the front window, debating whether or not the storm would pass in time for us to go canoeing. With the focus off me, I brought the mirror up to my face and peered into it until all I could see were my dark irises, the color reminding me of Javier's eyes. I cared about his happiness most, I realized. More than myself. More than my dreams of acting or my stupid plans for raising a little hell this summer.

I'd been so determined to get payback on my family that I hadn't stopped to see who I might be hurting in the process. That included Javier and me, too. Maybe this skit was a way for me to get the *right* kind of payback. The kind that meant redemption, not revenge—something Javier needed as much as me. Suddenly my confusion with Javier cleared as the rain slowed its rooftop percussion.

I guess I really did see something in that mirror— and I knew exactly what I had to do.

Chapter Seventeen

Javier

"Shouldn't you be on your way to the dock?" Helena tugged the dish towel from my hands as we finished up in the kitchen after lunch. "I thought you were supposed to be doing more socializing and less work?"

"Learning how to kayak with a bunch of rich kids isn't going to keep me out of trouble." The only "socializing" I did was going back to my cabin to sleep. I wasn't here to build lifetime friendships the way Camp Juniper Point's brochure advertised. "The less I hang out with people, the less chance I'll get into a fight, right?"

Helena scowled as she hung up the dish towels. "Being a hermit won't improve your social skills, Javier. There are plenty of good kids here."

Outside the kitchen, a screeching sound drew our attention. We looked out the pass-through serving window to see Vijay scraping the legs of a metal chair across the floor before dropping into it. He was right on time for his daily dose of so-called punishment. What a joke.

"Sorry if I don't see it that way," I muttered.

A knock sounded on the kitchen door from the back. The garden entrance. Weird. The only people who used that door were Helena and me.

Helena shrugged while I pulled it open.

Alex stood there, the sunlight turning her freckles into spots of gold.

"Can we talk?" She fidgeted with her Secret Camp Angel bracelet, spinning the lanyard around her thin wrist. She wore a blue-and-pink tie-dyed T-shirt with the names of her cabin mates on it. I'd seen a few kids wear stuff like that this week, so it must have been a craft thing.

"Come inside before you let the bugs in," Helena barked at her.

"Good idea," Alex agreed, stepping past me into the kitchen. Since when did she quit fighting authority? "Thanks."

"Have a seat." I pointed to a counter with a couple of our prep station stools. "Your ex is out in the mess hall, so he won't see us back here."

"I saw him. That's why I came this way."

Helena went back to putting away pots and scrubbing counters. Last time I looked, Vijay had his headphones on. It was as private as things were going to get for us. I waited for Alex to talk. Since I'd already told her where we stood, I didn't have a clue why she'd come.

"Javier, please do the skit night with us."

I heard a brief pause in Helena's scrubbing. Yeah, not super private here.

"I told you, Alex, it's better if we don't hang out anymore."

"It's not hanging out. It's camp skit night. Twenty other kids and a counselor will be there." She looked down at her hands, and one pink clip-on lock of hair slid forward from the rest of her silky dark waves. "I understand we can't be together, but as a friend, I really want you there."

Guilt pinched when I heard the sincerity in her voice.

"I need to stay out of trouble. You know that. And when I'm with you..."

She frowned and stared at the ceiling as if she might find an answer there.

"I'm scared I took on too much. Scared of messing up something I really want to do well." When her eyes met mine, I couldn't look away. "If you're there though, I know I can do it."

"No pressure." I wondered if she took classes on how to wear down my defenses, because she sure was good at it.

"Look. I know you don't want to be with me." Her eyes went to Helena for a second, and she lowered her voice. "And I'm not going to...you know...try to get you back. I'm just asking as a friend. And because you promised me you'd help."

"Not fair, Alex—"

"Javi, please."

Everything inside me stopped. "What did you just call me?"

Alex played with the hem of the tie-dyed T-shirt, twisting it around her finger.

"Javi." She stopped twisting and shrugged. "I heard your mom call you that."

No kidding. Hearing the nickname on Alex's lips now was like...the voice of my conscience kicking in.

"Speaking of which," Helena cleared her throat and set her scrub brush aside, "your mom would want you to be a part of something like this. I know your mother well, Javier Kovalev, and it would mean the world to her if you'd have some fun and be a kid for a change."

"Let's not bring my mom into this." I kept my voice neutral, but tension wound through me so tight that I thought I'd throw something. I tried to remember the bogus anger management classes I'd taken for the sake of my previous foster parents. I focused on my breathing.

In.

Out.

Too bad without the layer of anger, hot tears stung my eyes.

"Javier, I don't mean to push you," Alex said. "You can do what you want. But you shouldn't work in the kitchen all the time, and you'd make a great Tony. You have a lot to offer, and I'm sad no one but me gets to see it."

She hurried toward the door. I swallowed a big lump in my throat and looked to Helena.

"Can you handle meals this week if I do the play?"

Alex stopped in her tracks so fast her sneakers squeaked on the floor.

Helena sniffled and swiped a weathered hand beneath her left eye.

"Definitely. And I know exactly where to ask when I need help." She jerked a thumb toward the mess hall where Vijay sat—oblivious and jamming out to some tune on his over-the-ears headphones. "I've got every right in the world to put him to work."

"Really?" Alex's eyes lit up, but I couldn't tell if it was because Helena was going to put the screws to her ex or because she'd gotten what she'd come here for.

Either way, it looked like I was going to do the damn play.

For her. For my mom. For Helena, who'd gotten stuck with me too many times to count over the years.

"I'll be there," I told her flatly, determined to keep the boundaries between us. But the happiness in her eyes was tough to ignore. "Bam-Bam told me I needed to hang out with friends more."

"Awesome." She smiled at me and gave a thumbs-up to Helena. "I'll see you at seven in the theater building for our preliminary meeting tonight."

When she left, the kitchen seemed smaller, emptier.

"I thought you didn't like her," I griped to Helena.

"I never said I didn't like Alexandra." Helena filled a clean pot with water, and I grabbed it before it got too heavy. "As long as you two are just friends, then it's fine. Besides, she doesn't seem interested in getting into trouble anymore."

"No?"

"A girl can change. And she seems like she has." She folded her arms and studied me with narrowed eyes. "And you could, too, you know. I want you to think about taking my brother's offer to cook in his New York restaurant after camp. He said you can work part-time, and he'll help you get in culinary school while you finish high school."

Right. I wanted to be a real chef someday, but I owed it to Mom to stick around and make her life happy for once.

I'd play the game for a few more weeks, take the intervention trip with Bam-Bam, and "socialize" more to make sure I could stay at camp for the rest of the summer. After that, Alex Martineau would go back to her *Wholesome Home* life and I'd go back to my broken one, doing my damnedest to forget all about her.

Chapter Eighteen

Alex

"We only have four days to practice for the first skit night, so the sooner we start rehearsing, the better," I warned my team as they sat scattered around the stage in the theater building.

Half of them were still talking, even though I'd been describing my plans for the last ten minutes. Geez. Did I need a megaphone for this job? Why didn't Victoria ever do anything helpful to keep everyone on task? My counselor advisor was deep in the pages of a paperback in the last row of the theater.

I put both pointer fingers in my mouth and let out an ear-piercing whistle. Brittany and Hannah quit arguing. Siobhan paused in her efforts to braid Trinity's hair. Even Eli stopped running around the stage with the Viking helmet he'd found in a box of costumes. He stood still and listened, clutching a wooden sword to his tinfoil breastplate.

"Thanks." I gave a tight smile. "I was just saying that I'm going to cast the parts right away so we can get to work learning lines."

"Shouldn't we *audition?*" The newest Diva, a YouTube singing sensation named Brooke, rolled her eyes like I'd overlooked the world's most obvious task.

"I'm dying to be Maria," Brittany announced. "And I have a great idea to change the Sharks and Jets to vampires and werewolves."

Even her friends groaned at that one, although Trinity seemed on board.

"Cool!" She started discussing how they could do the costumes for a version of *West Side Scary*.

They weren't serious?

"Dibs on Anybodys!" Jackie called, bounding up to my side, her long basketball shorts doing nothing to hide the most grown-up set of curves at camp.

"Who is Anybodys?" Devon's eyes roamed over Jackie.

"She's the tomboy," Jackie explained. "I'm a natural fit."

"I have a list!" I shouted, waving the paper to assure them I had a plan. I'd worked really hard on this already, and I shouldn't have let the chatter get so out of hand. "I assigned roles over dinner so we can get started right away."

"Seriously?" Brittany marched forward along the polished hardwood floor, Brooke at her side. "You just *gave away* all the parts without seeing what we wanted to do?"

Campers swarmed me. Brittany swiped the paper while twenty other kids circled us. Someone stepped on my foot. I got an elbow in my side.

"Hey!" I protested, meeting Javier's eyes through the crowd.

He and Yasmine were the only ones who hadn't joined the footrace to steal my casting sheet. Javier leaned against a pile of crates near the box of props I'd dragged out of storage to save time. He yawned. Stretched. Looked totally unconcerned.

Nearby, Yasmine quirked an eyebrow as she stared at me, then made a big show of checking her watch.

"Should we come back another time?" she shouted over the outbursts from the other crowd milling around my casting notes. "It doesn't look like you're ready for us tonight."

It took all my restraint not to snarl. I stamped my foot and whistled again, but no one heard me this time. Brooke seemed to be hyperventilating over not getting a speaking role and ordered another new Diva, Nia, to get her some water. Rafael was laughing and telling all his friends that the only Puerto Rican among us was cast as a Jet, not a Shark. Eli did an impromptu tap dance while singing "Officer Krupke."

One shrill voice rose above the rest.

"She cast *herself* as Maria?" From the center of the crowd, Brittany glared all around the theater until her eyes found mine. Even her friends backed away from her. Her normally pretty face was contorted in angry lines. "You not only direct this thing, but now you take the prime, juicy, starring role? For *yourself*? As if being the most famous kid on the Internet wasn't already enough?"

I flinched. That wasn't the kind of attention I'd wanted. Or had asked for.

"Heeeeeey," protested Brooke. She shoved the water back at Nia, splashing some on the younger girl's shorts. "I've got over thirty-two million views on my video."

Brittany ignored Brooke and stomp-marched closer to me, my notes on the skit crumpled in her hand.

Hearing Brittany put it that way made me wonder if I'd messed up. I glanced toward Javier, who shook his head and closed his eyes like it was going to be a long night. Yasmine—my personal critic—smirked and looked down at her shoes. It was the first time she'd let someone else lead the charge against me. Unlike me, I guess she knew when to let someone else be the star of the show. Then again, hadn't I been asked to step up? Hadn't Emily told me I was the drama expert, and I needed to head up the production?

I was only doing what Ms. Personal Growth and Development had told me to.

"The play was my idea." I took a deep breath. "I wanted to do it because I was inspired by acting after doing *Mine Forever.*"

"And that gives you the right to do everything yourself?" Brooke chimed in, her purple-tipped black hair shimmering across one shoulder.

I glanced at Victoria, but she simply turned another page.

Well, no one said this would be easy.

"We've got four days to rehearse," I reminded them. "Do you want to argue about everything or move forward so we have a performance on Friday?"

"You really want an answer to that?" Brittany tossed my production notes back in my face. "Good luck, Miss Know-It-All."

My friends rallied around me. Kind of. Jackie slung an arm around my shoulders. Siobhan pushed her glasses higher on her nose and tried to reason with Hannah. Trinity worked to hide her pout, but since she'd already retrieved a few sets of dog ears from the prop box in an effort to make *West Side Scary* come to life, I could tell she wasn't happy.

"That's fine," I forged ahead. "We've got plenty of help to get this skit off the ground, so—"

Brooke chose that moment to walk out, followed by Nia and the rest of the girls from Divas' Den except Kayla and Hannah. A couple of the Warrior guys held the door and then ducked out right behind them.

"Shit!" I shouted, my temper getting the better of me.

I crumpled my notes and threw them off the stage.

"Are we wrapping things up?" Counselor Clueless called from the back of the theater, peering up from her book.

"I guess so," I hollered back, feeling like an epic fail. My parents would love to blog about this. Alex the problem child messes up again. "Looks like there isn't anyone to direct."

"I'll lock up behind you," Victoria announced, peering around uncertainly.

"Fine." I dragged the prop box back to where I'd found it. "I'll be done in a minute."

"Want a hand?" Javier appeared at my side and gave the box an extra shove.

"No," I barked. "Guess you're off the hook now. Happy?"

Javier straightened, his face expressionless. Carefully neutral.

"I came here for you," he reminded me. "It's not my fault you couldn't get out of your own way."

He headed for the door while I reeled from the underhanded blow.

"So this is my fault? I poured more gasoline on the drama?" I yelled, anger and betrayal simmering inside me. "Is that it?"

No way could he tell me I didn't try, damn it. I'd come here prepared. I'd taken notes. I'd arrived early.

He paused.

"I know one thing." He turned around to look at me. "I'm not the one yelling."

He left before I could argue. But even I was tired of myself. Bad enough he'd only come here tonight to honor a promise. At least I had kind of counted him as a friend. Now? I knew Javier wouldn't ever want anything to do with me again.

....

I didn't cry until I got to the beach that night.

Somehow I'd walked back to Munchies' Manor and deflected the conversation from my colossal failure, even though I was in a total haze.

My cabin mates normally teased me about being a drama queen or dragging too many mirrors to camp or flirting with Javier too much. But they didn't say much about what had happened in the theater tonight. If they were this quiet about it, then they didn't even know where to begin.

I was a lost cause. After asking them to give me some space, I'd curled up on my bunk.

Now, hours later, I sobbed until I hiccupped. Forehead on my knees, butt in the sand, I didn't care if a den of bears heard me and came to make a meal out of me. I didn't care if Gollum heard and called my parents to take me out of camp.

I'd let Emily down. I'd let my camp mates down. And I'd definitely let myself down. How could I have begged Emily to let us have a full-scale play when I couldn't even pull off a skit night? Because I'd been selfish, of course, and wanted to show off my newfound acting talents.

"Alex?" a girl's voice whispered on the breeze, the sound mingling with the soft noise of water rippling against the shore. "Is that you?"

Sniffling, I squinted toward the tree line as a girl walked toward me. The shadows hid her, the moon mostly covered by clouds.

"Who is it?" I called. It didn't sound like Emily. Our counselor slept hard, so sneaking out of Munchies Manor wasn't difficult.

"Hey. Are you all right?" Yasmine came into view. She wore the long red-and-white-striped T-shirt that she normally wore to bed with khaki shorts and a gray hoodie over it.

"Actually, everything sucks right now, Yasmine. I don't need you to rub my nose in it."

"I come in peace." Her flip-flops sunk into the wet sand as she walked next to me. "I found a present for you back at the cabin."

"My Secret Camp Enemy strikes again." I ignored the little pink package she held out and tried to wipe my tears away before she saw. "I'm going to wait and open that another time, okay? I've hit my crap news quota."

Yasmine kicked off her flip-flops and sat on them. I wish I'd done the same since my butt was already soaked from wet sand. But seriously? What did she want with me?

"I don't mean to be rude—"

"So don't be." Yasmine tucked her knees under her chin and looked over at me. She smiled, her gold hoop earrings glinting in the moonlight.

"Is your mission in life to be mean to me? Are you like working undercover for my parents? Because if you are, you're doing a killer job. But I came down here to be *alone*."

Her bracelets jangled as she flipped her hair over one shoulder, and I wondered if she slept with that jewelry on. I'd never noticed. But then, I tried to ignore Yasmine as much as possible.

"Well, at least take the present." She tried to shove it in my hand, but I had something else crumpled in my palm. "What's this?"

When I didn't say anything, she set the gift on my lap and took the paper. She had to tilt it a few different ways to read the lettering in the dark, but eventually she must have caught a shaft of moonlight.

"A New Day Alternative Boarding School for Girls?" She unfolded the brochure that had arrived for me this morning. I hadn't opened my mail until after the skit practice.

"My new school. Conveniently located three hours from home so I pose a minimum inconvenience to my parents." They didn't even want me in the same state with them. My new school was in southern Georgia.

"Maybe it won't be so bad."

"It could be the best school in the world, but it still means my parents can't stand the sight of me." I snatched the flyer back and shoved it in the pocket of my hoodie.

For a long moment, she didn't say anything. Thank you, God. She stared out at the water while gentle waves sloshed along the sides of a few canoes pulled up on shore.

"You remind me of someone, Alex. A girl who was like a sister to me the year my family lived in West Africa." Her voice had lost the snotty edge. Maybe it was because she wasn't thinking about me but about someone she actually liked. Either way, she stared at the mountains and twisted the tie from her sweatshirt around her finger. "My dad was doing missionary work and my mom and I stayed with a host family. This girl—Leta—she was a few years older than me, and I followed her everywhere."

I stared at the moon. Listening to Yasmine was better than thinking about the girls' school or what a giant failure I was in everyone's eyes.

"People always smiled at Leta. She was fun and funny. Doing chores never bothered me when I was with her."

Since when was I fun or funny? I couldn't imagine why I reminded Yasmine of this girl. I was the bringer of trouble. The creator of drama.

Yasmine turned to look at me and hugged her knees tighter while a cool breeze stirred the leaves into a soft fluttering sound.

"Leta flirted with boys too much. At least, that's what her mother said. I thought it seemed like she just had fun with everyone—boys or girls—but at her age, in her culture, I guess she wasn't allowed to have too much fun."

"You think I'm boy crazy." I started to see why I reminded Yasmine of her friend, and it ticked me off.

"Alex, listen. I loved this girl like a sister. But she got caught alone with a boy and her father was furious. He called her a disgrace to the family and sent her out of the village. She was only fourteen."

Harsh. Poor girl. I could so relate. And she'd obviously made a strong impression on Yasmine.

"I'm getting sent from my village, too." The brochure in my pocket was proof, no matter what garbage my mom told me about camp being a trial. They'd already made up their minds like I'd thought. It was the reason why I'd wanted payback. For this to be the best summer ever…only it'd turned into a disaster.

"True. And there will be jackals and hyenas there, too, I'll bet."

I laughed so loud I had to cover it up with my hand.

"I bet," I agreed, still snickering.

"But it could be an opportunity, too. People like to be around you, Alex. You'll make friends no matter where you go."

"Um? Get around camp much? Because in case you hadn't heard, I'm this week's equivalent of poison ivy."

"But if you figure out how to fix the skit, your camp friends will help you pull it off. They were rowdy tonight because they were excited about doing it. It won't be hard to get them back."

I wasn't so sure. Javier, for one, wouldn't return. But what if I had given up too soon?

"What happened to Leta after she was sent away?"

"I don't know." Yasmine's voice hit a rough note, and I realized I'd never seen her even a little rattled, let alone unsure of herself. "My father wrote to ask his contacts in the village about her two years ago, but when they wrote back, they answered every question except for that one. I hope she's okay. Someday, I'm going back to make sure."

"She sounds like a fighter." I straightened, knowing I could be, too. "If she could make people laugh, she must have found friends."

Yasmine's smile was warm and maybe a little grateful.

"Are you going to open your present now?" She handed me the small package again.

"What could it be?" I shook it and started ripping the paper. "Toothpaste to get rid of my bad breath? Diapers because I act like a baby? A mask so the world doesn't have to see my crooked nose and freckles?"

"Whoa." She made a timeout symbol with her hands. "One issue at a time."

"Drops for swimmer's ear?" I held the white bottle up to the moonlight to see if I was reading the label correctly.

"Hmm." Yasmine tapped her chin thoughtfully. "Guess somebody is telling you to get the wax out of your ears and listen up."

I finally understood the answer that had been in my face all along. "It's you, isn't it?"

"I don't know what you mean."

"You've been giving me the presents."

She snorted. "Why would I give you anything?"

But she didn't fool me.

"This is your totally messed-up way of trying to help me." I thought back to the gifts. "I'm supposed to grow up. See myself more clearly. And now...listen to other people. I suppose you mean like *you*?"

I poked her in the shoulder—sorta hard, but mostly just messing around. This girl wouldn't have sat with me through my tears if she wasn't trying to cheer me up. Amazingly, she somehow had.

"Hey, it never hurts to listen to your elders." She still sounded prissy and stuck up, but I was pretty sure she just wanted to help.

"Well, if one of my elders ever says anything *helpful*, I'll let you know." I noticed she hadn't admitted to being my Secret Camp Angel. But then again, she hadn't denied it.

"What did you get for gifts this summer?"

Yasmine's teeth flashed in the dark, and she held out a wrist with a charm bracelet. A tiny elephant, trunk up, dangled from it, along with an owl and a bear.

"Wow. Very nice. Any idea who got them for you?"

"Someone with good taste," she laughed.

I got to my feet and held out my hand to help her up. I could make an effort.

She clasped my palm and stood, taking her time to put her flip-flops back on while I tried to squeeze the excess damp out of my shorts from sitting in the sand.

"All right, then. Here's a good piece of wisdom just for you." She grabbed my shoulders and spun me around so we faced the beach again. "The world would rather see the soft glow of a candle than the glare of a floodlight."

I tried not to roll my eyes. "Sounds like a *Wholesome Home* blog post."

"What I mean is, you don't always need to bring the full force of your Alex-ness to every situation." She ducked under a branch as we made our way through the trees back toward the cabins in the dark. "We're alike in that way, I think. We have strong personalities, and sometimes that rubs people the wrong way. But if we can be a little more subtle, maybe people will listen to us more."

"You think? I keep hoping maybe if I just shout louder..."

Yasmine giggled. It kind of made my night, hearing that unguarded sound from someone who seemed light-years older than me in a lot of ways.

"Let me know how that works for you," she said softly, but my brain was back on what she said about the play. About people being excited to take part in the skit.

I couldn't fix things with Javier, and I sure couldn't do anything about my parents kicking me out to go to boarding school.

But maybe it wasn't too late to salvage *West Side Scary*.

Chapter Nineteen

Javier

"Break!" I shouted the next morning before Bam-Bam disappeared around a trail bend up Black Balsam Knob Mountain.

My backpack thudded to the forest floor, sending brown leaves and pine needles scattering. I braced myself against a moss-covered log and waited for my unstoppable counselor to return. Damn. Did the dude ever get tired? I uncapped my water bottle and chugged, the lukewarm liquid doing nothing to cool me off.

We'd been at this "intervention hike" for two hours, and Bam-Bam had barely broken a sweat in the ninety-plus-degree heat. I, however, would have ripped off my sticky T-shirt miles ago if it wasn't for the swarming mosquitoes. For a trip supposed to cure my anger issues, it was frustrating.

The large Marine loomed into view. The guy was huge—a musclehead. Except he was more than that. He'd been cool about sticking up for me after the Vijay fight and had basically saved my ass by talking Gollum into this overnight trip. Not that it'd do any good. Sure I'd play nice. Say everything the guy wanted to hear. But I'd been at this "save the child" party for too long to learn anything. I knew what adults wanted to hear. But it wasn't the truth.

However, if being here meant staying at camp and not letting my mom down, I was in. Even if it sucked. I slapped at another biting insect. Man, did it suck.

"Want some gorp?" A beefy hand thrust a bag of raisins, chocolate chips, nuts, and granola at me. My stomach rumbled, and suddenly I was starving. I could toss it all in my mouth and swallow in one gulp.

"Whoa. Slow down there, kiddo," Bam-Bam cautioned as I stuffed my cheeks. "We've got another couple hours before we make camp."

I choked on a peanut. Two more hours? This was starting to feel like hell. After all, I was hot, being tortured by wild creatures, and being punished for my sins. What happened to the bro-bonding time in front of a campfire where I heard about his war stories and how I needed to "straighten up, soldier"? *That* I was ready for, but this *Survivor*-meets-*The-Challenge* episode? It was all too real and not what I expected.

"Thought we were almost there," I gasped when I got my breath back. "Isn't this the end of Flat Laurel Creek Trail?"

Bam-Bam's deep chuckle sounded in the dense woods, one of the waterfalls we'd passed trickling in the background. "Yep. But we're joining up with the Art Loeb trail now." He tossed back a handful of trail mix. "We've got a ways to go to the summit." His worn lace-up boots lightly kicked mine. "You quitting? 'Cause you don't look like the kind that gives up."

My back straightened, and my shoulders squared. I was no quitter. I had worked all my life. While other kids played Little League and indoor soccer, I did every odd job a boy my age could do. And it'd never been enough. It hadn't kept Mom out of jail this last time. My hands tightened into fists automatically at the thought. Why hadn't she told me how bad our bills had gotten?

I would have done something. Dropped out of school and taken a third job...

"You okay?" Bam-Bam's knees creaked as he squatted beside me. His hooded eyes bored into mine until I looked away and nodded.

"I'm no quitter," I muttered, then stood.

"Good man," grunted Bam-Bam. He shouldered his pack, handed me mine, and took off without a backward glance. Like he trusted me. Knew I could keep up with him. Wouldn't let him down. And as corny as it was, I felt something lighten inside me that I'd held heavy and tight for a long, long time.

....

Hours later, I dropped my pack and wove through the tall grass and rocks with Bam-Bam to the mountain's bald precipice. The wind whistled soft and steady like Helena's tea kettle before she snatched it off the range. The view looked like it could have been straight out of a movie—one of those fake sets that are rolled away once the director yells "cut."

As far as I could see, the world stretched below me. My fingers dug in my palms when I thought of how small it was. From six thousand feet, I could admire it. I was safe here. And it couldn't touch me.

"Freaking amazing, huh?" boomed Bam-Bam.

"Yeah," I said, my voice sounding as thin as the air. It was awesome. Trees rippled and waved below like an ocean of foliage. Shadows made puppets of themselves on the swaying green when clouds swam in front of the sun. Birds called and darted amongst living skyscrapers, their wings moving too fast to see. Everything was bursting, swelling with life. Yet there was a peace about it, too. A rightness. And suddenly I didn't want to hate this world. I wanted to be a part of what I watched, not at war with it.

"That mountain's called Tennent." Bam-Bam pointed at a large peak to our left. "Next time we come out, we'll camp there. It's got great views of Ivestor Gap."

I blinked away the sting in my eyes and pulled on my sunglasses. The glare off the surrounding white rock must be getting to me. Why did Bam-Bam mention a next time? It's not like he didn't have a million other things he'd rather do than hang out with me. But there was something in his wide grin, the gleam in his eyes that made me feel like he was having a good time. Like he wanted to be here. I pulled out the creased picture of my mom and dad that I kept in my pocket. If he hadn't lost his visa, would he be here with me?

I don't know why I thought about stuff like that since it always reminded me how much life sucked. I turned my back on the world I'd never get to see with my father, the world I'd hardly got to see with my mother. Life didn't give a crap about me, so why should I care? A vision of Alex's green eyes came to mind, but I pushed it aside. I'd had too many disappointments to set myself up for one more.

"You hungry?" Bam-Bam knelt on a patch of tan grass, pulling tons of stuff from his backpack.

"Sure. Want me to cook?" I took the skillet he handed me and then grabbed the economy-sized can of beans from my bag. I'd brought some chili peppers from my garden, along with cilantro, green onions, and tomatoes. We might be roughing it, but that didn't mean we couldn't eat well.

"Looks like you came prepared." Bam-Bam tossed me his pocket knife.

"An Eagle Scout is always prepared." I crossed my fingers over my heart and couldn't keep a straight face at Bam-Bam's smirk. Yeah, I wasn't exactly a scout. Just appreciative of good food. The garden at camp had been great for my cooking.

"All right then." He roughed up my hair, then gave me a small shove toward a lone tree line. "Let's get some wood and start the fire."

I broke off a branch, then lowered it at Bam-Bam's frown.

"We need old wood," he said. "The drier and scruffier it looks, the better. Got it?"

I nodded and threw down the limb. After twenty minutes of searching, we barely had a bundle of twigs. Then I spotted it.

"Look!" A leftover campfire lay half-hidden behind a rock. Who'd ever camped here must have left early because most of the logs were in pretty good shape.

I staggered under his shoulder clap. "Way to go, champ. With that, the wood I brought, and this kindling, we should have ourselves a good old-fashioned campfire. I may even sing."

"Please don't," I said, my mouth moving faster than my brain. But Bam-Bam only laughed.

"You haven't heard me yodel yet, kiddo. And I only do it on special occasions."

"Like before they take you to the loony bin?" I was more comfortable joking around now. Bam-Bam wasn't uptight like a lot of adults.

"Maybe." He slid me a sideways look so serious my mouth dropped open.

"I, uh, I'm sorry. I didn't mean to make fun of—you know—like that post-war stuff and all, and—"

Bam-Bam's wide smile flashed, and he punched my arm. "Hah! Got ya, kid."

I punched him back. "You son of a—" And before I knew it, we were pretend-sparring on the empty mountaintop, our kicking, hitting, and shoving in plain view of God and anyone else who cared to watch.

At first it was just fun, but every time Bam-Bam landed one, then danced out of reach, my anger started to rise. The fight reminded me of my life, blows coming at me when I least expected them. And me—powerless me—unable to stop it. It didn't matter that Bam-Bam was barely tapping me.

Eventually my temper boiled over until I lashed out hard. I didn't realize his lip was bleeding until he pulled out a handkerchief. I'd split it. Damn. I sprinted away and got as far as the trailhead before Bam-Bam tackled me.

I turned, swung blindly and screamed, my fury at myself a tangible thing. I hated being out of control. Hated being me. Bam-Bam pinned my arms at my side and knelt beside me, his face calm despite the red dripping down his chin.

"You got a nice uppercut there."

I stopped thrashing and stared. What? No recriminations, no lectures, no "Proceed directly to a foster group home; do not pass Go...do not see Alex"? Impossible. My heart thudded louder than the rattling cicadas.

"You're crazy, you know that?" I blurted, staring up into his scarred, craggy face.

"That's what they say every time they take me to the loony bin." His cut lip quirked, and guilt cut me even harder. "What do they say when you get kicked out of foster homes?"

I gaped at Bam-Bam. So he knew about that. Of course he did. "That I'm out of control. Won't listen to authority. Have anger issues. Potential for future incarceration," I quoted from a report I'd once seen in Helena's office, my voice thick. Unsteady. No matter how calm or cool I usually tried to act, I always knew the truth about myself. It was all there in black and white.

"Any of that bullshit true?" Bam-Bam looked me in the eyes as if he could see through my dark sunglasses, past my apathetic expression, to what was hidden behind it all.

And he'd called the reports bullshit. I sat up and wrapped an arm around my bent knees. Protecting myself. Always on guard. Bam-Bam was throwing me off my game. Did he actually want the truth?

"No. Yes. Sometimes."

Bam-Bam plucked a long strand of grass and put it between his teeth. He stretched out on the ground beside me, one ankle resting on his other knee. "Fair enough. Honesty isn't one of your problems." He cleared his throat, then eyed me again. "Loyalty either. Helena says you've been running away from foster homes to visit your mother."

The way he said it. Straight out. No judgment. It made me want to share something I'd never told anyone before. Not even Helena. "My smile's the only thing that keeps her going."

His sigh mingled with the wind. "Keeping your mom happy isn't your job."

My hands balled in my lap. "The hell it's not."

"It's her job, Javier. Hers."

There it was again. That steady, matter-of-fact tone that made my world tilt.

"Yeah, well. I ruined Mom's life. If I hadn't been born, she'd have gotten a college degree and would probably be working in a nice office. Instead she's wearing orange and behind bars." It was my fault. Mine.

Bam-Bam tossed aside the grass and rolled over to lean on an elbow. "Did you ask to be born?" He stared up at me until I shrugged.

"Like I had a choice."

"Exactly." He lay back down again and crossed his arms behind his head. Casual. Like we were talking about the weather. Nothing major. Nothing that blew my mind apart.

My mouth opened and closed. I struggled to argue back, to deny what he suggested. But after a moment of looking like a fish out of water, I flopped back on the rocky dirt. I had nothing.

Seriously.

The dude had a point. And if he was right, then that meant...my mind shut the valve off of that possibility. It was too much to process. Taking care of Mom was all I knew how to do. That and cooking. Maybe I'd make her a big meal when she got out of jail. Show her what I'd learned at camp.

"Your situation is not your destination, Javier," rumbled Bam-Bam.

"Huh?"

The ex-Marine sighed. "Just think about it." He stood, brushed the dirt off his camouflage shorts, and headed back to our packs. "I'll get the fire started," he added over his shoulder.

His boots crunched away while I gnawed on the idea. What if I didn't stay in North Carolina? What if I moved to New York like Helena wanted? Worked in her brother's restaurant and earned enough to go to culinary school?

Did I deserve that? After the mess I'd made of Mom's life—no way. But another voice whispered that Bam-Bam could be right. Those were her choices. Not mine. Maybe I deserved a chance, too.

Lightness filled me as I stared up into the darkening, early evening sky. The emptiness was vast, and I breathed it in until it pushed out my anger and guilt. I wasn't mad at Bam-Bam. And I wasn't mad at the world. I was mad at myself, and that was something I could control. As for the rest, I didn't have to figure it out today.

"Sorry," I said when I finally joined Bam-Bam. He took the log I offered and nodded. "I'm going to do better."

He was quiet for so long that I wasn't sure he heard me. At last he grunted, struck a match, and tossed it on the pile.

"I believe you."

And just like that, I did, too.

Chapter Twenty

Alex

My spoon clanged against my glass until the mess hall quieted after lunch. The meal had been less interesting with Javier gone on his hike. I tamped down my disappointment at the thought of him and my disastrous first rehearsal last night. Hopefully, this announcement would fix all of that.

"Hey look, it's the dictator—I mean, the *director*," called Brooke. Laughter filled the room, especially when Brittany snorted milk out of her nose. All right, then.

"Enough, people," boomed an unrecognizably loud voice. We all turned to see Victoria, the Divas' counselor, propped against one of the vertical wooden beams that ran in rows the length of the room. "Alex has got important news about our skit."

Whoa. I'd told her my plans on the way in to lunch, but since she'd only nodded, I hadn't thought she'd heard.

"Yes." I cleared my throat and stood on my tiptoes since some of the taller boys blocked me. "We've renamed the skit *West Side Scary* after hearing Brittany's excellent suggestion that we update it to a vampire/werewolf love story."

Some of the Warriors booed until the Divas' crossed their arms and glared them back into silence. Brittany grinned and stood, taking a bow that revealed enough cleavage to earn a smattering of applause.

"She'll also be co-directing it with me and helping me hold an open audition call this afternoon. Hope to see you there."

"We'd better see you there!" Brittany warned, her flirty smile making more than a few male campers scurry over to the sign-up board and rewrite the names they'd crossed off.

I sat down and returned Yasmine's approving smile. "Phew. That went better than I expected."

She speared a turkey meatball with her fork and pointed it at me. "Good work, Alex."

I couldn't help but glow a little. She'd been right. Including other people, using their ideas and input, might not be what I wanted, but that didn't mean it wasn't for the best.

"Wonder what I'll be?" Trinity dumped her meatballs and bit into her saucy bun.

"A vampire," we chorused, laughing and pointing at the red running down her chin.

"Ewwww. I don't even like meat." She swiped at her chin and tossed a stray dreadlock over her shoulder.

Jackie held up her sub. "What do you think werewolves eat?"

Trinity shuddered and turned to me. "Are we doing anything graphic like that?"

I glanced at Siobhan, but her attention was riveted on Rafael, who seemed to be debating something with Julian at the next table. "Ummm. Not too much. Siobhan helped me rewrite the final scene this morning. Just a beheading, I think."

Piper clapped her hands. "Awesome. I so want to be a werewolf."

Emily pulled up a chair, an overstuffed folder tucked under her arm. "And I want to be Dr. Drew. Sheesh. Do you have any clue how much work it is to help girls these days?"

Yasmine nodded. "You are doing a good thing, Emily."

"What would I have done without you this summer, Yasmine?" Emily high-fived her.

I opened my mouth to say, "Had some fun," but closed it. Yasmine might not be the life of the party, but now that I'd started reevaluating things, maybe that wasn't important. In fact, she was starting to feel like a friend.

"So when does your skit meet? Sorry I'm not helping." Emily scooped up one of Yasmine's meatballs and popped it in her mouth.

I shrugged. I was getting used to this go-it-alone thing. Actually starting to like it. "It's okay. We start in..." I checked my waterproof watch. "Ohmigod. Ten minutes."

I stood and scanned the room for Victoria, but she'd disappeared. That figured. "I've got to go set up the theater building. I'll see all of you there, right?"

A chorus of fake snarls and gnashing teeth erupted from my friends as I wove through the tables toward the door. I smiled. They'd need a little voice coaching if they were getting parts.

Brittany met me at the door. "You weren't leaving without your co-director, were you?" Her fingernails, painted in ladybug patterns, tapped on the wooden frame. "I was so excited when you picked me as your partner."

My forehead beaded. Oops. I had promised to include her. "Of course." I handed her the rewritten script. "Here are the new pages—pending your approval."

Brittany smiled, gold-colored fangs on proud display.

Whoa.

"You like?" She tapped her "teeth." "My Secret Camp Angel got me a vampire grill. Emily's idea totally rocks. Now let's see that script." She turned the pages as we stepped out into a day so bright the camp looked like it'd been whitewashed.

A couple minutes later, she handed it back. "Looks fine."

I paused at the rec room door. "Did you read it?"

Brittany tossed her blonde hair into a high ponytail. "Duh. I have like a photographic memory."

My eyes narrowed. "So what's Camp Juniper Point's motto? You know, the thing on the brochure they give our parents every year?"

Brittany shifted her weight to her other foot and took in a deep breath. "At Camp Juniper Point, we embrace a holistic approach to reducing the fragmentation that exists in young lives. We empower our campers to be less busy, less formally structured, less overtly competitive, more committed to meaningful moments and attentive to the wonder that surrounds them. Our objective is to present opportunities that build into a series of personal accomplishments that accumulate during the time they are with us. The goal is that they return from Camp Juniper Point with bold hearts and strong character—"

I held up a hand. "Enough. I'm convinced." Wow.

Brittany brushed by me though the door, her ponytail swishing. "Good, because we need to make changes on pages three, seven, twelve to sixteen...to start."

O-K. I trailed behind her into the large space. Vampires and werewolves weren't the only beasts I'd unleashed.

....

After a chaotic activity period of tryouts, followed by an afternoon spent hammering out the script and casting, Brittany and I were ready for our first after-dinner rehearsal. Luckily, Gollum had given us this extra free time or we would never have finished. I owed a lot to Brittany. Who knew giving up things would gain you more in return?

I was sacrificing the limelight for a behind-the-scenes role. And it was...fun in a lot of ways, actually. It didn't feel like it did when my parents ignored me or told talk show hosts to pretend I didn't exist.

"Cut!" hollered Brittany for the eleventh time in the last ten minutes. We were near the end of our evening rehearsal, and from the tired looks around the room, most were ready to call it a night.

Rafael, a stand-in for our leading man, Javier, wiped his mouth with the back of his hand and glared at Brittany.

"I'm sorry, but I certainly did not expect tongue. It wasn't written in the stage directions." He pushed up his wireless glasses and squinted down at the script we'd photocopied. "Besides, won't I be wearing a wolf mask?"

"Certainly seems logical." Siobhan stepped in front of her fellow wolf pack members and tugged on a dog-ear flap to straighten her hat.

Brittany, who we'd decided to cast as Maria the vampire, tapped her black high-heeled boots. "When is Javier coming back? I can't work with a boy who's never been kissed."

Several gasps echoed in the large space.

"How dare you." Siobhan looked ready to stake Brittany on the spot.

Rafael hung his head, and my heart went out to him. He'd been a good sport to stand in for Javier when he clearly was more comfortable working the special effects we'd planned with him. But we'd all sacrificed today. I, for one, had given up my dream of starring in my own musical...and kissing Javier again. But Brittany had threatened to walk if she didn't get the lead—a part she said she was clearly perfect for—and take her impressive number of friends with her. If I'd had any chance of having my skit, she was it.

"Tell her it's not true, Rafe." Siobhan folded her arms across her chest, her eyes still locked with Brittany's.

"Enough." I moved out of the shadows and stood under the hot spotlight. Note to self: Ask Brittany to have Vijay, our tech wiz, to turn down the watts. Second note to self: What the hell had I been thinking in letting this creep on the set? But Brittany had insisted we needed his expertise. "Look. There's no tongue. Rafael's right. It's not in the script." I returned Rafael's relieved smile. "We're keeping this strictly PG for the kids in the audience."

"What's the dif? It's time we spiced up Juniper Point." Rachel, another Diva, bared her teeth in a fairly convincing vampire snarl.

"Look, time's almost up." I held my thick hair off my steaming neck. "We've blocked the scene, and everyone's read through the script."

"Everyone but lover boy Javier!" called Vijay from his state-of-the-art light and sound effects board. When he'd heard of my idea for the show, he'd had his parents express mail it from home. "How did he get the lead and not even show up?"

Murmurs of agreement sounded. Brittany held up a hand, and the group quieted. "Yeah, Alex? Why does Javier have to play the lead? We all know you wanted to kiss him, but since you're directing—maybe it's time to reevaluate?"

Despite my hot face, I marched up to her and blew a bubble so close to her nose she flinched. "Because we agreed he's best for the part, remember? I'll fill him in on what he missed when he gets back from his trip with Bam-Bam."

Vijay snickered. "I just bet you will."

"Shut it, Vijay," Julian hollered. The rest of the boys from the Wander Inn jumped off the stage and crowded around him. "It's time we talked, bud." Julian looped a long arm around Vijay's shoulders and guided him toward a back room while the rest of his cabin followed.

"Bye, Alex!" called Brittany as she and the Divas wandered out the door.

"Wait!" I looked around at the room littered with props and the beginnings of co-opted costumes. I'd be up until "Taps" cleaning up this mess. But I couldn't stay, not when there was a chance I'd see Javier at tonight's senior movie night—mine and my cabin's favorite: *Titanic*. For the first time, Leonardo DiCaprio wouldn't be the one I stared at. I really missed Javier, even if I could only be with him from a distance.

"We'll help," offered Trinity. She peeked at Jackie's watch, then frowned. The rest of the group shuffled around, beginning to pick up items. But I could tell from their worried glances they wanted to make the movie. It started in five minutes.

"It's fine, guys. Victoria will help." I pointed to our dozing counselor who woke at her name, wiped the wet from her cheek, and sat up, holding her head.

"See—we'll be fine," I continued. "Plus, I think Siobhan and Rafael are staying." I gestured to the couple talking quietly in the corner.

Piper hesitated while Jackie continued gathering up bits of fur.

"Really. Go." I pointed at the door. I was over being the needy, selfish person who only wanted fun. It was hard to believe, looking back at the start of camp, that "payback" had been my goal for the summer. Now I wanted to pay back my friends by letting them shine in the skit and by staying away from Javier, giving him the trouble-free summer he deserved.

"We'll save a seat for you!" Trinity called as she followed Jackie and Piper outside. Yasmine paused at the door and gave me a long look followed by a nod that could have passed for approval.

The crowd was thinning. I wasn't sure where the Wander Inn guys had gone, but hopefully they'd taken Vijay back to the cabin.

"I just don't see why you had to let her paw you like that." Siobhan's whisper was now audible in the nearly empty room.

"Technically, I was the one with the paws," Rafael pointed out matter-of-factly. His lips quirked slightly, as if enjoying this flustered, red-faced version of Siobhan. I had to admit, I did too. She was always so calm and cool. What a switch for someone else to be in the emotional hot seat for a change.

"And the tongue." Siobhan poked Rafael's chest with an eraser she'd been using while helping Trinity draw the sets.

Rafael's laugh rang out. "Now that was hers."

"Whatever." Siobhan brushed by me and stormed out the door. "Oops. Sorry," she said when she bumped into a departing Victoria.

The door shut with a click behind them. Rafael scratched the back of his head and peered at me. "Girls are completely illogical."

I grabbed a few sets of claws and stashed them in a box. "And boys are easier to understand? Please."

Rafael stacked some leftover scripts and put them on a table. "I just don't understand why Siobhan's so mad about Brittany."

"No?" I wanted to tell him so badly, but that would be a major breach of girl code.

"Something isn't computing. Siobhan doesn't like me, does she? She—" The paper fluttered to the ground between us. "She likes me?"

I shrugged, doing my best to keep my grin at bay given his shocked expression.

"She likes me." His voice rose to a squeak at the end.

"Umm." I blew a bubble. It was the only way to keep my mouth shut.

"That's why she didn't like me kissing Brittany." Rafael took off his steamed glasses and wiped them on his shirt.

I nudged his shoulder as the last of the stage lights dimmed. "Why don't you go talk to her, Sherlock?"

Suddenly I was caught in a tight embrace and released just as quickly. "Thank you, Alex. You're awesome!" He raced to the door, passing another, shadowed figure on his way out.

"Have I been replaced?" spoke a deep voice I instantly recognized.

"Javier!" Although my heart leaped, I stayed put while he crossed the room. Though the spotlights were off, the dim overhead fluorescents couldn't hide his sinewy, athletic walk.

"Hey, Alex." His smile gleamed against his tanned skin, the color darker after his mountaintop camp out. Maybe it was not seeing him for a couple days, but he looked handsomer than ever, his brown eyes sparkling, his hair so thick I wanted to run my fingers through it. "Look. I'm sorry for walking out on you the other night. If you still want me, I'll help any way you need."

Wow. That trip with Bam-Bam must have been a game changer. He stood taller, had a firmer set to his chin and an open look in his eye. I couldn't quite put my finger on it, but he was different. Better yet, he wanted to be around me by choice, not because I'd begged.

"Of course I still want you," I breathed, stepping closer. "We changed things a little, but you're still the lead."

His fingers laced in mine, and he leaned in. "Do I still get to kiss you?"

Our foreheads touched. His breath smelled like something spicy I really wanted to taste. "No. I gave Brittany the part."

"It's too bad I won't get to kiss you in the play."

"I could show you how that part goes," I whispered.

His hand cupped the back of my head. "I might have a few ideas of my own."

And suddenly our bodies and mouths fused. It was like we'd been separated for years instead of days. His hands roamed down my back, squeezing my hips and drawing me close. Our lips pressed against each other, then opened, his tongue on mine. I slid my hands along his back, and he pushed me against the stage wall.

Suddenly a pinpoint spot of bright light cut through the dimness, followed by an unmistakable sneer. "And cut!"

We froze, and I looked over Javier's shoulder to see Vijay race toward the door, his right hand clutching some kind of electronic device. A phone, I guessed, judging by the square of blue light that flashed near his hand as he ran.

Oh, God. He'd been in the building the whole time.

"Was that—" Javier shook his head, his eyes still fuzzy.

"Vijay?" My heart sank as I imagined the possibilities. "Yes."

"Why is he so obsessed?"

I shook my head. The better question was, what did Vijay intend to do with that video? All this time, I'd been on a payback mission. It'd never occurred to me that my ex might be on one, too.

Chapter Twenty-One

Javier

"We've got to get that phone."

The objective flashed into my brain with perfect clarity.

Setting Alex aside, I shook off the last of my hot-for-her haze and sprinted toward the exit.

"Wait." She held me back, her fingers clutching my forearm. "Don't go."

"Are you kidding me?" I shook my head. "All the times you've gone tearing headfirst into trouble and now you want me to wait? You realize that bastard is going to post that video all over the Internet, right? That your parents will see it? This is not the way for them to find out about us."

"I'm already going to boarding school, so what's the worst they can do? Plus, it's not like I haven't been humiliated on the Internet before." Alex put herself between me and the door. "It's my fault you almost got ejected from camp before, and I'm not going to let that happen again."

"That wasn't your fault." I unhooked her fingers from my arm. Gentle, but firm. "Alex, I'm not going to lose it, okay? I know that now after my trip with Bam-Bam. Besides, it's time someone confronted that kid and found out what's wrong with his lame ass." He held up his hands. "I'll use words, not fists."

I was going to control myself if it killed me.

"Then I'm going with you." She took off like an arrow from a bow, making a straight shot for the door.

"Seriously?" I caught her, tugging her back. "Go home, Alex. I'm ending this tonight."

She shook her head fast, her face white.

"No."

"Yes. I get distracted when you're around because I worry about you and want to protect you and...hell. I can't think straight. This time? Please. Let me do this my way."

She hesitated only a moment. Then she nodded, the movement jerky.

"Okay."

Whoa. Hadn't seen her agree that quickly before. I was already running by the time she shouted, "Good luck!"

Yeah. I'd freaking need it.

I took off into the dark, wondering where the creep would go with the video. Gollum? One of the other counselors? Or would he try to embarrass Alex by showing it off to his friends before using his 4G to post it?

Banking on the last option, I ran through the woods, ignoring the paths in case any counselors were out. When I arrived at the boys' cabins, the lights were on in Wander Inn.

Score.

Leaping up the steps onto the porch, I pounded on the door frame. The door was open, with only a screen between me and the Wander Inn guys. Three of them were scattered around the floor.

"Vijay?" I shouted, willing myself to stay calm. Focused.

"Not here, dude." Julian slid off his bunk and padded across the cabin floor. "He took off for the movie when we tried talking to him about—uh—what's up?" Julian quickly changed the subject.

"The punk snapped a picture or video of Alex and me at the theater building after the skit." I levered open the screen door and looked around, half-convinced they were hiding him somewhere. "He's been harassing Alex all summer and even during the school year. It's going to stop now."

After weeks of worrying that BLISS Network would pop out of some bushes and catch us, it was ironic that Vijay had been the real threat.

I waited for Vijay to step out of the bathroom or otherwise show himself. The kid never backed down from a fight that was for damn sure. But his cabin mates were the only ones here.

"The rest of the cabin is at the movie night." Rafe put down his cast notes from the play and looked up. They were a copy of the set tucked into my pocket.

"I need to find Vijay. Who's going to help?" I wasn't backing down on this. Besides, I was running out of time to stop this jerk from doing major damage to Alex's life.

"Whoa." Bam-Bam's voice echoed through the room as he arrived suddenly on the front porch. "What's going on here, Javier? I could hear you from two cabins down."

The warning note in his tone was obvious.

"Vijay spied on Alex and me—" I didn't say we'd been kissing. "And took pictures or video. I'm not sure which. But the kid is out of control and someone needs to talk to him."

Bam-Bam muttered under his breath, and I was pretty sure it wasn't anything good. "You kids stay here. *Titanic* has got another hour to go, I think, but I don't want you guys roaming the camp alone." His jaw flexed as he tucked his shirt in and changed from leather sandals to sneakers. "I'll circle the campus and see if I can find him."

"Will do, boss," Julian agreed, holding open the door for the counselor.

Bam-Bam was half-out the door when he called back, "And no fighting, Javier."

Umm...yeah. I sure as hell hoped not. But the longer it took Vijay to return to the cabin, the more amped I got. What was he doing all this time? Julian tried to show me some of his survival gear and asked about my hike with Bam-Bam. Rafe challenged me to chess, but I couldn't sit still. I'd prowled the Wander Inn for at least fifteen minutes before the door opened.

Vijay stood alone, an iPhone still in one hand.

"What the hell are you doing here?" he snapped at me, his lip curling.

Did the kid have no idea how hard I worked not to throttle him? I took a deep breath. Then another.

"Where is the picture of Alex?" Julian asked, coming to stand by my side. "You've gotta leave her alone, man."

I willed my fury into submission so I could speak reasonably. Normally.

"She doesn't deserve the way you're treating her." I sounded as smooth as a social services caseworker. Steady as a freaking camp counselor. "Hand over the phone and let your friends delete the photo."

Vijay shrugged. He tossed the phone to Garrett, who sat off to one side as if unwilling to get involved either way.

"Fine. But it's a video and I already got it on YouTube in spite of the slow-as-shit cell service up here. There's no deleting the thing now."

No punch had ever hurt as much as that news. I couldn't even catch my breath. Anger surged. I saw red. Damn, damn, damn, I wasn't going to be able to hold it together...

"What the hell is the matter with you?"

Rafe, the chess player, got up in Vijay's face. Nose-to-nose. *Mano y mano.*

"Chill," Vijay laughed and tried to push Rafe back, but Rafe didn't budge. "Seriously, man, get off me."

"You don't mess with people's lives like that," Rafe shouted. "All summer, you've been a jerk, and your friends have taken it. But you're screwed in the head—"

"What's going on?" Bam-Bam exploded into the cabin, inserting himself between Rafe and Vijay. "Two steps back, guys. Pronto."

The tension was thick. Veins popped on the sides of Vijay's forehead. Rafe's cheeks were red, his eyes narrow. And me? I had my fists jammed in my pockets so I didn't plant them in Vijay's teeth.

"Vijay took video of me and Alex and posted it online."

"I commented with a link on the *Wholesome Home* blog, too," he bragged. "Right where Alex's daddy can't help but see."

"You worthless sack of—"

My curses got lost in the obscenities shouted from virtually every guy in the room, except the dumbass smiling like he'd just won the freaking lottery. For once, I was hurt too much to be angry. I didn't know how to stop the world of pain about to descend on Alex. Though I did know pummeling Vijay wouldn't knock the stupidity out of him. And for the first time, I was pretty sure it wouldn't make me feel better either.

"Hey," Vijay shouted over everyone. "It's time her parents knew what kind of girl—"

"Shut up!" Rafe shouted while my chest burned with a new hole in it.

"What is wrong with you?" Bam-Bam shook his head, disbelieving.

"I'll tell you what's wrong with him," Rafe snarled. He dove under a bed and came out with a black drawstring pouch.

"No way," Vijay sputtered. "That's private."

He dove for Rafe, but Rafe was already yanking open the bag. As Vijay reached for it, he knocked it out of Rafe's hands. A vial and a needle rolled out, clattering across the floor.

"What is it?" Garrett put his feet up on the bed as if he didn't want them contaminated.

"Steroids." I'd seen enough juiced-up guys muscle their way through foster care. Had gotten my eyebrow scar because of one of them. If I hadn't been so focused on Alex, I would have recognized the signs weeks ago.

"Give the man a prize," Rafe murmured. "He got it in one guess."

"That's bullshit!" Vijay screamed, his face going purple as he scrambled to pick up the drug paraphernalia. "You have no right to touch my stuff."

"Keep it down, son," Bam-Bam urged. "You had no right to bring this to camp in the first place."

"I had no right?" Vijay shouted, only marginally quieter. "I had no right? Who are you to tell me what rights I have?"

Bam-Bam scrubbed a hand over his short buzz cut. "I'm an adult, a veteran, and your counselor. Let's start with that."

"Yeah, start there. But bottom line, no one messes with you, and you know why?" Vijay sneered. "Because genetics made you six-foot-four. You won the chromosome lottery that guarantees no one will ever push you around or call you weak or trip you in the lunch line just for the hell of it."

Vijay had lost it. Purple face. Veins bulging. Tears leaking out his eyes. I'm pretty sure he didn't know about the tears. Or else he was beyond caring.

I swallowed hard. Pissed off as I was with Vijay, I didn't like where this was headed.

"Maybe we should go to Mr. Woodrow's office—" Bam-Bam offered.

"So he can send me home? Back to where I was the runt of the junior class? Back to getting bullied by guys bigger than me? For being a tech-geek? For being Muslim?"

The silence that followed felt louder than the shouting. My ears rang with it.

"The answer to being bullied isn't to bully someone else," Bam-Bam said quietly as he picked up Vijay's iPhone.

"Tell it to my dad," he spat back. "The 'roids were his idea."

"That's messed up," Garrett muttered, shaking his head.

Bam-Bam's eyebrows shot up. "Your father got these for you?"

"He sent them underneath a box of cookies from my mom. Along with the iPhone so I could update him on my summer workouts."

Julian whistled low under his breath. The fight seemed to have gone out of Vijay, his face pale, his control wrecked.

"Seems like you should have been mad at your dad instead of Alex." I don't know why I said it. The kid was having a bad day and maybe I was a jerk for rubbing his nose in the ways he'd messed up. But Alex was going to be the one who paid for his choices, and I was still pissed about that.

"I don't know what I'm doing half the time." Vijay shrugged, his eyes vacant. "I thought it would be good to come here and get away from everything back home, but it just followed me anyhow."

"You think you can talk to Woodrow?" Bam-Bam talked to him with a patience I admired. He'd calmed a high-octane situation, and he'd never raised his voice. Never got angry.

Nodding, Vijay shuffled toward the door.

When Bam-Bam followed, I was right behind him. Stepping off the porch onto the soft carpet of pine needles, I turned toward the girls' campus rather than toward the Warriors' Warden.

"Not an option," Bam-Bam barked at me over one shoulder. "Lights out is in ten minutes."

"I've got to warn Alex—"

"Not tonight." He turned to stare me down. "Back to your cabin, Javier. We'll deal with the rest tomorrow."

I wanted to argue. But hadn't I just decided to control my defiance? My temper? Besides, Bam-Bam was one of the good guys. He'd looked out for me so far.

"Understood," I agreed, dragging leaden feet back toward my cabin.

I just hoped Alex would, too.

Chapter Twenty-Two

Alex

"I think Bam-Bam might be hotter than Rob," Jackie announced the next morning after we got back from the showers and were dressing for breakfast.

"Sacrilege!" shouted Piper, winging her pillow toward the window where Jackie stood, staring out at the common area at the center of the girls' campus. "Rob didn't get the nickname the *Hottie* for nothing. He is the hottest counselor here."

Distracted by the muddle in my head, I wasn't paying much attention to the half-hearted argument that broke out or the pairs of rolled socks girls lobbed like grenades at each other. Someone's blue cotton bra hit me in the shoulder, a slingshot missile gone wide.

"Is Bam-Bam out there?" I asked suddenly, wondering what he'd be doing here so early.

"Yeah," Jackie shouted, waggling her eyebrows at me. "And I'm starting to get what Emily sees in him. Hey, where are you going?"

I heard her shout to me, but I was already out the door. My hair was still wet, but I was dressed and I needed to know what went down with Vijay the night before.

"Excuse me?" I called, waving a hand to snag Emily and Bam-Bam's attention. "Can I—"

"Just who we wanted to see!" Emily whipped around fast to look at me, her movement jerky. "Gollum—I mean, Mr. Woodrow—would like to see you. Would you mind running down there before breakfast?"

My eyes darted to Bam-Bam. Had he brought this news? But his stony face gave away nothing. My stomach knotted.

"They kicked out Javier, didn't they?" I just knew it in my gut. My heartbeat skittered into high gear, and my face felt hot. "How could they—"

"Javier is heading down to see him now, too," Bam-Bam offered. "Maybe you can catch him if you hurry."

I was already running. Wet hair, no makeup, my sneakers colored with brown magic marker. I didn't care about anything but setting Gollum straight. Whatever had happened last night was my fault. Vijay's fault. Anyone's fault but Javier's, who was finally coming around to seeing a way we could be together after all.

"Alex."

Javier's sleep-scratchy voice warned me a few seconds before I would have collided with him. He stood on the path in front of the administration building, close to the director's door.

"Javier." I launched into his arms, not thinking. But he scuttled back a step and took my hands in his instead. "You're still here."

"I haven't gone in to see him yet," he explained. "By the time we found Vijay last night, there was a big blow-out in the Wander Inn—"

"You got in a fight?" I looked him over for evidence. If he had any bruises, I was going to pummel Vijay.

"No." Javier tugged me closer to the edge of the trees as a couple of staff workers strode past us into the administration building. "Rafe got in his face more than I did. Vijay's been on steroids. That's why he's so bulked-up and pissed off all the time."

My jaw dropped. "Vijay is taking drugs?"

I don't know why it felt so unbelievable. It made sense. But he'd always been a super smart kid. A tech-wiz who would get into engineering school or some high-tech program where he'd make big-time bucks. He wasn't supposed to mess around with steroids. Then again, maybe I was more of a *Wholesome Home* kid than I realized. Drugs just weren't on my radar. "Vijay left with Bam-Bam to talk to Gollum last night, but I haven't heard anything more since then." Javier peered past my shoulder as the door to the camp director's office opened with a squeak.

"I'd like to see you both, please," Gollum called, looking more serious than I'd ever seen him.

My heart dropped.

Javier let go of my hands. We turned to walk toward our doom, and out of one corner of his mouth, Javier spoke quietly.

"Vijay posted a video of us kissing online. He put it up on YouTube and added a link to the *Wholesome Home* blog in the comments section."

"Oh my God." I stopped in my tracks. My heart bottomed out and hit the ground. The news knocked the wind out of me, and I couldn't breathe.

I looked from Javier to Gollum and back again.

"Come inside, Ms. Martineau. We have a lot to discuss."

I'd imagined it was possible. Had acted like it didn't matter if the video got posted so Javier wouldn't chase down Vijay. But the reality. Holy crap. I was done. If not dead, I was at the very least disowned. Worse yet, Javier would lose his job for kissing a camper.

Javier walked back to me. In front of Gollum, he threaded his fingers through mine and drew me forward, past the director and into the small office lined with awards, photos, and flyers from camp events.

"Have a seat," Gollum urged, clearing his throat and gesturing to two gray folding chairs.

I lowered myself to the cold metal chair, already shivering from the news and the feel of my wet hair on my back. When Javier released my fingers, it was like I was unmoored.

"I want to assure you that the person responsible for this is being sent home even as we speak." Gollum stalked over to his computer monitor and turned it so we could see the screen.

The color video image was paused to show Javier's hands on my waist. My face tipped up to his. Our mouths sealed together. And that wasn't the worst of it. The worst was the fact that the image was embedded right in the comments section of my parents' blog, with all the cute, happy images associated with *Wholesome Home* surrounding it. A spotted puppy. A small house with a white picket fence. The iconic photo of my parents' faces pressed cheek-to-cheek and smiling.

Amid all that heartwarming bloggy goodness was dark and grainy video footage and a crude header that read "Not so Wholesome at Camp."

When a tissue box appeared in front of my nose, I realized I was crying. Gollum, of all people, extended the offering. I clutched it to my chest. I'd need an industrial-sized container to get through this.

"Please say Javier is not in trouble." Those were my first coherent words. "This is all my fault."

Javier started to speak, but Gollum interrupted.

"My hands are tied here." He toyed with his whistle as he sat on the edge of his desk. "I honestly would have preferred if we could have handled this at camp, but this situation has become as much a problem for the camp administration as it is for you."

Even now, I noticed his old-fashioned desk phone blinked with messages or calls or whatever it was that made those phones' buttons light up.

"Alex, your parents are leaving Honduras as soon as possible. They wish to speak to you in person to decide the next course of action." He cleared his throat a few more times, and I just knew my father had raised holy hell with him, probably threatening a lawsuit.

Yeah, that was easy to picture.

"I will make sure they know Camp Juniper Point isn't to blame for this." I tucked my dripping hair behind one ear. "I promise you, I take full responsibility for this. But what about Javier?"

Gollum's eyes went to Javier, and something passed between them I couldn't interpret. Whatever it was, it made Javier put his head down for a second. He closed his eyes and nodded as if he already understood.

"What is it?" I blurted, the tension so thick I could choke on it.

"Mr. Kovalev was well-aware of the stakes for another infraction." Gollum cleared his throat and turned the computer monitor away from us. "I'm sorry, son, but the social services department was very clear when I signed off on you that you had to follow all employee rules. They've already seen the video and contacted me with concerns about your lack of supervision. I'm to fill out an official report explaining that you behaved inappropriately with a camper, ignored direction to be in either your cabin or at the approved nightly activity, and used an unoccupied facility without permission. You're a good kid, and you've worked hard. I wish things had turned out differently, but my hands are tied."

Javier nodded again. Accepting. Quiet. How could he just accept that B.S. excuse?

"You can't kick him out." Anger evaporated my tears. "I kissed him! He had nothing to do with—"

Javier laid a hand on my forearm. "It's okay."

"It's not okay. You're not going to some group home with people who don't even know you or care about you." I couldn't believe he wasn't arguing his case. I looked back to Gollum. "He's brought so much good to this camp. The cooking. The garden. Helping figure out Vijay's problem, which no one else here even acknowledged."

"I agree, and for what it's worth, I will note every positive change I've witnessed in Javier when I file my reports. But I can't ignore what's happened here." The camp director frowned down at some papers on his desk. "Word will spread quickly and I can't–I won't–misrepresent the truth. Transportation will arrive to bring you to your new home on Sunday, Mr. Kovalev." Gollum stood, and even though he looked genuinely disappointed about the whole situation, it didn't change the fact that he was going to screw Javier over.

"I can't believe this," I whispered to myself. "I can't freaking believe this."

"It's all right." Javier looked so calm. Not defeated, exactly. But like he'd already moved on and left camp in his rearview mirror.

How could he have a temper all summer and then not fight when it counted most? I tried to plead with my eyes, but he shook his head at me.

Gollum cleared his throat. "As for you, Alex, I'll let you know if I have any advance notice from your family, but your mother hoped to arrive Friday evening. You can continue participating in your activities until we decide how to proceed."

"What about the play, Mr. Woodrow? Can Alex still direct? I know a lot of kids are counting on her." It was the most Javier had said since we'd come into the office.

But what did skit night matter now? I shook my head, thinking about how much I'd wanted to produce the skit and prove myself as a director. For what? And to whom? I'd be more famous for a lip-lock caught on tape than anything I did with the play.

Gollum frowned.

"It doesn't matter." I stood, my legs not quite steady.

"I think you should honor that commitment." Gollum's eyes were surprisingly kind. "The other campers are really looking forward to seeing what you've come up with, and for myself, I think it would be good for the camp community to remember the message of *West Side Story*."

"I won't do it without Javier." I folded my arms. I thought all the fight had drained out of me, but something rallied inside me now. "If he doesn't do this—"

"That will be fine, Ms. Martineau. Javier can join the cast on Friday." Gollum clapped me on the shoulder. "Good luck to you both."

He strode out of the office and held the door for us to follow him. Javier gave him a nod, a man-to-man thing that bugged me since Gollum had just singlehandedly consigned Javier to a group foster home. Who knew what kinds of troubled kids he'd be living with?

I stumbled out of the administration building into the sunlight.

"You want some breakfast?" Javier asked.

"I lost my appetite." I felt so empty inside. I wanted to go somewhere and just cry. Nearby, I heard the hum of voices in the mess hall and the clatter of trays on the tables as kids sat down with their meal.

Familiar sounds. The sounds of summer.

I breathed in the pine-scented air and knew I'd miss this place so much. Not for a second did I think my parents would let me stay after their ominous "visit." Javier and I would both go back to lives we resented. Only his would be much, much worse than mine.

"Come on." Javier gave me a lopsided grin and pulled me through the trees toward the lake. "The good thing about being kicked out of camp is they can't punish me with anything worse." He waggled his eyebrows. "Guess I can get away with anything now."

Following him blindly, I knew he was trying to make me smile, but instead his warm-hearted charm just made me want to sob even more.

"You belong here." I hugged him, fast and hard. "I'm so sorry I got you into trouble. I feel like I'm always saying that, but it's always true."

"Stop." He halted in the middle of the trees on a small hilltop. The water glistened less than a hundred yards away. "Don't you dare apologize to me for anything."

"I got you into trouble the minute you set foot in this place, and I just keep on making things worse, even though you've tried to tell me and tried to tell me—"

He kissed me. Caught my lips with his. Covered my words. I lost my train of thought. Frustration sighed out of me until I felt a soft, languid sweetness steal over me. I knew it was fake and fleeting—just the kiss at work on my biology—but still...he kissed the anger away until it was a smaller knot inside of me instead of a red cloud that covered my whole body.

When he eased back, his brown eyes looked straight into mine.

"You're the best thing that's ever happened to me."

My heart caught tight. I shook my head.

"No."

"Yes." He held both my hands. His work boots straddled my flip-flops. We stood that close. "This summer, however short it's been, was amazing."

"But now you can't be with your mom when she's released. You said you both had to have good behavior for her to regain custody." Even if Javier didn't understand how much I'd messed up, his mother would.

I'd hurt her unforgivably. "You won't turn eighteen for six more months."

"Still, I made the choices, Alex. I chose to kiss you, and I don't regret it. I'm in control of what happens to me. And I'm responsible for myself. Bam-Bam taught me that. It's the reason why I kissed you when I got back. I didn't want to waste another minute worrying about what other people thought." He touched his nose to mine, his eyes so close I could feel the brush of his lashes against my forehead.

"I'm so sorry you were embarrassed in front of tons of people and it made trouble with your parents. But for my sake? I wouldn't change one thing about what's happened between us."

My heart ached and ached. His words seeped deep into me, but no matter what he said, I wished I could turn back time. I shook my head sadly.

"Look." He pointed toward the beach where Siobhan and Rafe were holding hands. "Your play brought them together."

I squeezed his hand tight, grateful to him for trying to cheer me up. He had no way of knowing it was an impossible task.

"It's going to be the best damn skit ever," I sniffled.

"Everything will work out, Alex, you'll see. The scene will be a hit. And you're going to be a star at the boarding school just like you are here."

"Yeah, right," I muttered, punching him lightly in the arm. "Can't you see the disaster I've created? The fallout from that video is going to be crazy." I knew he'd have some kind of record from foster care. Going to a group home wasn't like going to juvie, but it would be noted somewhere in some caseworker's files forever. Not exactly what college admissions offices wanted to see...if he wanted to go to college. But if he didn't, what would happen to Javier?

"Give us credit. We're tougher than that." He reached down to pick a spindly violet from the base of a pine tree. "I want you to pack that glitter letter A of yours and hang it in your dorm room at school. Claim your territory. It'll make me happy to think about that when..."

"Sure." I was being selfish. He was being so strong, picking me up while I complained and cried about stuff we couldn't change. "I will. We both will. Make the best of it."

Javier nodded. The noise level nearby increased as the mess hall doors opened and kids started flooding out onto the flagstone paths to their next activities.

We headed back toward our friends, not bothering to hold hands now. I guess we both knew there was no point. We'd be leaving on the weekend. Would probably never see each other again.

And although we'd try to make the best of it, I'd screwed up more than ever before. I didn't need my parents to tell me. It was as clear as the strong, silent boy walking beside me.

I'd known I'd get him into trouble from day one and had cared too much about getting back at Vijay to worry about it. I never guessed it would hurt so much.

"Alex!" a shout from the exiting mess hall crowd caught my attention while Rafe and Julian jogged over to Javier.

Emily waved at me while snippets of conversations peppered my ears.

"...parents picked him up."

"...can't believe he was taking drugs."

"He was a lot smaller a year ago, remember?"

The gossip—obviously about Vijay—ticked me off as I moved through the crowd. Weird since I'd spent so much time hating him. But I'd had a reason to be upset with him and that reason didn't matter anymore.

"Alex!" Emily pounced on me, slinging an arm around my shoulders. "Mr. Woodrow asked me to find you. He said your mom's calling him back in a few minutes and wants to talk to you. Can you hustle over to his office?"

"My mother?" I could envision her now, her iPhone in hand, checking her blog's page views while updating her Twitter stream and simultaneously dialing the number for Camp Juniper Point. "Maybe she needs some quotes from me for a blog on disciplining a rebellious teen."

"Hey! Someone needs to march back to the Kindness Cup for a refresher course." Emily squeezed me tight before letting me go. "I'm sure she's just worried about you."

Um. Sure.

"Thanks, Em." I hurried away, not wanting to miss the call. All that anger I was feeling now had the perfect outlet.

I might suck at archery, but this was one target I wouldn't miss.

Racing through the trees toward the director's office where I'd been crying just a short while ago, I knocked on the closed door.

"Come in!" Gollum answered.

"Hi. I came because..." I stopped when I noticed he was on the phone.

"Here she is now." He stood behind his desk and passed the phone so fast it could have been a hot potato. "Your mom," he stage-whispered and stalked toward the door. "Just close the door when you're done. I'll be just outside."

It seemed like a lot of equipment to trust me with, but then, I wasn't a first-year camper and he wouldn't be far away. Grateful for a little privacy, I picked up the heavy handset.

I drew a deep breath, tension coiling in my chest. "Mom?"

"Alex, I'm coming to camp—"

"So I've heard." My heart thumped hard as I paced the tiny office. "I'm sure Dad couldn't wait for a reason to yank me out."

"Actually, your father—"

"Whatever," I cut her off and stared out the window at a couple of skipping, junior campers. "It's time we talked about what's bugging us instead of pretending to be a happy, *Wholesome Home* family."

"I agree."

Ignoring her, I plowed ahead, dodging the corner of the desk as I walked around it. "While you've been resenting me for being such a sorry excuse for a daughter, I've resented *you*. You used me as your token problem child since the moment I turned two and knocked over Gram's orchid." When my brother had been a kid, they'd blogged about the joys of helping his growth and development. As for me, I'd spawned a whole new archive category called "Toddler Messes."

"Alex." Mom's voice turned stern. Clearly she wanted to take over the conversation. But didn't she always?

"No. Listen to me." I pounded my fist on Gollum's desk, making a framed photo of Mrs. Woodrow jump. "I'm tired of being the problem child. Don't deny that posts about my mistakes have been way more popular than blogs about Andrew. You think I haven't noticed that the columns about me get more hits? My kiss with Javier will probably spawn a whole new book deal for you. So...you're welcome."

Something wet hit my hand, and I realized it was a tear. Another splotch joined the first.

"Alex, I—"

"You what?" I sobbed, then didn't give her a chance to answer. What could she say that would make anything better? "One of these days I'll be famous on my own...and not because of that stupid blog." I kept on talking since she didn't even try to interrupt this time. She was probably on a whole different screen on her phone, my whiny phone call minimized to a tiny icon in the corner of the big window of her life. "Of course, you have no idea I like acting and I'm actually good at it. And you don't have any clue that an assistant director said I might have some talent and that if I could go to New York for a few more readings, I might be able to clinch a spot at a performing arts high school in New York. I didn't bother to tell her that—too late—my parents can't wait to make a big, splashy deal of shipping me off to boarding school this fall."

"We can talk about it when I get there on Friday," Mom started, her voice soft. I wondered if she was trying to hide the conversation from Dad. Dad would probably have her hang up on me to teach me a lesson.

"I used to act out to get *your* attention, you know. Not the whole world's." I sank down into one of the metal chairs and wished Javier was still sitting in the other one. "Now, I've hurt someone I care about."

"The boy?" At least, I think that's what she said. The connection broke up. "In the video?"

"Javier." I wasn't sure I wanted to share anything about him with my mother, but how much more could the Martineau family hurt him now? "He came here to turn things around for himself and I messed that up so many ways..."

"I heard he's being kicked out of camp." In the background, I could hear what sounded like a public address system at an airport—muffled flight numbers and times spoken fast and low.

"That's not the worst part, Mom." I laid my forehead on the edge of the wooden desk and stared at the floor. "While you guys have been prancing around looking for photo-ops, Javier has been trying to stay out of trouble so he could help his mother when she gets out of jail. He hasn't lived with her for three years, but she was finally getting out and now–" God, I hated this. "Instead of being with her for his senior year of high school, he'll be sent to a group foster home on the other side of the state."

"Do you know her name, Alex?" A babble of voices swelled in the background behind her.

"Her name?" I shook my head and straightened. "Sofia, I think. But you're missing the point. Javier needed to stay out of trouble this summer to get that chance and now–"

"What's their last name?" Mom shouted through a sketchy connection.

My anger surged. "Ko-va-lev. Have you been listening? She's not even a criminal. She wrote some bad checks and had a hard time raising her kid in a bad economy. Javier's been stuck in foster care. But he really turned himself around and he's this great cook–"

"Alex, I'm boarding now and have to go, but I'll be there on Friday. We'll talk more then." She hadn't lectured me, but had she listened? At all?

I wanted to smash something with my fist. I had so much emotion welling up inside me and no place to go with it. I swallowed back some of it with an effort and took a deep breath.

"Sure, Mom." Why did I still try getting through to her? To either of them. "See you then."

Hanging up the phone, I snagged a few more tissues and marched out of the office. I couldn't think about Mom or boarding school or anything else right now. Because talking about Javier's mom made me think about a very different phone conversation I'd had with her.

She'd wanted Javier to have fun while he was at summer camp. I only had two more days before my parents swooped in to drag me home, but between now and then, I was going to make sure he got to make some camp memories. Not so much with me, but with the rest of the kids.

I was going to make *West Side Scary* the best, most fun and exciting production Camp Juniper Point had ever seen. And Javier was going to be the star.

Chapter Twenty-Three

Alex

Something tall and furry brushed against me in our makeshift backstage Friday night.

"Way to go, Alex!" Jackie thumped my back with her werewolf claws. "The show's awesome."

I put a finger to my lips and shook my head. With only a thin curtain between us and the audience, there was little to muffle sound. Besides, I didn't want to miss Javier and Brittany's kissing scene. Luckily Gollum had agreed that Javier's treatment was unfair, and allowed him this romantic acting scene. It'd hurt to watch them practice these past few days, but it was an important moment. For the sake of the scene, I wanted them to get it right. Preferably without tongue.

My nail polish tasted bitter as I gnawed on what was left of my thumb nail. Javier's rich singing voice filled the room with a final note, and then he grabbed Brittany, pulled her close, and pressed his lips (muzzle, really) to hers.

"Breathe, Alex," whispered Jackie.

But I couldn't. Seeing him kiss another girl ripped a fresh hole in my heart every time. Yet when his eyes lifted, they met mine through the mask holes, their expression tender and full of longing. I melted a little inside. He meant that kiss for me.

Air rushed out, and I sagged against Jackie. How bittersweet. Now that Javier was finally ready to be with me, we were being separated. It'd be easy to blame Vijay or my parents or even Gollum. But I knew who was responsible for this mess. Me.

I blew Javier a kiss from the shadowed sideline and pulled the curtain closed to thunderous applause. The jabbering actors rushed off stage. With stern looks and hand gestures, I quieted them and got them back in place. After a quick set change organized by Trinity and special effects arranged by Rafe, Brittany was back on stage in no time. In the gloom, a strong hand slipped in mine and squeezed. Javier. He didn't go back out for another couple of minutes. His breath was warm and close against my ear.

"Still wish you were my Maria," he whispered.

"The show's better with Brittany in the lead. That's what counts." I kept my voice quieter than the coughs and cleared throats in the audience.

He cupped my chin and brushed my mouth with his. "I'm going to miss you."

"Me, too."

We jumped apart when Rafe tapped Javier's shoulder.

"Here's the head."

Javier put on the replica head that added height since he was now looking out of the wolf's snout.

"Remember to scrunch down and squirt the blood bag if it doesn't go off automatically when Julian cuts off your head. Got it?" Rafael repositioned a Ziploc bag of ketchup and cherry JELL-O inside the snout.

"Got it." Javier's voice sounded muffled. It must be super-hot in there, and for the first time, I could see some benefit to not being in the spotlight. Directing wasn't so bad.

I glanced at my watch. When I looked up, I caught Rafael giving Siobhan a kiss. Aw! I felt so happy for my friend.

"Places," I hissed, and a few other cast members raced on stage with Javier.

I peeked through the slit between the wall and the material and spotted my mom during the West Side Scary climactic fight scene. She was here! I hadn't been able to see her earlier, but then again, I'd been big-time distracted getting the production off the ground. Weird to be thinking about my mother when I was still at camp with my friends—but it felt strange to see her here solo. My parents never went anywhere alone, so this must be a serious 9-1-1 for her to have shown up by herself. Then again, maybe Dad was already in New York negotiating a new book deal over my latest life drama. Either way, it worried me. Mom looked smaller and less confident. But that might have been because we'd made everyone turn off and stow their cell phones. She must be going through serious withdrawal.

My attention returned to the stage, and I smiled at my friends' theatrics in the wake of Tony's—aka Javier's—death. They growled and snarled and somehow still managed to sing and act like pros. Brittany delivered her final cautionary words with passion and a fierceness that made me glow with pride. For a moment, I imagined what it'd be like to take a bow as the scene ended, soaking in the enthusiastic applause and cheers now filling the room. But that wasn't my role this time. This day belonged to the stars, and mine had definitely dimmed.

"Hey!" Brittany exclaimed when Javier dropped her hand, ran off stage, and into my arms. Before I could react, he dragged me on stage and planted me front and center.

"Everyone. This is our co-director Alex. Please show her your appreciation," shouted Javier. He held up my hand like we were Olympic relay racers...and maybe we were. We'd run a marathon this past month.

Brittany gave me a hug and a bundle of pink roses and lavender. "Alex is the amazing director behind *West Side Scary*," she said to the clapping assembly. "None of this would have been possible without her."

If anything, the hoots and hollers got even louder. Tears threatened, but I swallowed them back. No way would I fall into a sobbing mess right now. This was my big moment. Maybe I didn't deserve it, but even my mother had leapt to her feet, cheering loud enough for me to tell her voice from the rest.

Javier led me off the stage and into the milling crowd. Emily shouldered her way through the throng surrounding us, Yasmine and Brittany behind her.

"Way to go, home girl! That so didn't suck like *Twi*—"

A gasp drowned out the rest of her sentence. Brittany's eyes glowed from behind her vampire contacts. "You were so not going to say what I thought you were about to say."

"She meant the *Twilight Zone*. Isn't that right, Em?" Yasmine raised her eyebrows. "We were talking about it the other day. Remember the episode with the guy stuck outside the moving train..."

"It was a plane." Emily's gums flashed in a toothy smile, and Brittany relaxed. "Dr. Spock was on the wing dressed like a baby Wookie and..."

"Trippy," Trinity murmured before wandering off to talk to Seth and his grandparents.

"No. Not Spock," Rafael interrupted. He slung his arm around a glowing Siobhan. "It was Captain Kirk. I mean, William Shatner." He held his fingers in a "V" sign. "Live long and prosper." Siobhan's adoring look earned her a kiss on the tip of her nose. "That's the Vulcan salute. I'm a bit of a Trekkie."

"Me, too," sighed Siobhan. She plucked a tuft of leftover fur from behind Rafael's ear.

Jackie and Piper made gagging sounds, but I only smiled. Even if my love life sucked, it felt good to see my friend so happy.

"Anyhoo." Emily grabbed my hands and squeezed. "I'm proud of you, Alex. You did an amazing job tonight, and you are an inspiration to all the girls here. I think you'd be the perfect keynote speaker tomorrow night to introduce next week's Girl Growth and Development seminar."

I took an involuntary step back and felt Javier's arm tighten around my waist. "I think you might have that twisted. Remember...I'm the girl *leaving* camp because of being punished. That's hardly inspiring."

Yasmine's wooden arm bracelets clanked as she reached for me. "Alex, you are leaving a different person. You should feel so proud. Look at all you've accomplished."

Her dark eyes locked on me, full of Yasmine-forcefulness, and I couldn't hold back a smile. Yasmine had grown on me this summer. I'd miss her lecturing, do-gooder ways. They reminded me of the person I aspired to be some day. But really, who was I kidding? The girls at the seminar would laugh me off that stage.

"Yasmine should be your speaker. I'm definitely not qualified."

Shaking my head, I backed away from the full-court press of pressure from Emily and Yasmine and accidentally bumped into my mom.

"What's this about not being qualified?" Mom swept me in a hug. "I'm so proud of you, sweetie."

I blinked over her shoulder at Javier. Had she lost wireless service? Why the sudden affection? And the compliment?

She squeezed my shoulders and pulled back, the dark circles under her eyes and her hollowed cheeks making me feel guilty for the long flight she'd taken. "You can do it, honey." She reached over and shook Emily's hand. "I'm Alex's mother, Grace, by the way. And I agree with you. The younger girls can learn a lot from Alex."

"From my mistakes." I hung my head.

Mom tipped up my chin. "That's how we grow. And we'll talk about them later." She exchanged a few quiet words with Emily for a minute before looping an arm through mine. "Please excuse us. We have a lot of catching up to do."

Emily shooed some campers to make way for us. "Clear out. Mother-daughter heart-to-heart coming through."

I cringed at the stares and cast Javier a despairing glance over my shoulder. His warm smile softened the regret I felt at leaving the rocking cast party we'd prearranged. Some of the cast members carried in the food and drinks we'd stowed backstage while others strung lights. One of the boys cranked some music, and vampires, werewolves and campers shuffled, swayed, and grinded as I walked an endless path out the door. Parting from Javier now was only a taste of what it would feel like later—when we said goodbye for real.

And wow. It would hurt.

Now, I had to deal with Mom's come-to-Jesus talk, no matter how supportive she acted publicly. Time to face the music, not dance to it.

"How about over there?" Mom gestured to some picnic tables appearing through the trees near the lake.

I couldn't make out her features in the softening gloom, but she looked serious. Didn't we always have our family blowouts behind closed doors? Public disagreements weren't part of the *Wholesome Home* image.

I followed her down the path and sat on the worn wooden bench. The evening air smelled pine-fresh with possibilities, even though I'd run out of them. My arms gave each other a hug. Now that we were alone, I wouldn't be getting any more.

A soft, hiccupping sound came from Mom's direction across the table. I stared at the tears streaming down her cheeks. I'd been ready for the lecture, prepared for the blame, braced myself for the punishment...but this...this I hadn't expected. And it hurt. I'd wounded Javier. Was Mom another of my casualties?

I groped for her left hand, and it felt lighter than usual. She'd lost weight. But more than that...I noticed her wedding and engagement bands were missing.

"Mom, where are your rings?"

Her shoulders shook harder, and I rushed to her side of the table. With my arms wrapped around her, my face pressed against her trembling back, I felt her fragility for the first time. Strange how I'd always seen her as this tower of strength. But her foundation seemed to have crumbled. Were her rings off because my parents' marriage was over? Had my actions made them fight and break up? Guilt flooded me. I'd wanted to pay back my parents for sending me away to school and publicizing my screw-ups on their blog, but I'd never wanted *this*. For the first time I realized how much I wanted a family—wholesome or not.

"Your father and I have separated." Her tremulous voice sounded younger and less sure than I'd ever heard it.

I squeezed her tighter around the waist, and her cold fingers laced through mine.

"Mom, I didn't mean to cause you guys so many problems. Please don't split because of me. You're great parents. I'm the failure. Me." My voice lodged in my throat at the end, my last word louder than the rest as I forced it out.

Mom shook her head, then let go of my hand to grab a tissue and blow her nose. I rested my head on her shoulder, and we both stared out at the lake, watching the rising moon mirrored on its inky, calm surface. Pretty on the outside with unpredictable currents lurking below. I felt one begin to drag me under.

After a long sigh, Mom twisted around to face me. "My problems with your dad aren't about you, Alex. If anything, you kept us together longer than we would have made it on our own. The blog gave us a common purpose. But it was a partnership more about business than love."

My chest felt heavy. Like I had slipped under those placid waters and swallowed a mouthful of pain. "But you two have always been so tight. A team."

Mom nodded, the lines around her mouth deeper than I remembered them. "A team, yes. A couple, not in the real sense. This summer we argued a lot about what to do with you this fall."

And here I thought Javier had suffered the most because of me. At least he'd be out of the group home in six months. My problems could ruin my parents' marriage forever.

"Why would you argue about that? It's already done. I saw the application filled out. I know I'm going to boarding school." I brushed a moth away from my cheek and realized, when my hand came away damp, that I was crying, too. "I know you and Dad are ready to get rid of me. I just...hadn't understood how many problems I was causing until now."

But now? I got it. Seeing Javier's life fall apart because of me had spelled it out perfectly. I was trouble.

Soft fingers wiped away my tears, then smoothed a damp strand of hair behind my ears. It was a familiar gesture, one that brought back memories of Mom soothing me when I'd woken from a childhood nightmare or fallen off a bike or gotten in school trouble. Always Mom.

Where had Dad been all those times? He'd been quick to jump on the computer to blog about things that happened to me but not to actually help. I guess that was a difference between my parents. Here was Mom, facing me with this harsh news, soothing me as best she could, while Dad stayed behind for more photo ops and blog posts.

"Alex, I never wanted you to leave us. I don't want to speak poorly of your father. No matter what, he's still your dad. But we couldn't see eye to eye on your schooling, and when it came to fighting for my daughter, I couldn't back down." She squeezed my hand. "It's too important. You're too important."

Wonder filled me that Mom loved me as more than a career booster, more than a publicity opportunity. She loved me for real. My heart pounded, and I put my hand across my chest, marveling that this was real and the fake-life I'd lived for so long might finally be over. But what would happen to Mom without *Wholesome Home*? Without my dad?

"I don't want to cause all of this, Mom." I clutched her arm tight, needing her to listen to me. "I've done a lot of thinking at camp, and I know the boarding school will be fine. I'm fine. Please don't end things because of me. I—I couldn't take it if you did."

Javier said I'd be all right if I went away to school, and I believed in him like I'd never believed in anyone else. But more importantly, I'd come to believe in myself.

"Oh, sweetie." My mother gathered me in her arms. "This is between your father and me. We both love you very much. We just don't love each other. I'm not leaving until tomorrow, but I want you to think about what you want to do and who you'd like to live with when you've finished camp."

Everything else fell away when she mentioned camp. My mouth opened and closed like a creature under that placid lake. "Aren't I leaving with you?"

Mom's lips twisted upward in a small smile. "After watching you with your friends, how well you managed the skit, I don't want you to leave when you're happy and thriving. Juniper Point is good for you, and if you help Emily, you'll be able to do some good for other people, too."

Relief rolled through me like a wave on the shore. I wasn't leaving. I had another month before boarding school. Time to make sense about how I felt about the divorce. Most of all, it was a second chance to be the person I'd finally learned I could become.

I kissed her cheek, tasting the salt of her tears—or mine—and gave her a bear hug. "Thank you, Mom. I won't mess up again before going to boarding school." Oh my God. I was really going to get to stay here.

If only Javier wasn't leaving...

"Mistakes are how you grow, sweetie. Even at my age," Mom whispered in the near dark. Something small and darker than the air swooped overhead, and we both ducked. Mom scrambled to duck as she shrieked.

"Was that a—"

"Bat? Yep." I shuddered at how close it had come, but we were facing something so much more sinister than this that I couldn't, wouldn't be afraid of flying rats. "For a minute, I thought it was BLISS Network surprising us with a TV crew. Now that would have been scary."

A ghost of a smile flitted across Mom's face. "I cancelled them before I got here. No family, no show."

"So what are you going to do?" I covered her twisting hands and pulled them onto my lap.

A short laugh escaped her. "Write a final post on the *Wholesome Home* blog, then shut it down or sign my share of the rights over to your father for a small fee." She winked at me. "I'll find a job, a place to live... actually, it's kind of a long list."

"Oh, Mom." I hated hearing her sound so uncertain. I watched a small group of younger campers trek out onto the dock to stargaze and remembered when the Munchies did that once. It felt like another lifetime ago.

"Honey, it's fine. Better than fine. It's good and long overdue."

"At least you won't have to worry about where to put me." Suddenly going away for school, which I'd come to accept, seemed like a decent alternative after all. With so much changing, it'd help my mom to have me settled. I would focus on that instead of how I felt about it. "I'll be away at boarding school."

I stared up at the sky, wondering if the campers would see any shooting stars so they could make wishes. Mine would be for Mom. And Javier, too.

"About school..."

I leaned forward. "Yes?"

"After we spoke, I contacted the assistant director of *Mine Forever.*"

So much had happened since my angry phone call to Mom, I'd forgotten I even mentioned it to her. What was more surprising? She'd actually been listening.

"You did?"

"She spoke very highly of you and strongly recommended you spend your last year of high school at the performing arts school she graduated from in New York." Her eyebrows lifted. She smiled. "Alex, she said you showed great passion for the small role you were given. That you reminded her of herself when she was starting out. I had no idea you were so talented."

My face heated at the compliment, and I traced patterns in the beach sand with my toe. It was one thing to hear kind words from a stranger, but to know that my mother believed it, too. Wow.

"The director promised to contact the school and get back to me. There aren't any guarantees, of course. But there's a chance she can help you get in if you would like to attend."

The words blew me away. The idea floored me. But Mom's strained face yanked me back to reality. If I didn't go to the boarding school, then I should stay with her. "I want to be with you. Help you."

Mom stroked my hair absently. Tonight was the most we'd touched since our obligatory Christmas photos last December. I'd missed this contact. Hadn't realized how much until now. "Alex, seeing you happy does help me. And besides, one of the jobs I've applied for is in Manhattan working to match disadvantaged women with careers."

I pulled back and studied her. "Isn't that your charity?"

Her mouth quirked. "Yep."

"So you'd be hiring yourself?"

"If the board agrees."

The joy of new possibilities streaked through me. "We'll make them. You've done a lot for them. And if I get into the performing arts school, we can get an apartment. Personally, I like SoHo, but I heard the Meat Packing District is really trendy and—"

Mom held up a hand. "Let's not get ahead of ourselves. Lots to figure out before then. I'm glad you're staying here for the second half of the summer while I get things settled. I just feel bad that Javier can't stay, too."

I startled, stunned she'd remembered him and his situation. So much had changed in my life, but everything was the same for him. He'd still leave camp the day after tomorrow to start over in a group foster home.

"It's not fair. Javier's tried so hard to be there for his mom. And he's smart and a really good cook, and now he'll be stuck in a group home without his family. With no options."

Mom pulled my head down to her shoulder and rested her chin on top of it. "Maybe there's more in store for him than you think."

Chapter Twenty-Four

Alex

Free period the next day felt like a death sentence. I lay on my back with my feet propped on the wall behind Jackie's bunk, my hair dangling over the edge of her mattress. In just a few hours, I'd deliver my speech to the girls who'd signed up for Emily's class, and I still had no clue what to say.

"Hey, isn't that another Secret Camp Angel gift?" Yasmine pointed to a small, tissue-wrapped object peeking out from my pillow. She sprayed something floral around her neck, transforming our musty cabin into a tropical garden.

"Probably." I rolled over on my stomach and dropped my head in my hands. My after-dinner talk was going to be an epic fail. What did I have to say to girls about growing up and becoming mature? Like my parents had written, I was the cautionary tale, the girl who wandered into the witch's candy house or fell asleep in bears' beds. Sure I'd learned a lot lately. But with Javier leaving, it felt like too little, too late.

"Aren't you going to open it?" Jackie's bunk squeaked when Piper jumped on beside me.

Something weighty dropped in my lap. Would this be an insult masquerading as a gift? Or had my Not-So-Secret Camp Angel decided to take it easy on me?

Yasmine's expression gave nothing away.

"Come on, Alex. Open it." Jackie scrubbed a towel across her damp head and joined us on her bunk. She'd showered after playing some pick-up basketball.

Bracing myself, I hoped for the best. The tissue paper came free, and a smooth silver pen lay in my hands.

"Ohhh," the group chorused.

"It's pretty." I held up the pen and inspected every angle. Was it booby-trapped or something? Would ink squirt out when I uncapped it? "I guess I could use it to write Javier."

"You should use it to write your speech." Yasmine gave me a knowing look, and I couldn't keep her secret to myself any longer.

"Thank you, Yasmine." I pointed a finger. "You wouldn't admit it the other night, but you're my Secret Camp Angel."

She smiled and shrugged. "Guilty."

Emily strolled in, her neon yellow biker shorts brilliant in the sunshine streaming through our screens. "Where did you get that awesome pen?"

I handed it to Emily. She turned it over in her hand, a small smile playing on her fuchsia-coated mouth. "That's a Waterman pen. My father only used these. They're French."

"I gave it to her." Yasmine smiled. "I'm her Secret Camp Angel."

Emily handed the pen back. "No wonder Alex's gifts were so awesome." She held out a fist to Yasmine. "Way to get in the spirit, home girl."

"Thanks." Yasmine fist-bumped her, then made an exploding sound that was so lame even Emily laughed.

"Yeah, thanks, Yasmine." When I really thought about it, she meant well. "But I still don't see how it will help me with my speech. I don't have a clue what to write about."

"What about the other gifts? You could use them, too." Siobhan hurried across to my desk area and held up my first gift—A *Girl's Guide to Growing Up*. "There are actually plenty of good facts in here."

She handed it to me, and I flipped a few pages, loving the smell of a new book. I stopped on a chapter entitled "Self-Esteem" and scanned a few paragraphs. It wasn't all that different than the things my folks wrote about on *Wholesome Home*, but the tone was less...know-it-all.

Or maybe it just helped that it hadn't been written by...*a parent*.

"You're right. Thanks, Siobhan." There was a lot of good stuff in here that would help me get a speech started. If only I'd thought to read the darn book before I caused Javier so many problems.

"What about this gift?" Trinity left the bunk and returned with the mirror I'd tossed near my laundry bag.

I peered over her shoulder and caught both of our reflections. Her calm expression didn't do much to slow my bumping heart. "You don't need a third eye to see the truth."

"No," I sighed and wiped off a mascara smudge with shaking fingers. "Maybe I just needed to open the ones I have."

A warm hand rubbed my back. "Now that you see," Yasmine held up the bottle of ear drops she'd given me, "it's time to listen. We'll all help with your speech."

I looked at the circle of smiles surrounding me and felt the first twinge of happiness in days. No matter how much I'd messed up, camp friends were friends for life and would always have my back.

Heart squeezing tight, I leaped into the cluster of my friends, trying to hug everyone at once. We collapsed in a squealing heap. "I owe you guys, big time."

Piper swiped her hair off her face and straightened. "Can I start?"

I nodded, my heart bursting that they wanted to help me.

She strode over to her bed to retrieve a friendship bracelet she'd been braiding from material scraps she'd found in the arts and crafts room. "My advice is never to be wasteful."

We all groaned. Of course Piper would say that.

"What?" She flicked her hair over her shoulder. "Is there something wrong with not wasting yourself on things that don't matter—like boys who don't treat you with respect or friend drama or obsessing over your looks?"

That shut us up. In fact, I used the pen and took notes in the margin of the book. It was actually really good advice. I clicked off the pen and glanced up. My ears were definitely working now.

The swimmer's drops must have kicked in.

"Anyone else?"

Jackie hugged her scabbed knees. "Don't let others intimidate you or push you around. Stand up for what you believe and don't stop until you reach your goals."

"Oh, I love that!" Trinity exclaimed.

"Writing it down." I scribbled. Yasmine was right. I should have been listening all along.

"My advice is to go after what you want. You'll never know if you'll get it unless you try." Siobhan's bright cheeks left no doubt she was talking about Rafael.

I reached across and gave her arm a quick rub. Siobhan had, just last summer, lectured our old cabin mate Lauren about boys being a distraction. But here she was, keeping up with her summer school by studying with Rafael.

"Thanks, Siobhan. Anyone else?"

"Be open-minded to change because you'll go through a lot. The universe has a plan, and there's no rush to figure it out," Trinity mumbled over a mouthful of kettle corn.

"Yep."

"So true."

"Definitely."

The girls each took a handful when the bag was passed their way. I munched on the salty sweetness, thinking life was like that. Sugar and spice. There were good times and challenging times, but in the end, you always wanted more. I hated that Javier and I hadn't worked out, but I still got to spend a summer with my friends. If only there was something nice I could do for him.

The slanting afternoon sun glittered on the letter "A" hanging from my bunk. For so long it stood for everything I'd wanted in life: appreciation, attention, control. Most of all, it stood for me. A glittery A for Alex because I needed to stand out in a good way—separate from my parents. It practically shouted "MINE" wherever I nailed it.

But none of that mattered anymore. I didn't need to be noticed and have people like me. So what if the world thought I was the problem child and now troubled teen? What counted is what I believed. I'd let other opinions affect me too much.

Suddenly, I knew someone else who should have the sparkling "A."

Javier.

I paid no attention to the "Where are you going?" and "Swim starts in ten minutes!" shouted behind me as I grabbed the letter and bolted from the cabin. In less than a minute, I was on the Warriors' Warden porch. I bent over, my sides aching, chest heaving. Luckily, all was dim and hushed inside. Knowing Rob, he'd used the free time to take them on a run. Knowing Javier, he was in the kitchen.

The door swung open with a small tug, and I strode to Javier's bunk. Like me, he had a top one. Unlike mine, his was neatly made with no frills to perk up the sad-looking navy comforter he'd tucked in the corners. I grinned down at my final Secret Camp Angel gift. Time to change that.

I found some paper and used my new pen to write him this note.

Javier,

I'm sorry for what's happened this summer. But I wouldn't change a moment we spent together since it meant everything to me. I won't forget you, and I hope you won't forget me. But just in case, here's something to remind you of the crazy summer you met an even crazier girl named Alex. P.S. The "A" now stands for amazing—as in our amazing summer. It was short, but I hope you'll remember it for the rest of your life. I know I will.

xo, A

I tucked the note under the "A" and put both on his pillow. Hopefully he'd understand it wasn't goodbye. It was forever.

Chapter Twenty-Five

Javier

"You have everything you need?" Bam-Bam asked me before we walked into the mess hall.

I checked my watch again. I didn't want to miss any of Alex's speech.

"Yeah." I pointed to the video camera I'd borrowed from Mr. Woodrow. The camp director had actually helped me out with a few things in my last days at camp, so I couldn't really think of him as Gollum anymore.

Camp Juniper Point had been good to me. Mostly because it had given me Alex, if only for a little while. But I'd met more people here who gave a crap about what happened to me than I'd ever met anywhere else.

"Good." The counselor nodded, jaw flexing. "But I mean for your trip across state. Do you need anything?"

I wasn't ready to share my plans about that just yet. But I knew Bam-Bam meant well.

"Yeah. I'm good." I had my head screwed on straighter than it had been in a long time. "Thanks."

Inside the mess hall, applause made me wonder if it was time for Alex to go on yet. I'd gotten special permission to slide into the back of the room, even though Alex's talk was geared toward the girls. When I'd told Emily I wanted to record footage of Alex, she'd turned cartwheels.

Literally.

"You'll do fine, kid. Good luck." Bam-Bam clapped me on the shoulder while some giggling girls wearing face paint ran past us into the mess hall, whispering to one another about seeing the *Wholesome Home* star speak. ·

Alex must have a following with younger girls. I wondered if she knew her parents' blog had won her fans.

"Thanks. I know you did everything you could to help me." This was awkward for me, but the guy deserved the words. "I appreciate it."

Bam-Bam stared into the woods, his expression guarded. "You helped me out quite a bit with the Vijay thing. I should have seen the signs he was using."

"Rafael gets most of the credit." I tightened my grip on the video camera. I needed to get inside and start filming, but it wasn't often that anyone stood up for me. I wouldn't walk away from someone who'd believed in me even before I did. "And it's not your fault you didn't know. That's not exactly the stuff you expect at a place like this."

People sent their kids to Camp Juniper Point to get away from drugs and bullying and all the crap kids faced every day at school. Kids here still sang "B-I-N-G-O," for crying out loud. Sure, some of it was corny. But it was special, too.

"All the more reason it should have stood out. Vijay was never a bad kid before." Bam-Bam held the door open. "Come on. I'll find us seats."

We slid into a back row just as Emily introduced Alex. I hurried to get the video camera going because I had big plans for this footage. Alex might not need her glittery letter "A" anymore, but she still deserved some time to shine. I'd talked to her for a few minutes during breakfast, and she'd told me her parents were splitting and that she might be able to study at a performing arts school in New York. But Alex didn't know about the plans her mother had in mind for *me*. Mrs. Martineau had approached me this afternoon with enough ideas for my future to make my head spin.

For now, I messed with the zoom feature on the camera and tried to get the best possible footage in case it would help Alex get into that acting school. I walked closer to the stage, careful not to distract her or anyone in the audience. I took some crowd shots while Alex held up a bottle of ear drops and a mirror, talking about her Camp Angel gifts. I snagged an image of her mom watching with teary eyes.

That made me start listening. Keeping the camera balanced on a folded table off to one side of the room, I tuned into what Alex was saying.

"...I'd been so focused on getting payback for what someone else did to me, I was making myself miserable." She held up the mirror to all the girls watching her. "Guess I should have taken a good look in here instead." She put her hand on one hip. "And I don't mean to check out my eyeliner."

That got a laugh from her audience, and I could see how she brought her acting skills into play. Sure, she spoke from the heart, but she used that big personality to work the crowd.

Light up the room.

"I should have realized you don't look backward. I hurt someone I cared about this summer because I wanted the wrong kind of attention." She blinked. Paused.

My gut clenched, and I knew damn well she wasn't acting now. I felt bad for all the times I'd pushed her away. I wished I could have every last one of those moments back.

She cleared her throat. "What I learned this summer is that you pay it forward." She set down her prop on a stool beside her. "It makes you happy inside to do nice things for other people, like what Emily did with the Camp Angel bracelets."

She held up hers to show it off and waved Emily to stand and take a bow. While the girls cheered, Alex hollered the loudest.

"My Camp Angel taught me a lot, even though I was *not* always a gracious learner." She turned to stare at someone in the audience, her green eyes shining with tears. "Yasmine, I'm sorry and thank you."

More applause. I picked up the camera to shoot the crowd again, my heart in my throat. Alex was freaking magnificent up there, and these girls really responded to her. She'd be like her mom one day, helping out people who didn't have their lives together. I'd had a chance to talk to Mrs. Martineau earlier and she was... awesome. I understood where Alex got her generous spirit, even though her star-power was all her own.

"So if you want to learn how to deal with negative situations or if you just want to become a stronger, better, more kick-butt girl, you should take the Growth and Development workshop with Emily. You won't regret it."

The cheers were louder now than they'd ever been. I had to put the camera down, actually, so I could make some noise. Alex was more than just a hot girl. She was funny, smart, and talented. And yeah, I'd say she definitely fell into the "kick-butt" category.

I'd been an idiot not to see it sooner. Or not to help *her* see it. But then, I'd had problems of my own this summer. Still, it wasn't too late to change. To offer Alex something to prove that I'd never, ever forget her.

Chapter Twenty-Six

Alex

"You were wonderful, sweetheart," my mom gushed. I'd been mobbed after my talk, and it was really strange feeling like a rock star at camp. But sheesh. I guess the younger girls all knew the *Wholesome Home* blog—they'd been following my "issues" with the same devotion their parents followed my parents. Weird, right?

I'd been so isolated from pop culture, I had no clue there were kids in the world who wanted to hear my side of the story.

"I was so nervous." My backpack containing my props quavered in my hand. I could feel it moving against my leg where I held it like a purse. "I worried the whole time—"

"You were amazing." Javier appeared at my side to whisper the words in my ear. "Emphasis on *amazing*."

"Thank you." I met his deep brown eyes and wanted to fall into them. "This is my mom—"

"Mrs. Martineau." Javier turned to her with a smile as if they'd met a hundred times before. "Nice to see you."

I frowned. Since when was Javier so at ease talking to parents? He'd been worried about meeting my folks since he first found out I was the *Wholesome Home* girl.

Before I could ask about it, he was passing off my backpack to Emily and taking me by the hand. "Would it be okay if I stole Alex for a little while? We don't have much time left—"

"Of course!" my mother and Emily said at the same time before my mom kissed me on the check. "Go right ahead. I have a few things to see Mr. Woodrow about anyway."

Should that sound ominous? Would Gollum try to talk her out of leaving me at camp? And most of all, did my mother just agree to let me hang out, alone, with a guy she knew I'd made out with? I didn't have much time to think about it though, as Javier whisked me out of the mess hall and toward the kitchen.

"Are we cooking?" I asked, confused and overwhelmed by the reception to my talk. I hadn't expected it to be such a big deal, but it had felt really good.

Really right.

"Not now, though I did make Julian some apple-cinnamon empanadas earlier today. They're my second Secret Camp Angel gift to him. I'll mail him my third gift from wherever I am next week." He led me past the food prep area and the sink where we'd gotten into our first fight. "I thought we'd find some quiet back here." He shoved open the door in back, the one that brought us into the kitchen garden.

The dirt path through the main row was visible in the deepening twilight, but the plants were taller than the last time I'd been here. My eyes searched for the oregano flowers he'd picked for me that day I'd cried, but I couldn't tell one plant from another.

"Here." He pointed toward a new bench off to one side, a few simple planks bolted onto two posts. "I made a spot for Helena to sit when she comes out into the garden for some fresh air. I just finished sanding it today."

He brushed it off with his hand and gestured for me to take a seat.

"Weren't you supposed to be doing camper things during your last week?" I sat beside him and pictured him alone out here today while I'd been surrounded by my friends.

"Hate to tell you, Alexandra—" He drew out the "x" into a soft, rolling "s" that made my name sound like a song. "—but I'll never be Mr. Social."

"But you were so great during *West Side Scary*." Everyone liked Javier now that Vijay was gone. They'd probably liked him before.

"I'm learning," he admitted, taking my hand and folding it in his. "And I got Rafe to help me on the bench, so we hung out for a while and he told me more about Puerto Rico where he's from. I've been thinking I'd like to go to Venezuela one day and see the sights, even if I don't find my dad."

"Really?" I remembered the cookbook I'd given him and the photos of Venezuelan dishes from around the country. "You could test your cooking skills against the locals and see how you do."

"Maybe." He stared down at my knee where my hand rested on my leg. He didn't take it, but he traced the backs of my fingers—one by one—until I shivered from the gentle touch.

All my life I fought so hard for positive attention, but with Javier, I always felt like I had it without having to do a thing. Maybe that's why it was so easy to be with him.

God, I was going to miss him. The knowledge that he'd be leaving in the morning socked me in the gut so hard I could have doubled over with the hurt.

"I can't believe you're going." It sounded like someone else was speaking, my voice high and desperate. "I mean, I know that's selfish because I'm thinking about how much I'm going to miss you instead of how awful this is for you, but sitting here right now reminds me so much of that first day you talked to me and we came out here."

Javier's knee rubbed mine as he turned toward me. He lined up our fingers and then interlocked them, our hands woven together in a tight bond.

He lifted our hands to eye level. A dried, woven grass bracelet slid down his wrist. My gift to him.

"Will you look at that?" He gave me a sad smile even as a tear rolled down my cheek. "No matter what else happened this summer, I'm still floored this happened."

"What?"

"You and me." He released me and looked into my eyes. "Alex, I'm not the kind of guy who gets a girl like you."

"You're crazy." I shook my head, frustrated. "You're gorgeous and talented, and you make amazing food. Trust me, Javier Kovalev, every girl at camp wants you."

"You don't understand. You're the best thing that's ever happened to me. You left that note that said you wouldn't change a thing that's happened this summer. Well, I wouldn't either."

I should be grateful he said that. But his leaving was a giant, dark cloud that settled over me.

"I still can't believe you feel that way." I clutched his shoulders, raising my voice. "I got you kicked out of camp. I messed up this summer for you when it was your last chance with the foster system, your last chance to spend your senior year with your mom. Now you're changing homes, changing schools...my God, I've turned your whole life upside down. You should hate me."

"Alex." He took my face in his hands and held it. "You did turn my life upside down, but that was what made me change."

"Are you insane?" For so long, I'd been told I was a nuisance and a problem. I'd never imagined I could be the solution.

"Remember when you tossed the wet sponge at me and yelled at me for not speaking to you?"

"That fight in the kitchen when I lost it. Yeah, of course."

"That changed things for me." His fingers slid lightly down my cheeks and into my hair where he combed through the strands. "My whole life I've bottled up my anger until it exploded in my face. And I'll admit, I was pissed off at you that week for getting me in trouble in the first place. But when I saw you crying and I realized I'd really hurt you by ignoring you..."

He shook his head, and his hands dropped away. His shoulders fell.

"I don't understand."

He drew in a deep breath. "It's hard to control my temper sometimes. But shutting you out didn't work either. Going outside and talking to you...it made me realize, for the first time, that I could be angry and talk through it." He gave me a lopsided smile. "I know—sounds like some self-help B.S. from your parents' blog, right? But I wrestled with that stuff for a long time, and this summer, something started to click in my head. And when Bam-Bam took me on that overnight trip, I realized it didn't just have to work with just you. I could handle things with anyone."

"Wow. I—I thought I ruined your summer." And your life, I added silently. I would never have guessed I'd helped him that much. I wiped my tears away. This was our last night, and I didn't want to ruin it.

"I've got something else that might cheer you up." Javier picked a piece of tall grass growing beside the bench he'd built.

"Shouldn't I be trying to cheer *you* up?" I plucked the long blade out of his hands and gently tore it into three strands for braiding. "I get to stay at camp while you have to leave the garden and your new friends and cooking..."

"I'll miss you a lot more than the garden." He tucked a finger in between my wrist and the Secret Camp Angel bracelet that had his name written inside. "Besides, your mom has been doing a whole lot more than just helping you stay at camp."

"What do you mean?" I stopped braiding the grass.

"I guess she volunteers for some organization that helps struggling women get back to work?"

I nodded.

"Well she found a job for my mom—working at that restaurant that provided the mobile catering truck back on the movie set, remember?"

"They wanted you to work there," I remembered, marveling that my mother had come through in so many ways. Putting everyone ahead of herself. Getting our lives figured out before she started working on her own future.

"Right. And having met me, the owner was happy to give my mom a job." Javier's eyes were wide. There was a different kind of tension in him.

Excitement?

"So she's got a job when she gets out." I knew he worried about her, so of course that would make him happy.

"It gets better. Your mother also found some subsidized housing until Mom gets on her feet. Then she called the jail and suggested my mom was eligible for some kind of early release between good behavior and having a job ready and waiting for her."

"She did that?" I could easily picture Mom on the phone nonstop on the way home from Honduras. What blew my mind was she'd been using her contacts—maybe even her fame—to help Javier and me.

"She's a dynamo, Alex. Just like you." Javier shook his head, voice full of wonder. "She talked to my social worker and—based on my mom's solid set-up—she got a special hearing scheduled for me with the family court judge next week. My social worker is recommending I be reunited with my mom."

My brain worked fast to process all that, but I still could hardly believe it. Javier would finally have the life he'd dreamed of. Imagined. My heart glowed as bright as the lightning bugs twinkling in the tomato plants.

"No group home?" I had to say it. It wouldn't completely sink in otherwise. This was incredible.

"No. Effing. Group home." Javier's grin flashed a mile wide.

I hugged him so hard I pretty much tackled him. I nearly rolled us off the bench.

"Oh my God!" I rained kisses on his cheek. One landed on his ear. I lost my gum. Thankfully, it rolled into the grass and not in his hair. "Mom didn't say one word to me about any of it."

"We were still ironing out the details and talking to the restaurant this afternoon while you were working on your speech." Javier kissed my forehead. "Mr. Woodrow called me down to his office after breakfast to meet with my social worker, and your mom joined us. She had this whole speech ready to go about the importance of reunification of families and the success of this program she runs...by the time she was done, my social worker was on the phone with my foster family and the judge. It was incredible."

"So you'll be living nearby?" The trip into town was twenty minutes tops.

"For the rest of the summer." He gathered me in his arms and pulled me tight against his chest.

"And I'll be here for four more weeks." My voice was muffled, my mouth pressed against his thudding heart.

"I'm still kicked out of camp," Javier reminded me, easing back. "Mr. Woodrow isn't budging on that one."

"I'm sure he'll have some sticky P.R. to overcome with that video circulating of us kissing." I still felt embarrassed about it. Not the kiss, but that the whole world had seen a private moment.

"I've got an answer to that video that might help you." He picked up a video camera that he'd sat beside him on the bench. "I videotaped your speech today."

"Oh. Okay." I frowned. "I don't know if that will help me get into the performing arts school."

"Maybe not. But it can be the first upload on your blog."

"My blog? Hello? I don't have a blog."

"Well, maybe it's time you got one. Do you realize all the younger campers know who you are because of *Wholesome Home*? There's a whole generation of kids who have followed your life the same way their parents follow *Wholesome Home*. Why not tell your side of the story? Starting with this?" He waved the camera in front of my nose.

"Was this my mom's idea, too?" I couldn't decide if I wanted to springboard off *Wholesome Home* fame. I'd spent so much time resenting it.

"No." He set aside the camera. "This one was all me. I even set up the blog for you if you want to load it in."

"You?" I tried to picture Javier over in the computer lab.

"Vijay isn't the only kid with tech skills." He shrugged as he studied me with dark eyes in the moonlight.

"Besides, this is the right way to fight back. Not with fists but with, you know, words."

I fell head over heels for him at that second. My heartbeat quickened. I swayed closer. A warm summer breeze lifted a lock of my hair to tickle my cheek.

"I should have let you give the keynote speech instead of me," I whispered, my eyes lowering to lips I very much wanted to kiss. "Because you're saying all the right things tonight."

"Alex." He cupped my chin in his hand and tipped my face up, halting the kiss before it started. "I know you might be in New York while I'm in North Carolina this fall."

"I *hope* I'll be in New York." I liked dreaming big dreams with him, but wasn't it enough that we might still see each other sometimes during the summer? I was already plotting trips into town. "But there are no guarantees."

"Right. And I'll still have social services keeping an eye on me until I turn eighteen. But once that happens, I'll be able to go anywhere. Even culinary school."

"In New York?" The words were a squeak, a wish I hardly dared to speak out loud.

"I hear that's the place to go if you're serious about cooking."

My heart lodged in my throat, like I'd been on an elevator that went down too fast. I felt dizzy.

"Can you even imagine?" I could almost picture a future that would put us on the paths to our dreams. Paths that could intersect again when we were free to really be together.

"I don't expect you to make any promises now or anything. But this summer, if there's any way I can see you sometimes, maybe you could...be my girlfriend."

"Javi." Tears stung my eyes. I wasn't used to getting half the things I wanted in life, let alone everything. All at once.

"Just think about it," he said quickly. "I know I pushed you away in the past–"

I kissed him. Not just a little. I planted a kiss on him to end all kisses. Arms around his neck, lips sealed to his full, soft ones, I lost myself in the feel of Javier.

My boyfriend.

I saw fireworks behind my eyelids. Breathed in the spicy, sexy scent of him. Spread my fingers into his thick, dark hair.

"Alex," he whispered between kisses, "is that a yes?"

I laughed. I couldn't help it. "That is a yes so definite you won't forget it. Plus, I didn't want you to think I needed time to consider it. I already know. I'm yours."

Epilogue

Javier

One year later

I jogged around a pretzel vendor just past West Houston Street, ducked between a couple of dudes with briefcases arguing about who should pay for a cab, and cruised toward Lafayette and Bleecker.

I didn't want my delivery to get cold. My girlfriend was crazy about cinnamon triangles, but they were only good if you served them warm. Last night, I'd played around with a new chocolate sauce recipe I wanted her to try.

"Hey Javier," the doorman greeted me. Or maybe he was a bouncer. After three months in the city, I was still getting my New Yorker lingo down. "Got any more arepas?"

I held up the brown bag. "Homemade pastries today. Do you think they're taking a break yet?"

"You're right on time." The beefy dude pulled open the big side door where I'd been showing up a couple of times a week for the last month.

Stepping into the dim theater interior, I saw a few cast members milling around the front of the stage.

"Javi!" Alex separated herself from a crowd of teens who had small parts in *Pod-Cast*, an off-Broadway play that opened in two weeks. Thanks to her performing arts school teachers, she'd been able to get the audition that landed her the role as Maureen, a fast-talking, unfiltered vlogger. Clearly they'd cast completely against type. I grinned.

Her happy smile reminded me of that day in the garden back at Camp Juniper Point when I'd promised myself I'd make her laugh and smile again. I felt proud of keeping that promise, even though I'd had to follow her halfway across the country to do it.

"How's it going?" I held out the bag to show her my offering, and her eyes lit up.

"Better now that you're here." She ignored the food and kissed me first, her lips sweeter than the dessert. Her body warmer than the oven I'd cooked them in. She rose on tiptoe and pressed against me, her soft curves molding against my chest. I inhaled the bubblegum scent of her and ran my fingers through her hair, loving the way the strands curled around my fingers, the feel of her mouth as it caressed mine. We broke apart when a loud cheer rose from her cast mates.

Red-faced, she stepped back and took the treats from me. "Is this what I think it is?"

"Still hot, with any luck."

"Plus the homemade chocolate sauce?"

"You have to give me your honest opinion." I'd been working as a prep cook at Helena's brother's restaurant downtown for two months now, and the pastry chef had inspired me.

I'd graduated high school early in North Carolina and signed up for a couple of online college classes until I got into culinary school in the fall. I still looked at the acceptance letter every morning. Otherwise, I'd start thinking I'd imagined the whole thing. What did they call dreams that happened when you were awake?

"I'm always honest with you." Alex kissed my cheek while we walked toward the back of the theater. She slid into a seat, and I sat beside her.

"You always say what you think." I tugged a magenta braid she'd woven into her dark hair. "It's one of the things I love about you."

Her emerald eyes darkened. "I love you, too, Javi." Her soft hand folded into mine. "And I wouldn't have a successful vlog without speaking from the heart." She pulled out a cinnamon triangle and the container of sauce I'd packed. "Speaking of which, do you want to film this?"

She juggled the food to reach into her pocket and pull out her phone, which she passed to me.

"Sure." Used to this ritual every time we went out exploring Manhattan, I clicked open her camera and focused on her pretty face.

Like a seasoned pro, Alex launched into her welcome for *Home Grrl*, the video blog that had gone viral, particularly in the teen and college student demographic. Even her father had called to congratulate her when she reached her latest landmark of subscribers.

"Hey, guys, I'm trying Javier's latest creation today..." She talked up my cooking and dissected the finer points of the sauce, forcing me awkwardly into the frame to discuss what I'd done differently with the recipe.

At first, it had felt weird to see myself on the computer screen with her, but by now, I was used to it. I'd even gotten some fan mail, which Alex insisted would be good for the restaurant I'd open one day.

With Alex in my life, I'd gotten used to dreaming big.

Reaching for the camera with cinnamon-covered fingers, Alex ended the video snippet with a shot of her palm.

"It's amazing," she sighed happily between bites. "You're so talented. You should be teaching the classes at that school."

"You think so?" I took her hand, checked that no one was looking, and licked the excess cinnamon off her thumb.

"I know so." She fed me a bite of the pastry dipped in chocolate sauce. "What if you become a famous chef while I'm still a struggling actress and I can't afford to eat in your fancy restaurant?"

She was full of it, and I knew it. But it also felt damn good not to be the "foster kid" anymore. I was paying my own way these days. I had new shoes. My mom had taken a job doing prep work at a high-end restaurant, and she loved it. They were paying for a couple of college courses related to her job, so she was working toward a culinary degree, too.

Things were good. Life was awesome.

"You'll always be able to afford my cooking."

"Yeah?"

"If you can't afford my restaurant, I'll come over to your house and cook for you."

"Wrong answer." She poked me between the ribs and kissed my neck at the same time. "You won't need to come over because I'll already be with you. We're a package deal."

"Okay, okay." I couldn't argue with her, but sometimes it was fun to rile her up.

"I promised your mother I would make sure you had some fun," she reminded me.

"Next time I see her?" I kissed her forehead. "I'm going to tell her you're doing a hell of a job."

Acknowledgements

From Joanne

To authors who have made me laugh out loud, cry into my pillow, and wish for happy-ever-afters- whether you've delivered them or not! Thank you for making me believe in the impossible and making me care about characters that exist in our shared imaginations. Also, to my mentors who made me believe I could share that gift of story too, most especially the members of North Louisiana Storytellers and Authors of Romance who read my books long before I sold them and listened patiently while I justified all my mistakes. On that note, here's wishing the authors of tomorrow the persistence, patience and passion that it takes to hone their craft. I continue to learn from all the new writers I meet and I'm grateful to them for sharing their enthusiasm for writing with me. You keep me inspired for the work I do! Finally, to the ever-awesome Kate Kaynak, the always-insightful Patricia Riley and the mega-dedicated Cindy Thomas at Spencer Hill for believing in our books and giving us a wonderful, welcoming home for them.

From Karen

To Danielle –who's more Alpha than Beta when it comes to reading for me and in all of the other incredible achievements in her life. Thank you for sharing your talent and love with me. Thank you as well to my loving husband, Greg. There is no greater gift than knowing that I get to spend the rest of my life with you. I love you both so much. Thank you as well to my wonderful in-laws, my father, and sisters, Jeanne and Cathy, for being such a caring family to me. A hug and huge shout out to my mentor and friend, Cynthia Leitich-Smith who believed in me until I did too. Much appreciation as well to my wonderful and supportive writer and blogger friends like Amy Guglielmo, Lucy Cooney, Jacqueline Tourville, Kayleigh-Marie Gore, Gaby Navarro, Dale S. Rogers, Jen Cooke Fischer, Brooke Watts DelVecchio, Lola Verroen, Marci Curtis, Cindy Ray Hale, Rachel Harris, Trisha Leaver, Lindsay Currie, my writer family at Spencer Hill, and our amazing street team, The Rock Stars, whose talent, support and positivity have been a great source of inspiration and encouragement! Finally, I am incredibly grateful for the blessing of my amazing sister-in-law, writing partner, and closest friend, Joanne Rock. We've spent many years talking about books and swapping writing ideas. It's a wonder and a privilege to share this experience with her and I look forward to our future projects together!

About the Authors

J.K. Rock is the pseudonym for writing partners- and sisters-in-law- Joanne and Karen Rock. Sharing a love of young adult fiction, marathon shopping and men with the last name "Rock," the two teamed up to write *Camp Boyfriend* and found they had a whole lot more to say than what could fit in one book. Look for them in matching t-shirts at book signing events around the country or chatting with their Facebook street team, the Rock Stars. FMI, visit http://jkrock.net

In a quest to provide her eighth grade students with quality reading material, former English teacher **Karen Rock** read everything out there and couldn't wait to add her voice to the genre. In addition to co-authoring young adult books, Karen is a Harlequin Heartwarming author. Her second novel, *HIS HOMETOWN GIRL* is an April 2014 release, with more to come in the months ahead. When she's not busy writing, Karen enjoys watching Supernatural marathons, cooking her Nona's family

Italian recipes, and occasionally rescuing local wildlife from neighborhood cats. She lives in the Adirondack Mountain region with her husband, her very appreciated beta-reader daughter and two King Charles Cavalier cocker spaniels who have yet to understand the concept of "fetch," though they've managed to teach her the trick! Hmmmm... wonder how that happened?! Check out her website at http://www.karenrock.com, her Facebook page at http://www.facebook.com/karenrockwrites, and follow her on twitter @ KarenRock5. She'd love to meet you!

Joanne Rock fell in love with reading at a young age and stayed out of trouble- mostly-as a teen thanks to long stints at her local library where she routinely checked out as many books as a bicycle basket would carry. She still pronounces all the names of the Greek gods incorrectly because she learned them through reading- a small price to pay for the vast amount of knowledge she gained from books! She started writing when the voices in her head kept her awake at night, demanding she tell their stories. A successful romance author, she's penned many books for a variety of Harlequin series and has been nominated for the prestigious RITA award three times. Learn more about her work at http://joannerock.com or follow her on Twitter @ JoanneRock6.